"Final Exam" by Jennifer Roberson: A kidnapped princess needs to keep her wits about her to survive a stressed-out apprentice sorcerer—and a New Age dragon . . .

"Nightside" by Mercedes Lackey: New York's occult sleuth/novelist Diana Tregarde and her daemon lover Andre must stop a soul stealer's murderous rampage . . .

"The Palace of al-Tir al-Abtan" by Lawrence Watt-Evans: Abu the thief can face all the mystic curses, djinns, and afrits guarding the wizard al-Tir al-Abtan—but does Abu dare meet the deadly magician face to face?

"The Truth About the Lady of the Lake" by Phyllis Ann Karr: Sorceress Frostflower and the woman warrior Thorn are legends in their own time—but now they're in another time . . . and someone *else's* legend!

"Change" by Jo Clayton: Together, a raped, pregnant slave and a vengeful lake goddess must stop the conquerers who mined and despoiled Paradise . . .

"The Dancer of Chimaera" by Diana L. Paxson: A lovely young space station dancer holds the key to end the war between humans and the mysterious Shifters . . .

The Nebula Award finalist **"The Adinkra Cloth"** by Mary C. Aldridge: In the dark heart of the jungle, their dead mother's burial shroud holds the only power that can save three small children from an evil tribal chief's black sorcery . . .

plus tales by Dorothy Heydt, Laurie Sparer, Pat Cirone, Kit Wesler, Peter Manly, and many other authors from

THE BE‌**DLEY'S**

D0754158

The Best of
Marion Zimmer Bradley's
Fantasy Magazine

Edited and with an Introduction by
Marion Zimmer Bradley

WARNER BOOKS

A Time Warner Company

Enjoy lively book discussions online with CompuServe. To become a member of CompuServe call 1-800-848-8199 and ask for the Time Warner Trade Publishing forum. (Current members GO:TWEP.)

WARNER BOOKS EDITION

Aspect is a trademark of Warner Books, Inc.

Cover design by Don Puckey
Cover illustration by Braldt Bralds

Warner Books, Inc.
1271 Avenue of the Americas
New York, NY 10020

 A Time Warner Company

Printed in the United States of America

First Printing: November, 1994

In loving memory of my dear Don Wollheim;
Editor and more of a father than my own
Who discovered the editor within the writer
And let it out for a good run.

—*MZB*

CONTENTS

The Best of
Marion Zimmer
Bradley's
Fantasy Magazine

INTRODUCTION

I've been asked again and again why I, with a good deal of success in writing fiction, chose to become an editor.

This goes back to my early experiences in science fiction fandom. Like many of my predecessors in all kinds of fiction, including such disparate purveyors of fiction as Charlotte Brontë and Howard P. Lovecraft, my first experience in literature was editing and publishing a "fanzine." The self-publishing and editing endeavors of the Brontë sisters are too well known to need extensive comment, and Oscar Wilde found his first audience in a college magazine.

One of the ways in which science fiction and fantasy fiction differ from any other genre of fiction in which I've written (and I have written, over the last half-century, in every genre field except hard science fiction and hard-core detective fiction) is that fantasy and science fiction writers, almost without exception, regard one another not as rivals but as highly valued friends and colleagues, not temperamental prima donnas but like members of one large orchestra, or choir, whose allegiance is given only to the music.

About such art as is featured in my magazine, I know only enough to know I don't know much of anything. That is why one of the first things I did after the magazine was well established was to put the illustrative artwork into the very capable hands of Rachel Holmen, who *does* know something about the subject; and, judging by the feedback I've received, it was the best move I ever made.

But while art may not be my field of expertise, fiction *is* my field; so one of the most rewarding experiences, in this field or any other, is to discover new talent. This is one of the main reasons why I wanted to publish a magazine in the first place. (It was with amazement that I learned, by way of a convention's editorial panel, that all editors don't share my delight in the slush pile, many of them regarding it as no more than, at best, a necessary evil.) But from the very first I read every story that was submitted to the magazine, and I still do; the slush pile is the high point of my day.

The main criterion I use for choosing stories is: Can I see this story in print, do I want to read this in print? I look for what I call "the sense of wonder"—that thing which makes me feel that with every word of a given story I'm learning something, finding out something I couldn't find anywhere else; stories which make me feel curiosity, adventure, delight; which make me feel that my imagination is at full stretch, that there's nothing else in the world I'd rather be doing than reading that particular story right now.

I set up something called the Cauldron (I got the idea from *Analog,* which did something similar, and the name from the legendary cauldron of gold at the end of the rainbow), where the readers vote for their favorite stories (Rachel added artwork, beginning with issue #14) in each issue, and the authors and artists who win get a small additional payment. I don't always agree with the readers—half the stories in this volume were not in the top three places in the Cauldron votes—but I value the feedback. It's always interesting to see what grabs my readers' attention, what they particularly like and dislike.

I think of editing as Herman Melville professed (tongue in cheek) to think of whalers: they went out to get the best and freshest light in the very source of whale-oil fuel; I go out and hunt up writers at the source, not filtered through other editors. And I love it. Which is a good thing, or I could never do it long enough to discover all these great writers. And here are many of those it's been my pleasure to discover, to present, to encourage. It's such a pleasure to present them, by way of this anthology, to a mass market.

I trust you'll like them too.

About Dorothy J. Heydt and "Moonrise"

Although I've known her now for about thirty years, I can't claim to have discovered Dorothy Heydt; I believe she had been published elsewhere before I bought the first of many stories from her. I met her originally through the Society for Creative Anachronism, where she was a member of a Renaissance music group and the possessor of one of the finest singing voices I have ever heard. I know for sure that I published quite a few of her stories in *Sword and Sorceress* and in my various Darkover anthologies before I published her in the magazine. Whether or no, as soon as I read this story, I knew I was going to feature it in my first issue.

Before I acquired Rachel Holmen as a capable managing editor, I was working with another lady I'll not name here for various reasons, whose talents were substantial but did not include any previous knowledge of our field. Since I had kept control of the literary content of the magazine, while her talents were almost entirely in the production line, I was amazed to discover that not only did she not share my enthusiasm for "Moonrise" but that—as she told me after it was in print—she had entirely failed to understand it, to the level where she told me that she believed some penultimate paragraph must have been omitted by the printer; and it had no point whatsoever.

4

I don't know what they teach in colleges nowadays; because, although my friend had a somewhat better education in most ways than mine, I had to explain it to her in words of one syllable, that while "taking the magic out of the moon" might restore a werewolf to normal, "taking the magic out" of Mars by landing on it could be expected to bring fighting to an end—Mars being the God of War.

But in all the other comments I ever got about "Moonrise," *not one* complained about not understanding Dorothy's story; so I imagine that the average reader of fantasy is better educated than even a college-graduate nonreader.

When I was a kid there used to be a belief that fans were all intellectually superior to nonfans. I doubt if even those who used the notion really believed it, but maybe it was true, and is still true—insofar as any reader is at least superior in at least one way to almost any nonreader.

Moonrise

Dorothy J. Heydt

Martin put on his professional smile and walked through the press-room door. If CBS in its infinite unwisdom chose to assign him to the Mars landing, rather than to something crucial like the Senate confirmation hearings or the Pan-Arabian war, he would put a good face on it and acquire merit for future assignments.

This good intention lasted about ten seconds, or until he saw, through the wall/window that separated the press and VIP areas, the lean profile and pewter-colored hair of Senator Vilkas, three thousand miles from where he should have been.

Martin backtracked out the door and threaded his way between dignitaries to Vilkas's chair. "Senator? Martin Raymer, CBS News. Senator, what are you doing here?"

Vilkas's smile was his trademark, startlingly white against his tanned face. "Space Committee chairman. Rank still hath its privileges."

"Why aren't you at the confirmation hearings? If Davidson gets in as Secretary of State, he'll set American foreign policy back fifty years."

"I left a list of questions and a prepared statement with Senator McCartney. She can cope."

"India and Pan-Arabia could be at war by the end of the week," Martin reminded him, pulling his newsscan from his breast pocket. The Senator glanced at the headlines racing by, waved the scan aside.

"I know," he said. "That's why this is important."

"Vandenberg, Phobos," the wall speaker said. "We've picked up the *Bifrost* on its second pass. You ought to be getting the picture about now." The screen lit up, brick red from border to border, flecked with craters. A silvery triangle crossed it slowly from left to right, fragile-looking as a child's paper airplane. Vilkas muttered something in a language Martin didn't know.

"Senator," Martin began again.

"Marty, shut up," said the Senator firmly. "I said, this is important."

Berkeley in August was empty of students. Most of the street people had drifted into San Francisco in search of tourists' spare change. They had taken the fog with them, and the sun was setting through clear air. Soon the moon would rise, and he was still on Telegraph. Nearly two miles to go. *Damn you.*

As he crossed Durant a gust of wind blew a fragment of newspaper into his face. He caught it and looked at it: a piece of an old *Chronicle,* with Herb Caen's column in it, from the day Apollo 11 had lifted off. "Today begins the violation of the last virgin . . ." He crumpled it and threw it back into the street.

Serve you right. Two weeks old, it would be, because they had lifted off at the new moon and tonight was the full.

He turned east onto Bancroft and began to climb, with the University on his left and a row of frat houses on his right. Both looked nearly deserted, the University left to faculty who were getting some work done, the frats left to caretakers who could relax and party every night. (Somebody would have to come and clean the plastic cups out of the bushes.)

He cut between International House and the football stadium and followed quiet hill streets to the beginning of the fire trail. The moon had risen by now, but he was sheltered by the hills for a few minutes yet. *Damn you. Why won't you let me be?*

He climbed the fire trail at a half-run that took him deep into Tilden Park before the moonlight began to discolor the evening sky. He met no other human on the trail, only a nearly grown doe that ran away at the sight of him. People never came here at night, and the deer would have to take their chances.

Soon he reached a big bay laurel that stood in the ravine deep between two branches of the road. Nobody would be scrambling all the way down here, not even to answer any calls of nature. He undressed swiftly, stuffed his folded clothes inside the hollow between the branches of the bay laurel, and dropped his shoes and socks on top. That was the only thing he had any control over: to see to it that his clothes would still be there when he was done. Once, when he'd been late, he'd run off with his shoes on, kicked them off somewhere, and never seen them again. *And I'd had them only a week. Damn you.*

It had begun when he was fifteen and still living in Placerville. He'd woken from a confused dream, the kind of dream they'd told him in health ed was only natural and normal, to find that he wasn't in bed anymore. He was out in the foothills a mile from home, wearing nothing but the legless shreds of his pajama bottoms. It was four o'clock in the morning with the moon going down, and a sheep was lying between his feet with its throat torn out.

He had managed to get home and wash without anyone's seeing him. His mother eventually asked after the missing pajamas, but had taken "I dunno; I put them in the laundry and that's the last I saw of them" for an answer. By then it was a month later, and it had happened again.

After the third time there was an article in the local paper: somebody had seen a big timber wolf among the sheep. He had fired both barrels of his shotgun into it, but it had run away as though it hadn't been touched.

Of course not, stupid, he'd thought when he read that. *You need a silver bullet.*

They might have figured that out too, eventually, but at the end of that year he graduated from high school and went to Berkeley. It was easier to cover up there; nobody knew what you did or where you went, and not even the University challenged you on it so long as you kept your grades up. His roommate was an engineering major who wasn't into noticing little things like a roomie who never came home one night a month.

He never remembered afterward what had happened, though sometimes there would be clues left behind: a line or two of newspaper story, a sheep or deer or dog lying half-eaten at his feet. Never a human being, not yet; thank God.

Once he had gone to the Newman Hall just before moonrise, hoping—he didn't know what. Maybe that the holy influence would subdue him, or that some traditionalist priest would have the presence of mind to read an exorcism? In any event, he'd woken up in Tilden anyway—apparently the holy influence had been enough to send him running like hell into the hills. Occasionally he still toyed with the idea of telling one of the chaplains what was going on. They might even believe him—the Paulist Fathers were pretty practical types, and this was Berkeley, after all. Or he could go join a peace march and get himself arrested—but they might not put him in solitary, and God help anybody they gave him for a cellmate.

Six to ten hours a month, moonrise till sometime after midnight. If clouds covered the moon it didn't last as long, but he'd make it up the following month. It was worse than being a girl. His sister had rotten cramps for three days a month; he fetched her aspirin when he was at home, and hot water bottles, and carefully didn't mention that he would have traded anytime. So far as he'd been able to learn—it wasn't the sort of thing you could come out and ask your parents about—he was the only one in the family.

But the family name meant "wolf," so maybe it had happened before. He spent his first couple of years as a biology major, and learned a bit about dominant and recessive genes, but nothing that helped. After that he'd switched to prelaw, figuring he might need it.

Maybe he should have chosen premed instead, as an excuse for doing nothing at Berkeley but study. It went without saying that he had no social life. He had few acquaintances, no close friends, and he'd never dared to get close to girls. Rumors were beginning to circulate—lurid ones no doubt, but soap-opera stuff compared to the truth.

He'd wanted to make something out of his life—something still fuzzy and unclear to him at fifteen, and since then he hadn't dared to plan for anything better than staying alive. He found he was leaning against the bay laurel, his fingernails dug into its bark, the pungent smell of its leaves strong in his nostrils, while the light of the cruel moon poured down on him.

Something strange was going on: or rather, it wasn't going on. He looked up at the moon, down at his hands: white under the moonlight, fragile long-fingered things with flimsy nails. He was standing manshaped on two legs, while the full moon rode on high overhead, and even for August the air was cold against his naked skin. Something had happened.

He pulled his clothes out of the tree and got dressed. Slowly, not quite trusting his luck, he walked back down the path.

"The moon like a flower in heaven's high bower, with silent delight sits and smiles on the night." The speaker was invisible in the shadows where he stood, but easy to trace by his voice (and a wisp of pot smoke that reached out and grabbed one by the nostrils).

"What did you say?"

"I said, wow, man, look at the moon. You wouldn't think, from here, those bastards had been walking on it. America's hero, Neil Armstrong," he said bitterly. "He's taken all the magic out of the moon. Hey, you got any spare change?"

"Will paper do?" He fumbled a bill out of his wallet, saw it was a five, and gave it to him anyway. He paced down Telegraph, avoiding curbs and power poles by dead reckoning, thinking hard. He would go into the space program—no, he couldn't, spacemen had to be small enough to fit into the capsules, and he was already six feet two and probably still growing. He'd go into engineering like his roommate; no, by God, he'd stay in law and go into politics—

"Fifty meters," said the speaker. Chin balanced on his clasped hands, his eyes fixed on the readout screen, Senator Vilkas looked like an elderly abbot in prayer. Completing the image, his lips were moving silently: not "Pater Noster," but "seventeen, sixteen, fifteen . . ."

"In fact, the *Bifrost* landed about half an hour ago," Martin was saying, while his autocamera panned slowly between the screen and his face. "But their signal, traveling at lightspeed, takes half an hour to reach us. In a few moments we should know whether they made it. Senator Vilkas, do you have anything to say on this historic occas—"

"Hush," Vilkas said. "Let's listen."

There was a burst of static that flared up and died away. "The *Bifrost* has landed. Our touchdown time was 06:22:14"—but the room had erupted into cheers.

"The *Bifrost* has landed safely on the surface of Mars," Martin told the autocamera. "In about an hour, if everything checks out, Commander Hunter will open the hatch and become the first man to set foot on Mars—really, in half an hour, but because of the time delay—"

"That's a point," Vilkas said, suddenly taking notice of him. "Does it count when it *happens,* or when we find out about it? Marty, let's see your scan." He glanced over the headlines: war in Pan-Arabia, rioting in Calcutta, chaos in New York. Half an hour till man set his impudent foot on Mars. He settled back in his chair and waited for the fighting to stop.

About Jennifer Roberson
and "Final Exam"

I can't claim credit for discovering Jennifer Roberson; that honor, like so many others of discovering writers, belongs to my friend and mentor, Don Wollheim. He was, during my first years in science fiction, one of the few who always tried to publish fantasy, as opposed to the hard-core hard-technology fiction preferred during the forties and late fifties by John W. Campbell, and the (mostly young white male engineering) students who were the majority of articulate readers of science fiction in those days. Of course, many silent non-participating readers and writers of fantasy or weird fiction, as opposed to science fiction, were women; the majority of readers of hard-core science fiction were male, or if female, obsessed or themselves engineers or scientists, or would-be writers. But they didn't usually edit it (excepting the very knowledgeable Cele Goldberg at *Amazing Stories,* and one or two of John Campbell's assistants).

Don, perhaps freed from fears about his own masculinity by one of the few remarkably stable marriages in the whole of the genre—he alone among the noteworthy editors of his day remained married to his first wife (who is now, with his daughter, at the head of his DAW Books)—Don, like me, never lost his delight in discovering good writers. In the last year of his life, stopping in at DAW to pay my respects, I found him chuckling with delight at something he'd just discovered in the slush. He discovered more writers than anyone else in the field, and while he once spoke very dismissively of a well-known fan publisher, saying that he "was and always would be an amateur," as opposed to a professional, he never tired of discovering new talent. I freely admit that without his belief and help, there would be no such writer or editor as Marion Zimmer Bradley. And if they wanted to tell the truth, a lot of other writers would have to say the same. Of course, almost all of them deserted him for other publishers as soon as they could get bigger advances elsewhere. And I must say that he encouraged them all to spread their wings.

So Don, who was a father to all of us in the fifties, must take credit for formally discovering Jennifer. Due to the accidents of the schedule, I actually published her first short story while her first novel was in production at DAW. But it was he who suggested I get in touch with her.

I think this is a fun story. I'll bet you will, too, after you read it.

Final Exam

Jennifer Roberson

He was, she thought, a rather ordinary man. Certainly unremarkable in looks, although his eyes were rather nice. Warm, brown eyes, but just a trifle myopic; he peered back at her worriedly. She found this rather amusing, in view of the circumstances.

A distinctly common young man, she thought, nodding to herself. Nice eyes, yes, but then eyes weren't everything, were they? His other attributes, such as they were, were clearly nondescript. Mousy brown hair (clean but in need of cutting); features of a distinctly average cast (although the nose was a *bit* too long); and the height and weight of at least half a hundred men who inhabited her father's castle, which made him utterly ordinary and not in the least heroic.

But then, he wasn't a hero, so she supposed it didn't matter.

She chewed her bottom lip, thinking of her father. No doubt he would worry, once he came round to it. After all, his youngest daughter had disappeared through no fault of her own. It was entirely likely right at this very moment he was summoning up all the royal armies, since there was nothing else for them to do and setting them to the task of

14

combing the woods for her, threatening whippings for one and all if they didn't turn her up.

Well, they wouldn't. *He* had made sure of that.

He. *He* sat there peering at her myopically, wondering, now that he had her, what to do with her.

She sighed. Rearranged her skirts. Crossed her legs beneath the table and gazed straight back at him.

He also sighed. He didn't know what to say. And so he said the very first thing he could think of: "You *are* a virgin, aren't you?"

At home she would have been shocked, because being shocked was expected of her. But she wasn't at home at present and therefore the expected responses were completely unnecessary, which meant she could say whatever she felt.

What she felt was laughter; *this* wasn't what she had been warned by all of her chamber ladies to expect from ravishers. Supposedly, ravishers never asked such things, regarding virginity as unimportant, since, if she were one, she wouldn't be for much longer, and therefore it really didn't matter.

But he hadn't ravished her yet.

She lifted red eyebrows (not auburn; *red*) in the eloquent manner she had been most carefully taught. The peculiarly feminine language of elegantly arched brows was *meant* to convey carefully measured, outraged condescension. But she hadn't practiced much, and she wasn't very good at it; besides, her eyebrows always mutinied and remained rebelliously straight.

Still, it was up to her to *try*; her women had labored so hard.

"I beg your pardon?" She used the fluting, plummy tones all the other ladies of rank employed.

He blinked, reddened, attempted to loosen the high collar of his wheat-colored apprentice's tunic. "I'm sorry. I'm not doing this very well. I'm new at it, you see . . . you're my first victim."

"Am I?" She brightened. She was never first in anything, having four sisters in front of her.

He nodded gravely. "But I had to ask, you know. The spell requires a virgin."

"Spell?" She brightened still more. "You mean—magic?"

"Oh, yes." His embarrassment faded, replaced with indulgent self-confidence, which she thought alien to his open, boyish features and therefore looked a trifle odd. "It's all in the books, you know: the virgin daughter of a king."

Ah. Well, she *was* the daughter of a king. And she was a virgin. But she didn't tell him yet, hoarding it for herself. "A *gentleman* never asks."

The confidence disappeared. "He doesn't?"

"No."

"Then how does one find out?"

It was a fair question, she thought. But she didn't have an answer. "Perhaps one just *knows*."

"But I *don't* know." He was looking worried again. "It has to be a virgin. Otherwise it won't work."

She considered it a moment. Then leaned forward and asked, carefully, "*What* won't work?"

"The spell," he said testily. "I told you that already."

"Yes, well, you have . . . but you haven't told me *why*." She set an elbow against the table and leaned her chin into the heel of her hand. "I think it's only fair, me knowing why. After all, you *did* bring me here against my will."

"I did, didn't I?" His tone and expression were glum. "Well, I'm sorry if I frightened you . . . but I was only doing what I was told."

"To steal women."

"To steal *a* woman," he clarified. "Specifically, the virgin daughter of a king." He shrugged. "I might have asked—I'm the sort who would *rather* ask, really—but the books all said it was quite impossible to find a *willing* virgin princess, so I'd better be ready to steal one." He sighed. "If I wanted the spell to work."

"Which, of course, you do." She nodded angrily, then leaned farther forward yet. "What is this spell *for*?"

He brightened. Apparently even this young man, caught squarely between boyhood and adulthood, enjoyed doing the one thing she'd learned all men liked to do: talk about himself.

"It's for my final exam," he explained. "I'm only an apprentice wizard, you see . . . but I'm behind all the others. If I fail this time, they'll dismiss me from school and I'll *never* graduate."

She frowned; she herself disliked lessons, preferring instead to sit in a window seat and dream. Or to read a book, which, she had been told numerous times, was really quite the same.

"Would it be so bad if you *were* dismissed? I mean, what kind of a school expects young men to steal young women simply to satisfy graduation requirements?"

He sighed heavily. "This one does, I'm afraid. It's stated clearly in the catalogue: 'in order to graduate, all spells must be completed according to the requirements of the various courses included in the student's specific curricula.' "

She nodded; an exacting requisite. "Which course is this one you've stolen me for?"

He drew himself up on his stool. "I am not allowed to say."

She was astonished. After all, he'd *stolen* her—the least he could do was say why.

Explicitly, she told him so.

He was visibly deflated and visibly depressed. "You have a point," he agreed, "but it says nothing at all in the books about the virgin princess knowing about the spell."

"Well, *this* princess wants to know," she declared, purposely leaving out the word *virgin,* which she was, but now thought it a distinct disadvantage, in view of the circumstances. "You really are being quite unfair, you know, regardless of what it says in the books. I mean, a lady likes to be prepared. She likes to know who—*whom*—she might be meeting, or where she might be going . . . will it be an intimate dinner, or a full-blown festive feast?" She smiled, trying not to sound terribly pompous; he was not the sort of young man who would know about feasts or intimate dinners. "You must understand, of course, that a princess has to know these things. It just isn't fair to surprise her, because she can't do her job."

He sighed. "But if I told you, and you didn't like it, what would I do then?"

She thought about it. "Well, you could put a binding spell on me so I couldn't run away. Or perhaps make me temporarily mute." She shrugged. "That's a popular spell, particularly with mothers-in-law."

He considered it, nodding thoughtfully. Then sighed dolefully. "It's a Dragon Summoning."

That set her back on her stool. "What?"

"I need you to summon a dragon. You know, like in all the stories." He nodded encouragingly. "Virgins are gourmet items where dragons are concerned. The spell is guaranteed."

This really was too much. "I've read those stories, too," she said. "The dragon *devours* the virgin!"

He refused to look at her. "Yes, I'm afraid so. That's the way it always works."

She drummed fingers on the tabletop. "I'd really prefer not to be devoured."

His expression was apologetic. "I'm afraid you have no choice. It's only *after* the dragon's eaten that it's safe to take a tooth, because then he's deeply asleep."

She frowned. "Why do you want a tooth?"

"To prove I summoned the dragon." He spread his hands ruefully. "The professors don't really want a whole dragon, you see—he wouldn't fit in the dorms and we can't keep feeding him people—but they need proof the spell worked."

"And so they want a tooth."

He nodded, saying nothing.

She sighed, frowning in irritation. "I really don't want to be devoured. I'm game for a lot of things, but that's not one of them." She saw the look on his face; a combination of dismay and determination. "Of course, it's all academic anyway."

Mouse-brown eyebrows lowered. "Why?"

Coyly, she batted lashes. "Because I'm not a virgin."

He was horrified. "Not?"

"Not."

"At all?"

"At *all*; either you are or you aren't." She began to smile, caught up in embroidery. "It was quite a scandal, you know. Here I was, the youngest of the king's daughters, and no virginity. My father threatened to beat me blue, but my mother said to ignore it." She shrugged. "I'm only a *fifth* daughter, which means they can marry me off to some liquorish old man who wouldn't know the difference between a virgin ewe and a virgin woman." She sighed dramatically. "It was really quite a to-do."

"Yes, I can imagine." He was plainly agitated. "What about your sisters? Four of them, you said?"

She scowled. Lying, she saw, didn't always have the desired results. And as much as she resented her four sisters for being born before she was (the hand-me-downs were already so badly worn), she didn't really want any of them devoured any more than herself.

"They're all married," she lied, "and some of them even have babies."

He sank into deep despair. "I'll *never* graduate."

She shook her head. "There may be another way."

"How?" he inquired glumly.

"Bring me this book of spells."

Aghast, he said, "I *can't*."

"Can't, or won't?" She stabbed the table with a finger. "Bring it here, *now*. I know you must have homework . . . well, then, you must have a textbook as well."

He sighed. Got up and went to a shelf. Brought back a battered book. "Used," he said. "All the new ones were gone."

"Show me the spell," she told him. "Maybe there's something you're missing."

He peeled back the pages, then pointed to one of the incantations. "That one," he said. "I have everything I need— except, of course, the virgin."

Frowning, she read the ingredients. Indeed, it did appear complete. But she thought there still might be a way. "Throw out the bat," she said. "Replace it with eye of newt."

"There already *is* eye of newt." His finger indicated the ingredient.

"Get *another* eye of newt—don't they have two, after all? But the bat's got to go."

"But that's what the spell calls for . . . right here. It says, 'one bat, stripped of hair.'" He shrugged. "I guess dragons don't like hair.

Her hand strayed to her own. "I've got hair."

"Maybe it's only bat hair."

She made a moue of distaste, wrinkling her nose. "Well,

anyway it doesn't matter. Get rid of that bat as well as the hair, and bring me an eye of newt."

"I hope you know what you're doing."

"Oh, yes; I'm a very good tutor, and *I've* already graduated." That too was a lie, but she thought it worth a try. She closed the book and rose. "Collect the things you need and let's go summon a dragon."

They went, but only after she promised not to try and escape. At length she agreed—since she knew he'd put a spell on her if she didn't—which made him happy, since *he* knew his spell might go awry and turn her into a toad, or something equally distasteful.

Not far from the Wall of Night, which encircled the school buildings and hid them from prying eyes, was a small clearing in the forest. The small clearing boasted very flat ground, withered vegetation, a post adorned with chains, and a carpet of gritty ash. It was a lab used expressly for Dragon Summoning, since not even the professors wanted a dragon inside the Wall of Night.

She stamped around the clearing, raising choking grayish clouds, and held up embroidered skirts. "This place could use a woman."

He looked pointedly at post and chains. "This place has used *many* women."

"Yes, well, you know what I mean." She ignored the post entirely, looking instead at his lumpy bag. "Shouldn't you get about it?"

He sighed and knelt, untying his bag with a spoken word that did the work for him. That spell he knew very well. And then, laboriously, one by one, he drew from the bag various bottles and packets containing ingredients.

"—and two eyes of newt," he said, then paused. "Or is it eye of newts?"

She waved her hands. "Just do what you have to do."

He thought about it. "Well, first of all I have to put you in chains."

"Skip that part," she said hastily. "Go on with the summoning."

He frowned doubtfully. "But these things have to be done

just so. In a special way, and in a specific order. If I skip anything . . ." His voice trailed off dolefully.

"All right, very well—if it's that important to you . . ." She marched over to the post, slipped her wrists into the chains, pointedly left them unlocked. "This will do, I should think. The dragon will never know."

He scratched his head and began to assemble the ingredients in their proper order, putting them into the mortar. He chanted as he did it, pestling carefully, but she couldn't be certain if he was performing the ritual or just going over things by rote.

At last he was satisfied. Carefully he transferred all the litter to his bag, being inherently a neat person, then poured the mixture into an enameled bowl, which he then placed in the center of the clearing.

"It should work," he said, more for his own benefit than for hers, she thought. "I've followed directions carefully. Of course, I'm not certain about that second eye of newt—"

"Never *mind* the eye of newt." Loudly, she rattled her rusty chains. "Just finish the silly spell so I can get out of here."

"It seems odd that an eye of newt can substitute for a royal virgin," he murmured. "I mean, if it were true, you'd think the professors would be more interested in saving lives than in saving face."

He really *was* a stubborn individual. She rattled her chains again. "Just cast the spell, will you? I'd like to be home in time for dinner."

"Well, all right." He backed up, knelt, prepared himself. Then began chanting words she'd never heard.

The requisite dragon appeared on cue, astonishing them both. A large, lumpy dragon, appropriately green, blinking at them in a mild, dragonish way, clearly as surprised as they were.

"Well," the dragon observed. "I'd *planned* on going to bed."

The girl observed him closely. Something, she thought, was wrong. "You're not smoking," she said.

"Oh, no—not anymore." The dragon shook his head. "The ordinance, you know."

The apprentice wizard sighed. "Then I *did* do everything right."

"Wellll . . ." The dragon tilted his head from side to side, "that depends on what you intended. "I *am* a dragon, yes, but not quite a normal one."

The apprentice wizard froze. "Not?"

"Not." The dragon chewed a toenail. "I'm a bit of a health nut, you know. No red meat for me. Which is why I came, of course—you left out that disgusting bat."

In her unlocked chains, she gasped. "You mean—"

"I mean I'm a vegetarian." The dragon chewed another nail. "It's really much better for you. No more brittle bones to worry about, no more unnecessary carnage." Thoughtfully, he smiled. "I should think the virgins particularly would be grateful."

"Well," she said finally, "no more need for these." And she shed her noisy chains and moved away from the post.

The dragon cast her a jaundiced glance. "Tricky virgin, aren't you? But what if I *did* eat meat?"

The apprentice gaped at her. "You mean you *are*—"

"Of course," she replied airily. "I'm a very *picky,* tricky woman."

"Now," rumbled the nonsmoking dragon, "what was it you wanted me for?"

"A tooth," the apprentice answered. "Have you one to spare?"

"Oh, several . . . at my age I lose a lot. But why do *you* want one?"

"So I can pass my final exam. I need it to graduate."

"A worthy cause." The dragon twisted his massive jaws a moment, did something with his tongue, spat out a large tooth. "Broken a bit, I'm afraid, but it should be enough."

Carefully the apprentice picked it up and tucked it into a pocket. "Thank you very much."

"Don't mention it. I'm in favor of higher education." The dragon worked on a third toe, spat out excess nail. "Why don't you ask a kiss of the lady? You're due congratulations."

The young man reddened. "Me?"

"It won't kill you, you know."

Startled, the girl shook her head. "I'd really rather not."

The dragon stared down his nose. "Too high and mighty, are we? Too good for the likes of him?"

"No, no—it's not like that—"

"Then give him a kiss, my girl. Won't kill you, you know."

"I really don't think—"

The graduate scowled at her. "You're only a *fifth* daughter."

She scowled back. "That really isn't the point—"

"Then come here and give me a kiss!"

My, but he *was* domineering. Not at all the polite young man he'd been before they summoned the dragon; she wasn't sure she liked the change.

"Very well," she agreed at last, "but remember, I'm still a virgin. I don't really do it right."

He crossed the clearing to her. "That's all right. I do."

It was not a long kiss. Her kisses never were.

The dragon's smile faltered. In shock he forgot the ordinance and blew a crooked smoke ring. "Oh," he said, "one of *those*."

The princess looked down at the frog. "One hundred and *four*," she sighed.

About L. A. Taylor
and "Counterexample"

After a quarter of a century I thought I had seen every possible variation on the *Star Trek* story. *Star Trek* was responsible for the entry of many women into science fiction because the first television series of *Star Trek* presented many women. Not only in starring but in supporting roles; perhaps it was the wholesale entry of such women as "Christine Chapel"—actress Majel Barrett (in private life Mrs. Gene Roddenberry) or the singularly beautiful black actress Nichelle Nichols, as Uhura, both of them there on the bridge of the *Enterprise,* every week, and whatever people said, they were doing more than "opening hailing frequencies." And both women were definitely people in their own right and not just love objects for the men involved—women found for the first time serious science fiction role models of their own, not just the array of wives, daughters, and little sisters of the men involved. Well, after that, women came into science fiction in droves. Many readers, many fans, many artists, and more to the point here, from the ranks of *Star Trek* enthusiasts many excellent writers both amateur and professional.

Star Trek and my own Darkover share one thing; it seems to be easier, especially among women writers, to write of already familiar characters—be they from Darkover or *Star Trek*—than to create one's own.

After a very bad experience I have most reluctantly had to close the Darkover universe to other writers, and now I belatedly understand Roddenberry's intransigence—like that of Conan Doyle—with his literary property.

However, this story infringes no literary copyright in *Star Trek*, nor, as far as I know, anywhere else. This story is just good fun about a young girl who went a bit far in her enthusiasm for the *Star Trek* characters.

Be all that as it may, I am presenting probably the most interesting spin-off of the *Star Trek* universe ever to come to my attention.

Laurie Aylma Taylor likes to explore that no-man's-land between genres; she writes mainstream fiction, mysteries, science fiction, and fantasy. In addition to her short fiction, she has published nine novels, and her next novel, *Cat's Paw*, will be out from Berkley Books in March 1995.

Counterexample

L. A. Taylor

"**W**hat? You mean you haven't told them?" Allyssa strolled toward me, thumbs hooked over her hipbones and fingers spread on her back. The old scowl creased her forehead.

"That's right." I leaned forward and set my glass of sherry on the coffee table.

"Don't you think you've left it a little late? Tammie's nearly sixteen already."

"No, I don't think I've left it a little late." Slightly cowed, as usual, by my big sister, I glanced regretfully at the glass I'd just set down. Too soon to pick it up, and I'd probably gulp the whole thing at a swallow if I did. "I'm not sure I'm going to tell them at all."

"What?"

We could be twins, if Allyssa weren't two years older than me. Does that mean we have to think exactly the same way? Not if I can help it. "Can you give me any good reason?"

"Well, but, but—"

"You aren't the one with children," I pointed out as she sputtered.

"I chose not to have daughters. You know that."

Allyssa sounded defensive. Maybe I'd get out of this yet. "So don't tell me how to handle mine."

Through her teeth, hissing, a threat: "Husbands. Lovers. Semen-engendered sons!"

Shaking inside, I raised one eyebrow casually.

"Women have lived with them for generations."

"Other women! Not us!"

The front door slammed. "Mom? I'm home," called my youngest. Allyssa whirled and pretended to be pulling dead leaves out of the spider plant hanging in the wide east window. A round red spot, like inexpertly applied blusher, burned on the cheek I could see.

Julie dropped a stack of books onto the coffee table and plunked down beside me on the couch. "Hey," she said. "What's up?"

"Nothing much," my sister said steadily. "Why don't you go find yourself a snack?" With Julie safely in the kitchen, Allyssa flashed me a glance that would have left me trembling twenty years before. "We will continue this discussion later," she said, and reached for the green sherry bottle.

I am still ill-suited to being the mother of three female Trekkies, which, alas, I am. Their discovery of, and enthusiasm for, what in my estimation is a rather mundane television series, its spin-offs, and endless, endless reruns, has led me into a year of serious self-examination, as I suppose was both inevitable and overdue. Still: what girls think significant is really quite minor—the two in love with Mr. Spock, for instance, are thrilled to have inherited my upswept brows, but are disappointed in my neat round ears; the one who favors Captain Kirk resents the browline she must carry but finds the ears quite pleasing. Amusing, in a way. When my hand falls naturally to lap or knee or over one of my daughters' shoulders, a space appears between the ring and middle fingers and the outer pairs of fingers lie together. Somehow none of them noticed this in pre-*Trek* days. Now—

"Will you stop making fun of Spock!" Tammie demands, with all evidence of the family temper.

"Mom, do you have to do that?" Kendra whines.

The one raised brow—a signal Tammie knew perfectly well at the age of three meant 'stop what you're doing this instant and mind your manners'—she now takes to be derision, directed at her hero. When enlightened I raised both eyebrows slightly, chin rising. When presented with a new idea, I am likely (like my grandmother) to murmur, "Interesting . . ." I am poker-faced. I am solitary. Need I say more? Any human mother of a teenage girl will know my Spock fans barely tolerate what they believe to be sneering at the Vulcan, and that the Kirk fan, for different reasons, likes none of it any better. Fortunately, when cut I bleed as red as any woman ever did. If my blood were as green as Spock's, they'd probably think I'd arranged that to mock the Vulcan, too.

And then, I am a scientist.

This gives me little trouble with my Kirk fan, who is mostly concerned to retrain the way her fingers fall when her hand relaxes. The—what shall I call them? Spockies? Spockettes?—are of the impression that their hero represents the highest reach of scientific endeavor known to man. True, Spock shows curiosity, essential to any scientist, but, so far as I can see in my occasional trips past the television when the nightly rerun is on, he does so only when convenient to the plot line. His celebrated "logic-alone" is a poor tool for real inquiry, which proceeds by hunch and hump, and drags in design and argument as necessary afterthought. The burning desire to know, to figure it out, Spock seems to lack. Through his example my daughters believe that science proves things, and remain quite unaware of the power of the counterexample to demolish an otherwise attractive hypothesis.

Infuriating. Well, I'll allow that science does establish facts, as I have established to my satisfaction that my mother's conjecture was correct: like summer aphids, I and mine are haploid in every cell.

Now you know: I'm a geneticist.

I have three haploid daughters—that is, they, too, have only twenty-three chromosomes in each cell, half the normal number for a human being. I can only conclude that our egg cells are formed through mitosis rather than the usual meiosis, which would more or less halve the number of chromosomes yet again: how else to explain generation upon generation of parthenogenesis? I suppose I might mate with a human male and conceive a child. The sexual act is not only possible but enjoyable, the number of my chromosomes would be correct, and so far as I can determine they would form the proper pairs. I have no direct proof of this. I can't exactly pop a laparoscope through my own belly button and prise out an egg to slosh in a dish with stolen sperm; the more direct form of the experiment does not appeal to me at the age of forty-five. Such a pairing would also be the end of the line of my kind, whatever we may be. Strangers who meet me with my daughters and turn, smiling, to say, "You must have strong genes," have put their innocent fingers directly on the problem.

I was born in April of 1943. My "father," a fictional creation, was supposed to have died in the Pacific. Wars have, historically, always provided us with good excuse for fatherless children. (My mother was born in 1917.) I used the Vietnam War to explain my oldest (1971); its extension, post-traumatic stress syndrome, to explain the "desertion" by the "father" of the middle one (1972); and plain brazened it out with the last (1974). Fifteen months apart is close spacing—ask anyone with three kids in diapers—but I wanted three, and I wasn't getting any younger. We, like normal human women, have our menopause, our imperfect copies.

Given present mores, my daughters, should they choose to have girls of their own—sons, you understand, are impossible—will have less trouble. Should they choose. The meditation needed is arduous even to learn. Perhaps they'll just find fathers for their children and our line will simply cease. As Allyssa discovered this afternoon, I haven't yet decided to tell my daughters how different they are from their friends. In a way I suppose I should be grateful to Leonard Nimoy for creating Mr. Spock to absorb the affections of my oldest. He's given me more time to dither.

Watching my children grow has proven—ah, hell, I'll say it—fascinating. I have filled dozens of notebooks showing the effects of nature versus nurture, studies on these clones of myself that I can never publish. Genes, for example, determine that moles will appear on the skin, but not where; they determine build, but not the fine detail of skeletal structure that sets one of my children off from the others; they determine the outline of personality, but not the ways in which it is expressed. All of us are intelligent although our interests vary; none of us has ever been tidy, not even those few adopted out.

"Well," Allyssa said when the door closed behind the last of the girls the next morning. "Have you come to your senses since yesterday?"

"Have you come to yours?" I coolly—I hoped—poured another cup of coffee and sat down with it. "And aren't those my jeans?"

Allyssa glanced down at her long pinstriped legs. "It's just until I get my laundry done."

"You could have asked," pressing my advantage.

"I didn't think you'd be so stingy." Parry and riposte. *En garde!* Mother of Trekkies.

I let my right eyebrow rise slightly, unhampered by cries of *Oh, Mother!*, and sipped at the coffee. Allyssa glanced at me and walked away, down the length of the kitchen, her hands cupped behind her back, head down. Like our mother, like our grandmother. Like every one of us forever, for all I know. Are family gestures genetic? Or something imprinted on the infant brain? I know no way to tell without giving myself away. At the end of the kitchen my sister wheeled on one heel and came back.

"Do you have any idea what you'd be ending?"

"No." I set the cup down carefully, willing it not to chatter against the saucer. "Do you?"

"Gramma had records back to 1512."

"1512 is not 1988."

"Not as easy," Allyssa flashed. "What they went through, those women, our mothers—drowned as witches, put to the stake, condemned as adulterers—"

"And because of their troubles you think my daughters should go on reproducing like—like gussied-up paramecia?"

"Have you no sense of history?"

"Maybe not." I got up, put the cup in the sink, and faced her. "But I do have children. And you don't."

"If Mother were here—"

"But she's not."

We both fell quiet. Mother's plane crashed into Boston Harbor, its engines stuffed with birds, just after I started college. Allyssa was a research technician in a hematology lab at the time; the cool blues and purples of the while cells she showed me through her microscope were what first pulled me toward genetics as a profession. That, and my own quandary as to what I am.

"If you don't tell them, I will," Allyssa said.

"Get out of my house."

She went, of course. I may be poker-faced, but I can be roused. I have the family temper. The family stubbornness. Pigheadedness, Gramma called it.

The family.

We are human, I am absolutely sure. Somehow, some centuries ago, some woman, our ancestor, yearned so strongly for a child that she learned to have one by herself. Perhaps she was isolated, alone, and too poor or proud to be married. Perhaps her husband preferred another. Perhaps she had access to some powerful form of self-shaping other humans have forgotten. I don't know. All I know is that her daughter was slender and agile, had neat round ears, eyebrows that swept upward at the outer end, eyes of a clear greenish brown, and hair that was glossy and dark. The girl would have tanned easily, if she'd exposed herself to the sun, and had a small straight nose and a wide mouth whose lower lip quirked inward as she smiled.

Here is my evidence: I have 0 positive blood (the rhesus antigen for which I am positive is D). I lack no other human blood factors. Put a drop of my blood between two coverslips and pull, stain the dried smear with Wright's, and under the microscope you will see biconcave red cells, polymorpholeucocytes in their infinite variety, the dull-blue stodginess of monocytes, lymphocytes with sky-clear cytoplasm. Hemoglobin prepared from what flows in my veins travels with normal hemoglobin A when electrophoresed. Doctors who order other biochemical assays for routine physicals have never found an abnormal value. My electrocardiogram is normal. The one chest X ray I had before they went out of style showed ribs, lungs, the dome of the diaphragm and liver, and spleen nestled beneath it. I nursed my babies, six months each. Nothing, other than a chromosome study, would show me to be what I am. Then, the long line of women so alike—we must be derived from human beings. What else could we be?

A month gone since those meanderings. Allyssa has sent me a copy of our grandmother's records. Just as I suspected, every third or fourth generation, the sad little note: someone got married, had a son, had a daughter that more resembled first one parent and then the other, in the ordinary way.

It has been nearly four months since I wrote those words. I am so furious, I can barely hold my pen.

Allyssa has made good her threat. How could she think she knows my daughters better than I do myself? Has she forgotten how stubborn we can be, the risks we sometimes take? How often we demand proof, the proof that things are as someone has stated them to be? She must be insane!

The upshot of it is that Tammie is pregnant. Her grades have fallen this semester; she's been spending her time in meditation. I have demanded that she abort. She refuses. She says, quite coolly, that the school has made provisions for girls who get pregnant and that she can continue to attend. She is due at the end of July; she will have the rest of the summer to make arrangements for someone to keep the baby while she is in school. Her devoted aunt calls me, crestfallen and apologetic, and what the hell good is that supposed to do? The other two are all agog: I suspect that Julie, at the age, God help us, of fourteen is also plotting reproduction. I have talked myself blue about the problems of teenage pregnancies—the greater probability of birth defects, the effects upon the mother's education and career, to say nothing of her health . . .

And to top it off comes the school social worker with a

sticky frosted pink smile and "If you could please just try to persuade Tamara to tell us the name of the father, we feel the boys need counseling too . . ." She was lucky to get out of my house alive, although she probably doesn't realize it. What, dear Allyssa, am I to do?

What could I do but continue to work? Go to the lab every day for the past four months, play with frogs, unravel their dumb DNA. Parthenogenesis has been known to occur in frogs. A clue. Hah!

And meanwhile, attempt to educate my child. I can't imagine what the schools in this country are coming to. Just before New Year's, during school vacation, Tammie came dreamily downstairs one morning and said, "I can't wait to see my son."

"Tammie," I pulled out the chair at her place. "Sit down."

She sat, with a sweet patient smile.

"You will have a daughter."

"No."

"Daughter. Girl. Female-type person."

"No."

"Look," I sighed. "In normal human beings, the sex of the child is determined by the father. He contributes either an X or a Y chromosome—X for female, Y for male—and one single gene on the Y chromosome, not anything that comes from the mother, is what decides whether the baby is a boy or a girl."

"I know that," Tammie replied, still sweet, still patient. "I learned that years ago, Mother." She got up and pulled the Cheerios out of the cupboard.

"We only have X chromosomes," I said. "So we can only have girls. It's always that way, throughout the animal kingdom. When parthenogenesis occurs, the children are always daughters."

"Are you going to tell me about aphids again? I'm not an aphid."

"Look," I said. Tammie poured Cheerios into a bowl, added 2% milk and put the bottle back into the refrigerator, sprinkled half the brown sugar she'd normally use onto the cereal.

"Mom," she said. "The trouble with you is that you have no imagination."

"Darling," I said—sometimes I can't help sarcasm—"I do have history!"

"History is what's done with." Tammie tilted her chair onto its hind legs and leaned back to open the silverware drawer for the forgotten spoon. "My son isn't history. Not yet."

"Don't do that. You'll wreck the chair," was what came out of my mouth. Tammie let it thump back down with a grin, and started to eat. Over the next few weeks I tried everything I could think of to shake her conviction. I brought books home from my office—"Mother, that's human biology," Tammie protested.

"We are human."

"How could we be?"

"How could we not?"

She smiled, so sweet, so patient I could have smacked her. I marshaled my evidence. My child—who is at least as intelligent as any of the rest of us—refused to be swayed. I discoursed upon the nature of inquiry. Upon inductive reasoning in general. I even took her into the lab and showed her my frogs, squatting droopily in their tanks, waiting for someone to toss a crumb of hamburger into the air for them.

Tammie enjoyed feeding the frogs.

Spring came. My daughter rounded out, first a thickening of her waist, then a gentle mounding below her navel, pressing ever higher. She studied dutifully, daydreamed about her "son," watched *Star Trek* with her sisters. Back around Valentine's Day she began signing her name T'Ami, Vulcan-style. Some of my fears were allayed: Julie remained her usual active self. She couldn't possibly have had time for the requisite meditation.

July 12—Tammie's water broke yesterday morning, two weeks early. She said nothing about it. Therefore, no one called the doctor. In the early stages of labor she was able to conceal the contractions long enough to camp in front of the TV for *Star Trek* reruns; once hard labor set in, she locked herself in her room. Only when the baby was nearly crowning did she drag herself off her bed and let me into the room to help.

I wish I hadn't. I wish I had sent her far away to have this baby, where no one we know . . . no. No. No, I don't.

My life, the whole structure of what I am, has fallen apart. The child, thank Heaven, lived only a minute or two. Why, I'm not sure. He seemed perfectly formed, from his tiny toenails to the tips of his pointed ears. The placenta was a sappy green; it smelled like sweet corn just torn from its stalk, the tang of crushed grass with a musty undertone. "Copper instead of iron in the hemoglobin," Tammie informed me smugly. "Type T negative," whatever that may be. Well, why not? If a plant can put magnesium where iron should be and get a type of chlorophyll, if a horseshoe crab can similarly use copper and come up with the blue blood of a nobleman . . . oh, Tammie! Is that it? Did you get the valence of the copper wrong?

Tammie also told me her son's heart would be where one would expect the liver; she was quite correct. About the other internal organs, she wasn't sure. They were rather a mishmash, but I saw no obvious reason why they shouldn't have worked. Everything connected.

Later, once she's rested, I'll try to get her to tell me how she did it. How she arranged the chromosomes she came with to construct this semi-Vulcan child born of a popular fiction and a—a what? Later, we will make a plan. How to conceal this birth, how to divert suspicion. Tammie can't help with that, not yet. Just now, she is upstairs, weeping.

Am I? All this time, these years, I've thought that somehow I was human, like all of you around me. That if I wanted, anytime I wanted, I could slip into the great stream of human history and take my place, like any woman with forty-six chromosomes in all but a few hundred of her cells. My own "normality," the long unimaginative line of women exactly like myself, the occasional fertile marriages among them, seemed proof enough. That's the trouble with scientific hypothesis, I tell myself bitterly. It is always vulnerable to the counterexample.

What am I? Where could I have come from, those generations ago? And why?

Women have had children alone since recorded time began. How many others, with other builds and other features, are like me? Do they know? They must!

Sisters, please, show me your faces! Soon!

About Mary C. Aldridge and "The Adinkra Cloth"

I have one secret hate; when someone describes a book or a movie to me as "heartwarming," I know it is likely to be soppy, saccharine, and otherwise not worth reading. I would never have so stigmatized this story from our third issue, which was one of the half-dozen stories in its year to make the final Nebula balloting. It also took first place in our Cauldron vote. It was, and is, a fine, strong story with the feel of an African folk tale.

In the final balloting, it did not win the Nebula. I have no idea what won it that year, but I'll bet a ripe peach—or plum, or any other piece of fruit you prefer—that it wasn't as good as this. I still consider this one of the best stories we've ever printed.

And if you should ask why editors always speak of themselves in the plural—"the editorial we" being used only by royalty, editors, and people with tapeworms—I can say only that I haven't the least idea.

The Adinkra Cloth

Mary C. Aldridge

Our mother was dying: grief ate her heart like a witch. On the night of her death, she called me to her side. "Oliasso, oldest of my sons, you have twelve years now, but you are not strong enough to fight your father's brother, and I am too weak to call my own brother to help you. When I am dead, you children will be defenseless. So do what I tell you: take my body into the bush, dig a pit, and wrap me in the adinkra cloth from my marriage chest. Lay a fire in the pit and leave me there for two days. The cloth will not burn; when you open it, you will find my ashes. Then take clay from the riverbed; rub my ashes into the clay, make a bowl and color it red. Wrap it in the adinkra cloth and lay it on my death-fire. In one day, the bowl will be cooked. Roll up the cloth and bring it out and say, 'Our Mother, we are hungry.' Then you will see what happens. Also, keep the adinkra cloth. Keep—" She stopped speaking and closed her eyes. Grief was done with her.

When I had wept, I opened the marriage chest that her twin brother, the Lord Mbanyo, had carved for her many years ago, in the far land of her birth. Inside the chest were things she had brought from her home, which belonged only to her: silver bracelets and rings, brass necklaces, images of strange gods done in bronze. There were three little stone jars whose contents I could not guess. At the bottom of the chest, neatly rolled, was the adinkra cloth. It was blue cotton, patterned with black spirit signs. I removed it, brought it to the bed, and carefully wrapped it around our mother.

I woke my little brothers. The four of us bent our backs to lift her. Even though we were but four children, our mother's body was light in our arms, as if the adinkra cloth were filled with gentle thoughts. We carried her out of the house. It was the dry season, and a full moon shone on the still compound that once had been our father's. Now his younger brother claimed all the goods and people in the compound. Most of all he coveted our mother for the magic he believed she had; but he would never have her now.

We crept in silence out the compound gate and made our way down the village street. The night was as hushed as if the moon had poured out a sleeping potion over animals and people.

Chami, the youngest of us, was afraid to go into the bush. He was only four years old. I told him, "You must come, our mother asked this. Don't you think her spirit is here, watching you?"

He dried his tears and came with us. The woods whispered as the dead who could not rest came to see what we were doing. We couldn't see them, but I felt their presence. I said, "Forgive us, dead people, for entering your home. I have a task to do for my mother."

The dead withdrew respectfully. It was not so bad after that. Ilomi, who was ten, carried a spade, and so did Kiwaso, who was seven. We dug the pit, not very deep, and I laid the fire in it. When the fire died, we lifted our mother's body in the adinkra cloth; again it was very light. We placed her on the coals.

Chami and Kiwaso began to cry. Ilomi and I comforted them; then we went home.

For two days, we left our mother in the pit. It was only the next morning after we put her there when Uncle came to the house. I stopped him in the yard. I bowed. "Our mother is no better; she can't see you."

Our uncle was a tall, strong man. When he was angry, he

looked fierce. "Tell her she must see me. I am her husband now. Tell her."

I went into the house and came out again. "Our mother has blood. She says you must go away."

Uncle looked disgusted. He hated such things and sent his own wives away when their bleeding came. "Tell her I will be back. I will be back as her husband."

When the two days were over, we went by night to the bush. We opened the cloth. It was not burnt. Inside were white ashes. I closed the cloth, and we went to the river, waded into the cool water, and dug clay. I sat on the bank and sprinkled the ashes into the clay, then worked the clay into a bowl.

Chami, squatting beside me, asked, "Why are you putting Mama in a bowl?"

"Shh," said Ilomi.

I painted the bowl red with seed dyes and wrapped it in the adinkra cloth. We went back into the bush and placed the bowl in the death-fire, which was still glowing.

The next day, my father's first wife came to our house. She was one of the brides his father had chosen. She was brown, like all my father's people. Only our mother was black. She said, "Tell my sister I have come. She must not continue to refuse our husband's brother. She is no better than the rest of us. I will speak with her."

I went in and came out. "My mother says she dreamed last night of a jar that would not open." The first wife retreated a step, for she was pregnant with our father's last child. I hardly had to say, "Mother does not dare speak with you until the dream's influence is gone," for our father's first wife was already hurrying down the path to her own house.

I went inside. The little ones were eating my meal-cakes, which had big dry lumps of raw meal in them. The other wives hadn't asked us to share with them after our father died and our mother became sick.

Ilomi said, "Oliasso, what will they do when they know our mother is dead?"

"And not here," added Kiwaso, putting down his cake. He gave it a sorrowful look.

I knew pretty well what Uncle would do, but I shrugged as

if it didn't matter. I sat down and took a cake. It was heavier than the ones our mother made. Only Chami was still eating, spreading his cakes with honey. I bit into the cake. Its crust was hard as coconut rind.

"Maybe," Kiwaso said, looking at his feet, "maybe Uncle will send a leopard after you."

Ilomi and I hissed together, "Never say that!" and Kiwaso looked frightened. Everyone except Chami stopped eating altogether.

We knew who the leopard was, who had killed our father.

That night, we left the village again and went to get the bowl. The night was inky, with clouds covering the sky. I felt spirits wandering unhappily and wished the other three boys could stay home. Surely something was going to happen. But mother would have expected us to do it together. I only wished the night felt less evil.

The bush spirits were whispering excitedly among themselves as we came to our mother's death-fire. Something brushed wetly against my cheek, and I jumped. It was only a leaf.

By the death-fire's glow, we unwrapped the adinkra cloth. The bowl was firm, and though it had been on the fire, it was cool enough to touch. I gave it to Ilomi to hold while I rolled up the adinkra cloth.

"I want to hold Mama," said Chami.

"You'll drop it," Ilomi said.

"No, I won't. Oliasso, please?"

"Yes, let him hold the bowl." I stuffed the adinkra cloth down my tunic and knotted my waist belt so it wouldn't fall. Chami giggled, dropped the bowl down his front, and tied his belt too. He looked pregnant.

"Stop playing," Ilomi scolded.

Kiwaso said softly, "Oh, Oliasso, look!"

He pointed.

Off through the trees, something was moving. Something black as the night around us. It came toward us, slinking through the brush; two green eyes pointed our way.

"A leopard!"

The same fearful thought held all of us rooted to the ground.

The leopard came into the clearing where the death-fire was. It was a big leopard, not spotted, but black from the tips of its ears to the tip of its tail. We could not move from fright. It circled us once, and I thought I felt its hot breath. Its green eyes glittered. It looked from me to Ilomi, from Ilomi to Kiwaso to Chami. Its tail switched. It began to stalk Chami, whose legs bent from fright. He sank to his knees and covered his face as the leopard came closer.

The leopard stopped. It gave a puzzled yowl and backed away.

Ilomi and I ran to Chami. I picked him up. The bowl in his tunic bumped against my chest. The leopard started to approach us again, then backed away very quickly and whimpered.

Ilomi grabbed Kiwaso's hand. We ran out of the clearing, back through the brush, all the way to the village and never looked back.

When we got home, I hid the cloth and bowl at the bottom of Mother's marriage chest, for my uncle had no claim on that.

Uncle came to us in the morning. He stormed up to the house, shoving me aside so I fell. I got up and followed him in as my three brothers quietly slipped out.

"Where is your mother?" he demanded, looking bigger than ever in our little house.

"Dead."

"Dead!" He seized the front of my tunic. A wild green light came into his eyes. "Where is her body?"

"I burned it in the bush!"

"Where? Show me!"

He dragged me out to the bush where the death-pit was, but it seemed to me he already knew the way. He looked at the empty, dead pit. He looked at me. "Where is the body?"

I looked away from his furious eyes. "Perhaps a leopard ate it."

He broke a switch off a thorny jitaio tree and began to beat me, saying, "Where is she? Where has she gone? Did she go back to that brother of hers? Tell me where she went!"

After a while we returned to the village. Uncle stood out in the street and complained loudly to the other men. "My foreign wife has run away! This boy claims she died, but there's no body!"

They all began to scold, demanding I tell them where my mother had gone. I kept repeating that she was dead and I had burned her up.

"She's run away," one of the old men said finally in disgust. "That's what comes of marrying foreigners. Your brother was ill-advised!"

"She's my wife now! I want her back!"

"But she's only trouble," the other men protested. "What do you want her for? You have her children, four fine boys. You have her pots, cloths, brass and silver bracelets. Take them and give them to your other wives, who are more deserving. And she was a hard worker, at least. Her granaries are full. Give that to your wives as well, and forget her!"

"I want her," Uncle said. "The young men must go to her land, to her brother Mbanyo, and bring her back."

"Oh, no!" the leader of the young men spoke up at once. "That's a great journey, and who knows what'll happen in a foreign land? Suppose we go all that way and Lord Mbanyo won't release her? Very likely she'll tell him a lot of lies about how badly she was treated here. They are twins; he'll believe anything she says. Who can win against a great lord in his own country? Besides, we have our own farms to think of."

"Yes, the land must be cleared!"

"Forget the woman," the other men urged.

Uncle's fists clenched; his face shook with anger. "And who is to feed her children? Why should my other wives work to fill their greedy mouths?"

"Someone has to feed children," the old men said. "Your dead brother's sons are your sons."

Now I clenched my fists. Never, never, never!

The old men said, "This is enough," and everybody walked away to go about their business. My uncle waited until they were all gone, then he grabbed my shoulder and dug in his fingers like iron talons.

"You know where she is," he hissed. "You'll pay!" He started dragging me to our mother's house in the compound. The bite of his fingers on my shoulder brought stinging tears to my eyes, and I had to grit my teeth to keep from crying. When we came to the house, he threw me inside and glared at all four of us.

"Does she think she can escape me? You are my sons now, and I shall use you as I please. And she will know. The witch will know, I'm sure. When she sees how I use you, your mother will come back and then she will do as I say!"

"But she—" began Chami.

Ilomi pinched him.

"She'll come," my uncle whispered. His face twisted with anger like a fearsome mask. "I will have the woman and her magic! My brother knew nothing." He sneered at us. I hid my fists behind my back. "He could have made you little princes. Far greater even than your uncle, the Lord Mbanyo, in your mother's country. When I have her magic, I can do that for you! Would you like to be princes and ride on fine steeds and wear gold, copper, and coral?"

"I would," Chami said breathlessly. "When?"

"When your mother comes back."

Chami laughed. "But she is—"

Ilomi slapped him. Chami rocked backwards with astonishment, and tears rushed from his eyes. He wailed, "Oliasso!"

I jumped up. "Shame on you, Ilomi, picking on the little one!"

"Yes, shame!" cried Kiwaso, meaning it. "Mama said to take care of our brother!"

Kiwaso and I continued to yell at Ilomi until our uncle got angry and shouted at us all to be quiet. But Chami wept and wouldn't talk to him anymore.

Uncle said, "Tomorrow you can all go out to the fields. The land must be cleared and broken for planting."

Ilomi looked astonished. "But that's men's work! We aren't strong enough to do that!"

"Do it or be beaten."

The next day we went to the fields. Uncle told each of us what to do. It was a grown man's work. The other men in the family muttered among themselves. Nobody dared speak up.

Years ago our uncle had gone to the city to study with the

magic men there. Now whenever something disturbing happened, people suspected him.

We had to clear the dry brush and chop up the land. It had been baking long months in the sun, hard work even for men. Ilomi and Kiwaso and I went first to work on Chami's part. My uncle watched us. By the day's end, we were able to finish Chami's work and part of Kiwaso's. Our uncle beat Ilomi and me. Then he turned to Kiwaso, who was trembling.

"Do you want this to happen to you? Tell your brothers to pray for your mother's return!"

"She's dead," Kiwaso whispered.

He beat Kiwaso. We all started toward our house. When we got there, he told us: "No. That's not your house anymore. From now on, you live in the goat shed."

I said, "I'll take our mother's marriage chest, then. That belongs to us."

"Nothing belongs to you!"

Father's youngest brother, overhearing, spoke up: "That was their mother's; it was Lord Mbanyo's gift. It belongs to his sister's sons now." Wild green light jumped in Uncle's eyes. Our other uncle stepped back quickly, but said, "Would you claim a twin's gift?"

The other men began to mutter against breaking a twin bond. Uncle said, "Take the chest, then, and nothing else!"

"They have to take some food!"

"Their mother can feed them," said Uncle, "or let them dig wild peanuts when they finish their work—which they did not do today! Go on, you boys! Get out of here!"

We went into the goat shed. At least it was clean. The door was made of sticks. I tied it shut. Alone we sat in the faint afternoon light that stole through the cracks.

"I'm hungry," Chami said. "I don't want to go and eat peanuts!"

"Hush." I was almost too tired and sore to be hungry. But of course, we must eat. There would be tomorrow. I went to the wall and peeked through a crack. Nobody was outside. I went back and sat down on the floor with my brothers and opened the marriage chest. The bowl was there, wrapped in the adinkra cloth. I unfolded the cloth and lifted out the bowl and set it on the ground.

Chami whispered, "What are you going to do?"

I ran my tongue over my dusty lips. "Our—" My voice broke from the dryness in my throat. I coughed and grasped the red bowl with both hands. I said softly, "Our Mother, we are hungry."

A wonderful smell filled the goat shed. A rich stew of meat and vegetables, such as our mother used to make, appeared in the bowl.

"Oooh!" Chami and Kiwaso said together. Ilomi swallowed hard and said nothing.

We had to eat with our fingers, for we had no spoons. We ate and ate, yet there was food in the bowl. Only, when we had enough, the scraps disappeared. The bowl cleaned itself.

I picked up the adinkra cloth to rewrap the bowl. The cloth felt good in my hands, cool and soothing. I had a sudden thought, and pulled off my tunic. I laid the adinkra cloth across the welts on my back.

All at once they were eased, and in the same moment I felt a sense of our mother's presence, filling the shed with her love.

"Come," I said to Ilomi.

I wrapped first Ilomi, then Kiwaso in the adinkra cloth, and the cloth healed their wounds too. Then Chami insisted on taking his turn, though he wasn't hurt. He smiled broadly when I laid the cloth over his shoulders.

"Mama's here," he said.

In the morning, before we went to the fields, we had a breakfast of delicious cakes with fruit and honey, and then the bowl cleaned itself and filled up again with fine, creamy beer. We drank our fill, and the bowl cleaned itself again. I wrapped it carefully in the adinkra cloth. Then I bowed to the cloth and bowl.

"Thank you, Our Mother."

It was a bad day in the fields, just as before. We did Chami's work first, then began on Kiwaso's. The sun was unforgiving. The dust flew in our faces, and our backs ached. When the sun was very high, Kiwaso fainted. Chami seized a gourdful of the men's water and poured it on our brother. At once Uncle struck him hard enough to knock him down.

"That does not belong to you!"

"But my brother is sick!" Chami was not very afraid of our uncle. But I was afraid when Uncle looked at him, silently, for a long time.

The next day, when we left the goat shed after our secret breakfast, Uncle was waiting for us by the compound gate. "You three go on. I'm taking Chami into the forest to hunt with me."

My throat closed with fear. I whispered, "I'll go with you."

"Yes. You would, to get out of your work! Go to the fields and make sure you finish what you have to do, unless you want another beating!"

"What are we going to hunt?" asked Chami, but Uncle did not answer him.

"Go on to the fields," I told Ilomi and Kiwaso as Uncle walked way with Chami.

I went back into the shed and opened the marriage chest. I gathered up the adinkra cloth. "Our Mother," I whispered, "I am afraid. I think our father's brother means evil to Chami."

My mother's presence touched me. I stuffed the cloth down the front of my tunic and tied my belt at the waist so it wouldn't slip out. I left the shed and ran after my uncle and Chami.

It was dark and quiet in the bush. I could see no sign of where my uncle had passed. I stood silent, listening to my heart hammer. Where were they, and what would he do to Chami? "O dead people who own the forest, have you seen a tall man and a little boy?"

"We saw a little boy pass," whispered a voice like wind tickling stiff leaves. "And one with him, but whether man or beast we do not know."

"A standing beast or a man with a tail," another voice sighed.

"With green eyes like a fire."

"Which way?" I asked. The underbrush ahead of me bent to one side.

"Thank you," I whispered, and followed the path. I walked quickly, into the stillness and the deep darkness. Then I heard a soft hopeless whimpering and ran to it.

Chami crouched by a huge old tree. Around and around

him, slowly, in an ever-closing circle, stalked a great black leopard.

Suddenly, its tail switched and the beast changed shape. Uncle stood over Chami, smiling with teeth that for a second were too long. "Weep, nephew," he said softly. Skin crawled on my spine. "Your mother will come when she hears you crying."

Chami moaned. Uncle again became a leopard, circling closer, closer.

I pulled the adinkra cloth out of my tunic and crept forward. I prayed the beast would not smell me. It put out a great hooked paw to touch Chami's face.

Chami screamed.

I jumped forward and flung the adinkra cloth over the leopard's face. The beast screamed louder than Chami. It began to struggle and claw at the cloth.

I snatched up Chami. His arms went around my neck tighter than a baby monkey's. I started to run, then stopped. The cloth!

The leopard was still fighting it. The cloth whipped around the beast's head as if lashed by a wind, though the air was still.

Suddenly the beast became a man. He struggled with the cloth, tore it from his head, sat up, and looked at us. His face was scratched and bleeding from clawing at the adinkra cloth. His eyes shone green.

"Curse you," he said softly. "How far away is she? Too far to hear the child cry out?" He stood and threw the torn adinkra cloth aside. "Perhaps she doesn't believe I'll harm him," he said, coming toward us. I backed away, but he seized my arm. His breath in my face was warm and rank. "I will have her. Come; we will go home."

I set Chami on the ground.

"Run and pick up that old cloth of our mother's," I told him casually.

He brought me the adinkra cloth, and we walked back to the village with Uncle. Anger and greed made him steam like a running beast. When we reached the compound, he shoved Chami aside and gripped my shoulder again. "Now," he said, "you and I will bring her here."

"She's dead."

"Dead or alive, I'll have her!"

He pulled me into the shed, leaving Chami outside. He left the door open for light.

"There's only one thing of hers that I don't have, and that is her marriage chest. So."

"That belongs to us!"

"And you belong to me," he said with a smile. He pulled the chest out of the corner and sat on the floor. My fists knotted. I felt my own weakness. He opened the chest. The red bowl was on top; he tossed it aside. "She never could make decent pottery." He lifted out one of the little stone jars. "What magic did she do with this, I wonder?"

"You have no right to touch those things. They are family things of my mother's."

If I were a man, I could seize the chest, I could strike him—but even in my thoughts, I faltered at striking my father's brother. In spite of all, he was head of the family.

He opened the jar and shook some of its contents into his hand. Even in the dimness I saw the red glow of a coppery dust.

"Aha! Copper for magic!" he said. He dipped a finger in the gleaming dust and stroked his forehead, cheeks, and lips with the copper. He sucked in his breath. "Yes! I feel it—power, hot as wine!" He unstopped another jar and poured out a white powder.

"Bone," he gloated. "Old bones from some magician's tomb, no doubt, to strengthen the copper's magic!" He streaked the powdered bone on his face beside the smears of copper. He laughed softly. . . . "She should have taken this with her. She—" He looked at me again. "Is she really dead?"

I nodded.

"Not much of a witch, if she couldn't even stop her own sickness."

I put my clenched hands behind my neck. "Mother died of grief after the leopard killed our father. Magic is too dangerous to use."

"Dangerous to fools, yes." He took out the third jar. "And what, I wonder, is this?" He smiled at the little jar. "Could it be blood? I wonder. Yes." He shook it. "Now I see. She isn't dead, you little liar. She put some of her blood in here, so you could call her." His eyes narrowed then. "And I think you will call her, Oliasso. I don't trust that woman."

"I tell you, our mother is dead!"

He caught my arm and jerked me close to him, forcing me to kneel between his thighs. With one strong hand holding my right arm twisted up behind me, he smeared copper and bone on my face. Then he opened the third jar and shook the contents into his palm

It was a powder, dark brown: dried blood.

He laughed again. "How good of her to leave all this behind! You will call her now, boy."

I shuddered. Why would our mother leave blood behind when she had left us the bowl and the adinkra cloth? I shook my head. "I won't."

He hurt my arm. I cried out, and Chami rushed into the shed.

"Stop hurting Oliasso!"

"All right." He threw me aside and grabbed Chami. "Do you want your little brother to call her, Oliasso?"

I sat up, shivery and cold inside. "I'll call."

He dipped his fingers in the dried blood and smeared it around my face. My features turned numb.

"Now call her," he said. "Call her by copper, blood, and bone!"

I made my mouth work. "Our M-Mo-Mother." My own blood beat like thunder in my ears. Would I see our mother's ghost—or some other thing? Whose blood was on my face? "I c-call by copper, b-bone, and blood—"

Something ripped. The dim air in the shed tore apart. A tall black man, dark as our mother, stood wavering in ghostly form before us.

Uncle breathed, "Lord Mbanyo!" and seized me, holding me against his chest. "Your blood!"

The Seeming of our mother's brother loomed so tall that his ghostly form stooped under the shed's roof. He wore brass jewelry and a long loose robe, patterned like the adinkra cloth. A knife hung from a belt at his waist. His voice when he spoke was soft and deep and echoed in my ears like our mother's voice. "Where is my twin sister?"

Uncle ignored the question. "You are in my power," he said. He smeared the blood off my face and rubbed some on his own. His voice was a little thicker when he spoke again. "I hold you by copper, blood, and bone, and I hold your sister's sons." One strong arm tightened around my throat. I found it hard to breathe.

Uncle said, "And I will hold you here until your body dies for lack of its soul, and then you will have no choice but to serve me forever or perish."

"Where is my sister?"

Chami said, "She's dead, and our father's brother is mean to us!" He ran to the Seeming and looked astonished when his hand passed through Lord Mbanyo's form. He jumped back. "It's a ghost!"

"Not yet," Lord Mbanyo said, "though I will be if my soul is kept from my body too long." His gaze settled on Uncle, and he added scornfully, "Just enough knowledge of magic to do evil!"

Uncle hissed. "Enough to master you, and everyone else when I have your power at my service!" His voice became taunting. "You, great lord, you will listen and poison and spread fear for me, like the basest servant!"

"Or I can perish," Lord Mbanyo corrected him, "which I prefer to do."

"Will you watch your sister's sons perish first, one by one, and very slowly, my lord? Have you ever seen a child's body torn by a leopard?"

Lord Mbanyo seemed to grow still. "You are a shape-changer?"

"He turns into a leopard and kills people," said Chami. "He tried to kill me, and Oliasso stopped him with our adinkra cloth!"

Lord Mbanyo said, "Ahh."

"Well, great lord?" said Uncle. "Shall I start with the oldest or the youngest? Which one shall be first?' His arm tightened again around my throat until black lights sparkled before my eyes. "It's so easy to kill a child."

"Let the boy live," Lord Mbanyo said in a voice like dust. "What do you want me to do?"

Uncle laughed. "What a fool, to sell yourself for children you've never seen before!" He eased his hold on my throat. "I want you to begin with the head of the council. Find out where he keeps his wealth, and when you do, frighten his household so they run away—and I'll seize his wealth."

I croaked, "Please let me go. My throat hurts."

"And mine is dry from so much talking," Uncle said. He let me go, leaned back, and grinned. "Oliasso, bring me some wine," he ordered. "You, Chami, come sit beside me while your brother fetches wine."

"No," said Chami.

I said, "Do as Uncle says!" The little one looked hurt and rebellious, but he went to sit at Uncle's feet. Lord Mbanyo watched them.

I picked up the red bowl and went outside. Standing in the bright sunlight, I whispered, "Our Mother—our enemy is thirsty."

I took the bowl back into the shed. It was brimming with palm wine. I knelt down and passed it to Uncle.

"I'm thirsty," said Chami.

Uncle grinned. "Share it with me." I had never seen him in such a good mood, and my heart nearly stopped.

I said sharply to Chami, "This is the best palm wine from Uncle's first wife. It's not for children!"

"But I—"

"Your brother grows wise," Uncle said to Chami. He put the red bowl to his lips and drank a long drink. He set the bowl down and grinned at me. "That is truly excellent—"

He screamed.

He clutched at his belly and clawed it. "Fire ants! Fire ants! My gut is crawling with fire ants!"

He struck at me. I jumped back.

Lord Mbanyo said, "Quickly! Wipe my blood from his face!"

I snatched up the adinkra cloth and dipped it into the palm wine. I lunged for Uncle, who was still clawing at his belly and batting at me.

I swiped at the dried blood on his face. Chami saw what I was doing and leaped to help me. Uncle tried to cover his face. He shouted and struck out at the little one. I climbed onto his chest and rubbed furiously with the wet cloth.

His fist knocked me backwards and made me see black lights again. I heard him groan. "Fire ants, fire ants in my belly!" Blinking, I saw him stagger to his feet. His face was clean.

"The adinkra cloth!" shouted Lord Mbanyo. "Lay it at my feet!"

I jumped up. Uncle made a grab at the adinkra cloth; it tore in two. There was a terrible shrieking noise as it tore.

Chami screamed, "You tore our mother!" He jumped at Uncle and struck him with the red bowl right between the legs.

Uncle sank moaning to his knees. I caught up the two halves of the adinkra cloth and laid them at the ghostly figure's feet.

Lord Mbanyo stepped down onto the cloth. He was as solid as I was. He drew his knife and went to Uncle and knelt down with the knife at Uncle's throat. "Go and bring the elders," he said to me in a very gentle voice, but I knew there would be no gentleness for my uncle.

The river was smooth and still by our camp; beyond the shore, the dark forest rustled with the whispers of the dead. Lord Mbanyo knelt by our campfire. He placed the red bowl on a flat piece of stone, lifted his hand, and struck the bowl with a rock repeatedly, until it was powder.

Chami sighed, and Kiwaso blinked at tears. Our mother's brother looked at them sternly. "Are you so selfish?"

They shook their heads. Chami leaned against my side.

"Oliasso," Lord Mbanyo said.

I took up the pieces of the adinkra cloth. For the last time, our mother's presence drifted through the world; a fragrant wind kissed me.

I placed the pieces of cloth on the flames. Lord Mbanyo carefully gathered up all the clay dust and dropped it into the fire; he dusted his palms over the flames. He said softly, "Go to the arms of our ancestors, my sister. Your sons are with me. Rest, now; sleep."

"Now she's gone," whispered Chami.

Lord Mbanyo held out his arms. Somehow he managed to get us all into his embrace.

"Now she rests," he said.

About Pat Cirone and
"To Father a Sohn"

I've published stories by Pat Cirone more than once in the Darkover anthologies and in *Sword and Sorceress,* and I've met her at more conventions than once. I remember once hitching a ride with her after Darkover Con in Baltimore, into Manhattan and the Plaza Hotel. Pat called this story by this name; but when we published it in issue three, we published it under the name of "A Flower From the Dust of Khedderide." I can't remember why; I usually don't change titles, although it was standard practice when I started writing for a living. Back then, editors would arbitrarily change titles, make cuts, etc., without so much as a by-your-leave to the writer. Nor did any of us ever as much as see a proof. No, not even of novels, far less of shorts before we saw them in print.

This story won second place in the Cauldron vote. I liked it because it takes a good hard look at social and sexual stereotypes, in an alien society, causing us to think about ours. If science fiction has any reason for existence and I think it has—it should be to examine our own social taboos and hang-ups.

I seldom print or write science fiction anymore; but this was in an early issue when we had not drawn clear lines as to what we wanted. Despite being one of the most clearly science fictional stories we ever printed, it's still a favorite of mine.

To Father a Sohn

Pat Cirone

Silivera walked, black robed, amidst the swirling colors others wore. While not the only southerner who had moved up here, to the mushrooming town of Khedderide, jhe was probably the only one who persisted in wearing the black, day in and day out. It was easy to ignore the occasional surprised comments.

With a bound, Silivera leapt up the last two stairs to the narrow level where the shops for their section were cut into the cliff. A mischievous smile flickered around the edges of jhes mouth and jhe entered the produce shop.

"Ah, Belder! I'll have some kuai fruit, a nice large portion of sketer root, and maybe some zircot grain." Belder leaned massive arms, clothed in filmy pink, on the bare counter and looked with Silivera at the colorful paintings of fruits, grains, and vegetables that lined the walls and provided such a stark contrast to the dusty, empty shelves.

"Would you like some puli-puli, too?" the grocer inquired genially, nodding to a picture of an exotic fruit difficult to obtain, even in the south.

"Yes!" Silivera exclaimed, enchanted.

The grocer leaned back, chuckling, and began to measure out the ubiquitous kwaicarat. It was the only crop that grew close enough to the edge of the desert to be delivered regularly. Everyone was sick of the black-and-white-striped grain, and Silivera was no exception. It was kwaicarat bread for morning, cold kwaicarat for midday, and fried kwaicarat for evening. And lucky to get that. If the population continued to outrun the transport, they'd have to start using a Gate to import food, and that was against the Code, which demanded that communities be self-reliant.

Silivera put the ration books down on the counter and began to slap at the pale dust clinging to the bottom of jhes knee-length black robe.

"When are you going to start wearing some sensible clothes?" Belder asked.

Silivera looked up with a rueful grin. "These do show the dust, don't they? But I just don't feel comfortable in colors. In the south, colors are never worn for anything but night-clothes."

"What do they do to you southerners to make you so rigid? You're what? Nineteen? Twenty? And already you're too old to change. Let go of all those petty rules you grew up with!"

"Next you'll be wanting me to forswear the Code!" Silivera retorted in mock horror.

"You don't wear the Code on your skin. I walk in as much honor as any crow-decked southerner!"

"I know, I know. Just call me eccentric." Silivera tried to soothe the grocer, who was starting to take this too personally. Sometimes jhe wondered if it wouldn't be easier to change to colors, make everyone more comfortable. But it wouldn't be honest. Jhe'd still be a southerner, no matter what jhe wore. Wearing colors wouldn't be right; it would be a deception. Jhe'd rather struggle through misunderstandings like this than be dishonest in the way jhe met life.

"Ah, you. I think you just want to stand out. Maybe you're young, after all."

"It doesn't hurt to stand out sometimes," Silivera replied, glad that the conversation had bounced back to a lighter tone. "You need something to be noticed in this sea of strange faces."

"Oh, I don't think you'd have a problem. But speaking of

strangers . . ." Belder reached beneath the counter and pulled a large sketer root up from the depths. Jhe plunked it down and waited for Silivera's reaction.

Silivera stared at it as if it were an off-world animal, before snatching the dusty tuber up and hugging it to jhes breast. "To think I used to take these for granted!"

The grocer chuckled. "Time brings a glow to all memories?"

"Rationing brings a glow to anything. Even sketer roots!"

"I've heard we might get some tapier grain in next week. Do you want me to set some aside for you?"

"Yes! I'll even give you the ration coupons now. Anything for a change from kwaicarat."

"No, no, keep your coupons until it comes in," the grocer said, handing jhe the bag of striped grain and subtracting just the day's allotment of coupons for a family of three from the ration books. Chimes rang and more customers came into the store, their boots swishing against the wooden floor. Silivera said good-bye to the grocer and left, plunging back into the sun.

The narrow sideway was hard beneath jhes feet; like all the paths in Khedderide, it had been carved right out of the cliff. Silivera angled across to the open side, leaned against the wall, and looked out over the city.

Khedderide always reminded jher of a jewel, basking under the sun, each tier one more carved facet. Facets that clung to the cliffs, narrow and rocky, with heartstopping drops between. Silivera loved it: its beauty, its newness, its row upon row of identical white houses with gleaming blue roof tiles that seemed to capture and hold bits of the vivid sky. It was hard to believe that just ten years ago there had been nothing here, nothing but a few halauks, circling, trying to wrest a meal from the barren desert.

That had been before kerillian ore, needed to maintain the busy Gates between all the worlds of the Sectors, had been discovered in these cliffs. Now dusty roads snaked in across the Kassian desert and Khedderide had sprung from nothing. Silivera leaned forward, trying to catch a glimpse of government center, wondering if jhe might spot Ricel's blond head.

But the angle was wrong, and jhe couldn't see even a corner of the large buildings hurriedly built to accommodate the citizenship needs of nearly seventy thousand people.

Silivera pushed back from the wall, grimaced at the streaks of white it had left on jhes robe, and started walking home. Little Dafire would be waiting. The thought speeded jher up.

"Vera!" The call spun Silivera around. Ricel was hurrying toward jher. Silivera's heart tripped into an extra beat.

Laughing, Ricel caught up and gave Silivera a quick hug. Silivera savored the moment, acknowledging to jherself the ridiculousness of feeling so breathless over someone jhe'd lived with for a year and a half.

It had been that way from the first sight of that blond head, back when jhe had thought blond hair was foreign and might even mean its possessor was male or female, from one of the dual-sexed worlds. Even that had not stopped Silivera from moving forward to meet the stranger.

Silivera had since learned that such blond-haired, tan-skinned beauty was common in the far north, where Ricel came from, and that Ricel was as androgynous as the rest of the natives of the planet Rocque. But the heady rush of that first meeting was still with jher.

"What are you doing here? And where's Dafire?" Ricel was asking.

"I left Dafire next door, with Soel. I was called for a job interview. And I got the job! A permanent one, not a temp, like I've been working!"

"Great. Where?"

"Up at Blue Shaft."

"Not in the mines!"

"No, no. Paperwork. Their supply manager left to lay the groundwork for the new shaft. They needed a replacement. The coordinator wasn't too happy that I was so young, but jhe said my credentials were the best of those that applied, so I got the job."

"Now you'll have a niche of your own."

"Ummm. I've been so frustrated, seeing everyone else working to build this city, while all I could get was fiddling temps. Thank God I've had Dafire to look after these last six months. That's one drawback—even though it's an office job, there's too much dust from the mine for a baby. I'll miss not having Dafire with me every second of the day. Perhaps Soel would be willing to watch Dafire for us, as long as jhe's out with that leg injury. By the time jhe's ready to go back to work, we'll have had the time to link up with a good trade-time group. But just think of all Dafire's 'firsts' I'll miss!" moaned Silivera.

"Like me. I've already missed more than I've seen," Ricel replied. Silivera nodded, but inside jhe was thinking that it wasn't the same. For all that Ricel had borne the baby, jhe didn't love jher as much as Silivera did.

When they picked up Dafire from Soel's, the baby was so anxious to nurse that jhe nearly squirmed out of Ricel's arms.

"Hey, watch that!" Ricel exclaimed breathlessly, laughing as jhe tried to juggle the baby. Silivera dropped the bag of kwaicarat and thrust a quick hand against the baby's bottom, until Ricel could rearrange jhes grip.

"Thanks, Vera."

"Quick, let's get in before the monster squirms loose again!" Silivera laughed. Jhe palmed open their door and they struggled in. Ricel quickly shed jhes working clothes, stepped into a nursing robe, and sank into a chair to nurse Dafire. Silivera memorized the sight, as jhe did every night, of the two blond heads nestled so near each other. Then jhe turned to the wall that passed as a kitchen, rinsed the dust off the grain jhe'd dropped, and threw it into a frying pan.

Silivera talked as jhe stirred the grain. "I think my blacks stood me in good stead today. The shaft coordinator was a southerner. I think the only reason jhe took a chance on someone so young was jhe felt I would be imbued with the ethic of doing things with grace and formality rather than the slapdash way you northerners operate."

Ricel laughed. "You and your 'southern traditions.' Did you explain your parents shunted you up here because they thought you were too much of a rebel?"

"No." Silivera grinned.

"A big mistake when it comes to you: judging by the black, instead of the mischief in your eye."

"Maybe not. Otherwise, why can't I switch to colors like other southerners do?"

"Because you know you look stunning in black." Ricel got up and nuzzled the back of Silivera's neck. Dafire gave an indignant snort, and stopped nursing long enough to push at Silivera's back with a chubby fist. Ricel laughed and sat down again. Dafire fixed an indignant blue stare on jhes parent's face, before the nursing made jhes eyes sink blissfully shut again.

"Seriously, though," Silivera continued, "sometimes it's disgusting just how much I have absorbed my parents' attitudes."

"I wouldn't worry, if I were you," Ricel laughed. "You're the least conventional person I know. Even your wearing of the black is a sign of it: no one else wears clothes because they're a sign of inner convictions! Only you, Vera, only you." Ricel shifted to start burping Dafire, and watched Silivera's quick, precise movements as jhe set the table. "You're just an interesting collection of odd quirks."

Silivera slid the steaming mixture of grain and sketer root down onto the table. "As long as you keep the word 'interesting' in there." Jhe glanced up. The laughter stilled, and they exchanged a long look. Silivera glowed as they sat down to eat.

After dinner, Ricel pushed up from the table and slowly started to stack the dishes, while Silivera mashed some of the food to feed Dafire.

"How soon do you start work?" Ricel asked.

"Next week. I don't suppose . . . do you think you could get some time off before then? Once I start work, it will be even harder to get together to sign contracts."

"Oh, Vera. You know the hours I keep. It's hopeless. Is it really so necessary to do it right now? I mean, we've signed intentions, I'm not avoiding marriage, but time off this week? When we've just started surveying a new tract? Impossible."

"Yes, I thought so," Silivera sighed.

"I know, Vera. You want to be married: contracts written and signed. I want to, too. It's just . . ."

Silivera looked as cheerful as possible. "Don't worry,

Ricel, we'll get to it eventually. This will just have to be one of my 'southern traditions' I'll have to change." Jhe scooped the dishes out of Ricel's hands and headed for the sink, missing the baffled, wistful look on Ricel's face.

After a short period of silence, Ricel spoke. "Did you hear they finished paving the road in from the north today?"

"So that's why Belder is expecting tapier grain next week!"

Ricel snorted. "I bet more people arrive before enough food does. I wish they'd put a limit on immigration here, at least until my department gets a chance to take care of the housing shortage."

"Forget it. Kerillian's too important. The more people they have, the more shafts they can open up," Silivera countered practically. "There's four already, and a fifth opening up. How greedy can you get?"

"With the deposits on Thuneau, Ridelle, and Actue mined out? Pretty greedy. Every transport gate and every transport bracelet made needs kerillian. And every newly joined planet wants to be on Sectors' net as fully and as quickly as possible. Especially those who don't follow the Arian way, and want a Gate every few blocks, so they don't have to do anything for themselves. No, the deposits here will be mined to the last inch, regardless of the cost."

Ricel sighed and sank into a chair. "I suppose you're right. I'll just have to get used to the pace."

Silivera leaned against the chair and passed a hand through Ricel's blond hair. "Rough day, hmmm?"

"God, yes. Norill came in screaming that Rylie placed half jhes markers wrong—you know Norill's pleasant manner—and Rylie swore jhe'd sunk them correctly, and by the end of the day no one in the department was speaking to anyone else, for fear of setting off more explosions."

Ricel shook jhes head and closed jhes eyes tiredly. Silivera gave jher an extra caress and sunk down onto the floor to play with Dafire. Ricel leaned over to pick up a half-made crawlie for Dafire that needed hemming.

"Look at that!" Silivera exclaimed a few moments later. "Dafire's stacked three of them together!" Jhe looked up, but Ricel's blond head had fallen against the side of the chair.

Silivera smiled ruefully. "Wait here, Daf," jhe said, patting the baby on the back. Silivera went over to Ricel's chair and, quietly maneuvering the sleeper into jhes arms, carried jher into the bedroom they shared. Ricel never stirred. Silivera stood there for a moment, looking at the tousled blond hair which had seemed so exotic to jhes southern eyes when they had first met. Then Silivera swung back through the door and walked over to where Dafire had stopped playing with blocks in favor of gnawing on them.

Silivera idly removed the block from the small mouth and watched with a slight smile as the baby promptly stuck a different one in. Jhes sohn. Precious, lovable, and half jhes . . . - and not jhes at all. Only if there was a marriage contract could a parent claim a child jhe'd fathered.

In the south it would have been a scandal to conceive, let alone bear, a child out of contract. But here, mores were less rigid. Ricel didn't see anything wrong, as long as they got married eventually. So they remained a couple living together, with a child born between them, and no marriage contract. It bothered Silivera to the depths. It seemed ridiculous to put so much stock into a piece of paper, but it was the way jhe'd been brought up. Jhe'd never forget the shock when Ricel announced jhe had gotten pregnant without that paper. And every time someone asked if Dafire was jhes sohn, jhe choked on the yes, knowing that, under the Code that was the law of all of Rocque, both north and south, jhe had no legal right to call Dafire jhes without that piece of paper. With a sigh, Silivera picked up the crawlie Ricel had dropped and finished hemming it.

Silivera waited outside the Records Hall for over an hour. Ricel had said jhe'd be able to get off early. Silivera had put in for an hour off and hurried over. They'd have the contracts drawn up, and arrange for a signing date. But Ricel never showed. When the whisper of the evening breeze began, Silivera gave up and headed home.

Ricel dragged home, dusty, later than usual, and discouraged.

"I tried, Vera."

"What happened?"

"Norill blew up. Said the last set of sites I'd surveyed were all crooked. I had to go out and do them all over again. I swear, Vera, I know I'm tired, but I'm not so tired I'm careless. They were so off you could tell by just looking at the flags marking the corners. Someone must have moved them."

"But that's beyond mischief! What if it hadn't been caught and the houses had been built wrong on the cliff? It could have endangered people's lives! That's a gross breach of the Code!"

Ricel looked as grim as Silivera felt. "It isn't the first time markers have moved mysteriously. I can't see how . . . it can't be kids. Those flags have to be drilled into the rock. And there weren't any other holes." Ricel shrugged. "Oh, maybe I am getting so tired I can't see straight. The only other explanation is the cliff moved. And that's impossible; this area is stable. If it isn't, we're in trouble. All those mine shafts." Ricel shuddered.

"Don't be so fast to dismiss kids. They can be pretty clever. And they don't always think too far ahead. . . . Still, they must have known they were going too far, even if they didn't realize their actions could be breaking the Code." Silivera shook jhes head. The Code was something learned from birth on; to break it was to say you disdained the rights of others. You walked outside of them.

Weeks passed. There never seemed to be a second opportunity to meet at the Records Hall to draw up the contracts, let alone sign them. Silivera didn't have time to let it depress jher; jhe was busy proving to the Blue Shaft coordinator that jhe had been right to hire a seventeen-year-old with only temporary jobs for experience. Despite the satisfaction the job gave, the best part of the day was going home, to Dafire and Ricel. That was the center of existence. When the evening breezes sighed along the cliffs, Silivera would plunge down from the cliffs into the fairy-tale tapestry of twinkling lights. Silivera's hours were almost as long as Ricel's now. It was pitch dark when jhe'd arrive at Soel's to pick up Dafire. Still, Silivera never seemed as tired as Ricel, so jhe kept the burden of most of Dafire's care, as well as the larger portion of the housework.

Ricel objected, but Silivera just laughed and told jher to rest while jhe could, because jhe planned to be the next one to bear a baby and then jhe'd be the one exhausted with nursing and working and child care. Truthfully, Silivera enjoyed having the excuse to hog the care of Dafire. As the youngest in jhes family, jhe'd never had the care of an infant before. Silivera was astonished at how much jhe enjoyed it, and was eager for more children, even if jhe had to do it without a marriage contract.

One night Ricel came home late, almost at Dafire's bedtime, but jhe looked happy.

"I wrestled a promise from Norill for the afternoon off tomorrow! No matter what happens, I'll meet you at the Records Hall; we'll draw up the contracts and sign them then and there."

Silivera looked up from cleaning the table and smiled all the way from the toes.

Ricel threw jherself into a chair and motioned for Silivera to come over. Silivera stopped to scoop up Dafire, plumped the two of them into the chair beside Ricel, and grinned at Ricel's blond-topped face. "What?"

"Let's celebrate!"

"Celebrate? It's almost Dafire's bedtime. We can't go out now."

"There's more than one way of celebrating. We hardly ever save any time for ourselves. Either I'm asleep or at work, or you're busy with the house and Dafire."

"I know. But we're together." Silivera's smile began to dance. "And we had a nice courtship."

"That was a year and a half ago. And it didn't last long enough," Ricel murmured, freeing Silivera's hair from Dafire's grasp to run jhes own fingers through it. "So let's celebrate the last night we'll be unmarried."

Silivera lingered under Ricel's touch for a moment before murmuring: "Let me settle Dafire down for the night." Ricel smiled and followed. Jhe watched, lazy eyed, as Silivera changed Dafire and tucked jher into the crib. Then Ricel closed the door softly and the two walked arm in arm into their own bedroom.

Dasday was clear and beautiful, the sky a blue so molten it was deeper than the tiles on the roofs. Silivera worked swiftly, sparking with the knowledge jhe'd be meeting Ricel at the Hall of Records in just four hours. They'd have to skip wearing the red: there was no time to shop for wedding robes. But Soel had promised to bring Dafire to greet them outside the private chambers after they had traced the ritual marriage signs on each other's faces. Silivera wished jhes parents could be there for the celebration feast—but of course then jhe'd have to explain the existence of Dafire, pre-contract. . . . It would be nice being just Ricel, Dafire, and Soel, too. Silivera smiled, imagining.

The ground moved beneath jhes feet, pressing against the soles, then fading away. Silivera looked up startled.

A low rumble built, became a thudding roar that shook both skull and chest. Silivera tried to stand. The ground jerked and bobbed.

Silivera staggered against the room. Made it to the doorway. A cloud of pale-gray dust was rising from the city below, obscuring the view. In a slow dance, it started to eddy, then settle with the breezes. Silivera's breath caught. Jhe clung to the door and stared, horrified, at the tumbled swaths of blue roof tiles and broken walls.

Another rumble. Silivera watched as the cliff face below Red Shaft shrugged and parted from the rocks behind, carrying houses and streets into dusty oblivion.

Silivera stood, in a state that felt like calm, and waited for the rumble that would carry Blue Shaft, and jher, away.

It didn't come. At last jhe left the door and walked back to the desk. Moving delicately, jhe gathered scattered paperwork into neat piles and filed it in the trays. Picked up the drinking glass that had fallen. Straightened the chart on the wall.

When there was nothing left to tidy, jhe had to let the knowledge seep in. Trembling slightly, jhe started the climb down to the city. The staircase from Blue Shaft was littered with rocks and cracked in places, but it was passable. Below was different.

Silivera had to scramble. The sideways were more rubble than street. In several places, slides had wiped out any trace of habitation. The rocks were quiet now, except for an occasional trickle of sand.

Cries filled the air. A figure erupted from the broken rocks beside Silivera, shook the dust from shock-blinded eyes, and stared at the scene; then turned and started scrabbling at the chaos behind, calling a name. Others were doing the same, up and down what had been the sideway. Silivera threaded a way through them. The closer to home, the swifter jhe hurried, breath rasping painfully, tearing jagged rents in the blanket of shock.

One last featureless slide. Silivera scrambled across, then stood and looked for landmarks. A shop sign was sticking out of the debris. Oh Honor! It was Belder's, all that was left of the produce shop. Silivera looked for the staircase that had wound down to their level. It was gone; covered or swept away, Silivera couldn't tell which. Bracing feet as best as possible, jhe slid down. A number painted on a jagged portion of a wall gave some bearings. Silivera turned right and counted along the heaps of rubble to Soel's number.

Hands tore quickly on the gritty, sharp-edged pieces. Silivera's began to leave a bloody trail. Jhe stopped, ripped off a piece of tunic and wrapped them. The hands became black flags moving among the rocks. Muffled crying spurred jher to frantic activity. Silivera called and called to Dafire as jhe scrambled and heaved. Jhes voice grew harsh; sobs came unbidden. Unknown hands began to help as jhe fought and wiggled and pushed a way through. First Dafire's foot was uncovered. Then a hand. Gently Silivera pulled the wildly sobbing baby from a miraculously protective triangle of broken walls. No blood. No injuries that jhe could see. Silivera hugged Dafire so close, the baby started to cry harder.

Silivera sat, shook, kept sobbing over Dafire while the others went on searching for Soel. A warden came by, passing out colored construction flags. Houses were marked: blue for those already searched or whose occupants were accounted for, red for all the rest. Silivera stuck a blue in the rubble that had been their home. Ricel wouldn't have been there, and jhe and Dafire were accounted for. Jhe went back to the seat on the sunny rock by Soel's home and hunched protectively over Dafire. Soel's body was found an hour later. Only then did Silivera feel free to walk to government center to find Ricel.

Silivera walked unhearing through a confused babble of sobs, hurried talk and cries for loved ones, doctors, help. Dafire took jhes head out of Silivera's shoulder and peered with interest at the milling crowds. Silivera tried to stop the tremors that still shook through jher. Jhe had the baby. Dafire was alive and unhurt. The tremors came anyway, as jhes sandaled feet traced their way over the rubble.

Silivera approached government center by the back of the Records Hall without even remembering this was to have been their marriage day. That special day seemed years ago. Silivera rounded the side of the building and dug sandals into the ground in a sudden stop. Jhes hand wavered as it reached for the wall beside jher, for support. A gaping wound of scoured rock met jhes eyes. The cliff had sheared completely away at this point, carrying half the Records Hall and the rest of government center with it. Silivera drifted forward to peer down at the featureless jumble of gray rocks and dust that spread to the valley floor. Tears choked throat and eyes: never to see Ricel's blond hair again! Without a sound jhe turned around and started heading up the cliffs to where the warden had said tents for the homeless were being erected.

Hope returned after food and rest. Maybe Ricel had been out surveying a site, maybe jhe had already left to get ready for the ceremony at the Records Hall. Silivera changed the flag on their house from blue to red and entered Ricel's name among the thousands of missing, opposite their own location in case Ricel was seeking them. Then jhe joined one of the search teams. Silivera knew jhes skills would be better suited to organizing relief efforts or helping Records in their efforts to reunite families and establish order among the lost and scattered vital records. But there was something numbing in the hard physical labor that satisfied a driving need. Jhe kept quiet and spent the days heaving aside the rubble of the red-flagged buildings, searching for victims, living or dead.

Each night Silivera arrived back at the tent, shaky with exhaustion. Jhe'd scan the message board hopefully, and then quietly strip off the grimy dust mask, rinse filthy, scratched hands in the shallow bucket of communal water, and pick up Dafire from those who had volunteered to care for the children, to free the more physically able. Carrying Dafire, Silivera would go over to their own small partition, feed the baby, then hold Dafire close.

Silivera lost track of the gray days. Numb surprise greeted the realization, upon asking the day, that a week had passed since the quake. That day Silivera found it hard to believe Ricel might still be alive.

The ache of that knowledge so filled Silivera that jhe barely heard what the caregiver was saying when jhe entered the tent that night. At first.

"I think you should stay in tomorrow and rest, dear. Your milk supply must be down, the way your baby has been taking it from the bottle during the day. I don't mean to complain, but we're so short of even the powdered milk, we want to save it for those babies who no longer have mothers to nurse them."

"Yes, of course," Silivera mumbled as Dafire was handed over. Jhe walked away swiftly. Once behind their private partition, Silivera trembled.

Dafire. Jhe would lose Dafire. Without a marriage contract there was no way jhe could claim the baby as jhes sohn. Wasn't it enough that she had lost Ricel? Now Dafire would be sent to Ricel's family. A family that had never seen or wanted to see the child. A family whose shock at Ricel's desire to marry someone they didn't know, and a southerner, had led them to cut off all relations with their sohn. It just wasn't fair!

Tears blurred Silivera's vision as Dafire squirmed free of a too tight grip and began to crawl around the cot. Poor Dafire. Mother gone, only a father left. Silivera wondered if the baby noticed what a drastic change had occurred. Dafire had been quieter, had clung to Silivera more in the evenings. Of course, Dafire had been missing the mother that had nursed jher! Silivera had been numb. Now the thought pierced. How could jhe have been so blind? How would Dafire react to losing Silivera, too? Silivera, the one who had loved and cared for jher from the minute jhe had left Ricel's womb.

When would jhe bring jherself to notify the officials of Dafire's position? Jhe'd wait for the bureaucracy to catch up with the fact that jhe wasn't the baby's mother.

For the next two weeks Silivera walked with but one refrain: jhe was going to lose Dafire. The tears that spattered the dust weren't just for Ricel now, they were for Dafire also.

The day came that Silivera was assigned to help clear the Records Hall.

Silivera learned that the birth records had been held in the section which had been sheared away. For the adults, like Silivera, it was no more than an inconvenience; another copy could be obtained from the place of birth. But Dafire had been born here. There had never been any reason to file a copy elsewhere. Silivera asked casually what was being done in such cases and was told new certificates were being made as fast as possible; parents, or the nearest surviving relative, gave the information.

Silivera returned to the tent that evening, and as jhe rinsed face and hands in the tent's gritty bucket of water, there was a whisper in jhes head. It would be easy. All jhe'd have to do was state Dafire was jhes born child instead of fathered child. . . .

No! That went against the Code. It even had a name and number all its own: kidnapping. Dafire belonged to Ricel's family and to Ricel's family jhe would go. In fact, to resist temptation, Silivera would go, first thing tomorrow, to the tent serving as a temporary shelter for the Hall of Records and start the proceedings.

The next morning Silivera reported to the regular work crew. The rescue work was more important, jhe argued to jherself. Even though it had been eight days since anyone had been found alive, there might still be someone clinging to life below the rubble . . . shame coiled inside Silivera's breast. Jhe knew that wasn't the reason jhe was sifting through dust and rocks instead of filling out paperwork.

That night Silivera had a headache from the thoughts that fought in jhes head. Honor, love, loneliness, and fear vying with each other, leaving only confusion. Was Right always right? One part of Silivera shuddered at the wrongness of what jhe was toying with; another part shouted it was not wrong at all. Silivera shook jhes head. It was impossible, so why even consider it?

But the whisper kept coming back. Was it so impossible? Was it? Jhe and Ricel had been too wrapped up in each other to have many friends—there were few who could be certain which had borne the babe. Soel, of course, but jhe was dead. Probably several of Ricel's coworkers had at least known jhe was pregnant. But could they swear that Dafire was the baby? Simultaneous pregnancies were rare, but not impossible, and Ricel had never taken Dafire in to work with jher. . . . They were probably all dead with Ricel, anyway.

And jhe had been too ashamed to write and tell jhes parents jhe had fathered a child without contract. Jhe could just switch to the equal shame of having borne a child pre-contract.

But, even if jhe managed, somehow, to fool all these people, would jhe be able to live with jherself? To go against the Code? To walk outcast? Even if no one else knew it, jhe would always know.

Kidnapping. It had an ugly ring. Under the Code it didn't matter that jhe loved the babe: other unwedded fathers had surely loved their children before. This did not change the law that said children belonged to those that bore them, unless a contract said otherwise. The hand of anyone who had ever borne a child, loved it, and guarded it from harm, would be against jher.

Would Ricel's family bother to trace jher? Silivera wasn't even sure if they knew of Dafire's existence. They had returned all of Ricel's letters after that one telling them Ricel had filed intentions with someone here. Without ever a meeting, they had condemned Silivera simply because jhe was not one of the few they had already picked as suitable for Ricel.

Honor had probably demanded they forget Silivera's name!

Umbrage turned to thoughtfulness. There was a good chance they didn't know Silivera's name. Ricel had so hated the name Silivera, jhe had always called jher "Vera." And if Silivera remembered right, Ricel had deliberately omitted Silivera's last name from that letter, wanting them to accept Silivera for jherself, and not for jhes family connection. So, even if they knew Ricel had had a sohn, they would be seeking a Dafire Tojer, sohn of Ricel Tojer and some unknown Vera. Not Daffy Aubochon, sohn of Silivera.

Silivera looked at the sleeping Dafire. If jhe walked outside the Code and took the baby, jhe would never be able to marry: it would be easy to notice that jhes body carried no trace of having borne a child. Besides, jhe would never ask someone jhe loved to step outside the Code for jher. Bad enough jhe was doing it to jherself. That was the question: could jhe spend jhes entire life alone, with just Dafire: no lifemate, no family, no more children? And always with the knowledge that jhe walked outside the Code, eating at jher?

Jhe stared again at Dafire's blond head and jhes heart wrenched. Jhe would never be whole, or at peace, again. Which was it to be: Love? Or Honor?

On Dasday, exactly four weeks after the quake, Silivera strapped Dafire to jhes back, gathered up their few belongings, and walked to where government center had stood. Jhe picked a desert aloene which had struggled up from a crack, maybe from what had been someone's garden, and tossed it down. A wildflower, like Khedderide itself, sprung from desert and dust and a bit of magic. And just as quick to die, thought Silivera.

Jhe stared down at the spot of color on the dusty gray rocks. Jhe wondered, if Ricel had lived, would they have stayed and worked for Khedderide's rebirth? Or would they have fled, as so many already had? Jhe watched the silent flower for a while. Not even a body to bury. The rocks had taken care of that.

Silivera turned and, still with some misgivings, walked to the Records tent. Jhe requested a new certificate, for jhes sohn Dafire Aubochon. With one extra copy to carry. Then jhe headed south. Back to the lands of black-clad formality, green fields, and old cities. To where the shame would be greater but the chance of exposure less.

Jhe would go to jhes parents for a while, until jhe chose somewhere else, as jhe had chosen Khedderide. Jhe would not tell them Dafire's true lineage; even Dafire must never know jhe was father, not mother. Somewhere on the long journey south, between the steady pace of walking and the intimacy of fending for just the two of them, Silivera found peace, and the conviction jhe had chosen rightly. Together, a mother and jhes sohn, they arrived at Aubochon.

Nonar answered the door.

"Hello, Mother," Silivera said.

Tears sprang to Nonar's eyes, tears that pride held, unshed, at the corners. Silivera knew these unshed tears were the closest Nonar would ever come to showing jhes joy that Silivera had returned alive from Khedderide. Nonar's gaze traveled over all of Silivera's figure, over the dust-covered robes, the unexplained baby on the hip. Jhes eyes flickered, saying that some things would have to be discussed soon.

"So. You still wear the black. I'm glad to see you're not so lost to Honor that you've adopted northern ways."

I've fallen much farther than that, Silivera thought.

"No," jhe replied simply.

About Susan Urbanek Linville and "Born in the Seventh Year"

This story could easily have been a cliché; instead, it features one of the few original insights into changelings that I've ever read. No story I've received in the years since has equaled this for insight into a theme that has been much overused and could so easily have been just another cliché: overdone, overused, or just soppily sentimental. It took second place in the Cauldron vote, so obviously my readers liked it too. It's also the only changeling story I've printed in ten years of doing anthologies.

Susan Linville is currently working on a Ph.D. in biology, specializing in animal behavior in birds. Between studying and working as a teaching assistant, she doesn't have much time to write at the moment, but she plans to do more of it once she finishes her degree.

Born in the Seventh Year

Susan Urbanek Linville

Myrica grasped the willow rungs in the ancient birth-ing stool.

"Please let this baby live," she cried. Another contraction ripped through her body. Sweat burned her cracked lips.

"It's time," said Rubra. The darkened room filled with the strong odor of rosemary and lemon balm, as the herbs were dropped into a boiling pot. "You must push now. Push the child out."

Myrica pressed her spine into the well-worn wood and dug her toes into the sod floor. Rubra's wrinkled hand moved along her swollen body, pressing against the muscles to relieve the pain. Bone pushed against bone and flesh against flesh. Myrica took a deep breath and bit her lower lip.

With a whimper, the child took its first breath.

"She's alive," Myrica laughed. "Thank the Earth Mother."

"One more push." Rubra brushed her graying red hair away from her face. "This is not finished yet."

Myrica hardly heard the words. The child lived! Her first two daughters had been born blue and still. They had been beautiful fairy creatures, with creamy dark skin and cat-green eyes, but had had only one nostril and no lungs with which to breathe.

"Let me hold her," Myrica said. Finally, she had a living child, an infant to hold next to her breast and nurture.

Rubra moved the infant to the hearth, where she cleaned it with herbal oils. She pulled a piece of old linen from the table and wrapped the child.

"I have a new cloth for my baby," said Myrica.

"He will not need it."

"No!"

"I'm sorry." Rubra pushed open the wooden window, signaling the arrival of a male child. Cool damp air crept into the room. Myrica shivered. She could hear the Wikkens, the witch fairies, rattling squirrel bones to keep pixies away.

"Please, let me hold him." Myrica wiped the tears from her face. "He's my only living child."

"It's better you don't touch him. The parting will be less painful."

"Less painful?" Myrica shouted. "How would you know! You've never had a child to lose!"

Rubra turned her back to Myrica and held the child closely.

Before Myrica could speak again, the door latch lifted and three Wikkens entered the birthing hut. Dressed in dark robes, they flowed into the room, smelling of holly and sweet incense. Each wore a long necklace of thorn and nightshade. Rubra handed the infant to the Wikken Elder, a short female with long white hair.

"He's my child!" Myrica struggled to stand, but fell in a pool of blood and afterbirth. "Go away, before I summon the wood magic against you!"

"He is lost," said the Elder. "Another will be found for you. A human child will fill the void now in your heart."

"No!" Myrica tried to crawl toward them, but Rubra grabbed her and quickly wrapped a blanket around her shivering body.

"Let them go," Rubra whispered, guiding Myrica to the sleeping mat.

"This is your brother's child too. He is part of your blood."

"It's the law, Myrica."

"I don't care about the law."

"You should!" Rubra's eyes were large and dark, like a wild cat's ready to kill.

Myrica's cheeks flushed. She looked away from Rubra.

The Elder held Myrica's baby in the firelight.

"Look at the bones protruding from beneath the skin. This male is weak and sickly." She held up his foot. "He is webbed between the toes. It's a sign of bad blood."

"I will make potions to strengthen him. I will find a human to nurse him."

"You know the law," said the Elder. "This is the Seventh Year. All males born in the Seventh Year must be given over as changelings. We need the strength of human blood. You must know, after the death of your other children, that the blood runs bad."

"You can make an exception to the law. My grandfather was Tanoak, high wizard of the wood. His blood is in this child."

"There are no exceptions." The elder took the child and handed him to the other Wikkens. They wrapped him tightly in dark linen and protected him with a necklace of silver fairy bells.

Myrica tried to stand again. She wanted to grab her son and run out into the darkness, to hide in the protective arms of the forest.

Rubra squeezed her arm. "Be still. Don't question the Wikken."

One of the witches pulled a glass vial of elderberry extract from her cloak pocket. Myrica knew the red liquid was to be part of the magic used to disguise her son. His new human parents would never know he was a fairy child.

The Wikken poured two drops into her palm and drew a pentagram with it on the child's forehead.

"Ashem balic sabin," she chanted in an ancient fairy tongue. "Cilim balic Sabin."

"Stop! You'll not change my son with the Fay-erie. By the gods of the forest realm, I name this child Cedrus, Son of Myrica and Tallowman."

"Myrica, don't do this," Rubra pleaded. "Let him go."

"In the name of Ostrya, I bring him in as a forest brother."

The Elder turned and lifted her wooden staff as if to strike. Anger flashed in her amber eyes. "Do you curse our race?"

"In the name of Tamarack, I protect Cedrus within the Seelie Court," Myrica shouted her petition desperately. By naming the child, she proclaimed him to be a fairy and under the gods' protection. The Fay-erie would not work on him now.

"You are a fool." The Elder hissed like a snake. "A fool who thinks nothing of her child and the Fay. We must still take him in accordance with the law."

"What?"

"You have doomed your child. He must be given to the humans without benefit of the Fay-erie. He will surely be left to die by them."

The Elder spat on the herb-covered floor. "May the curse of bones be upon you for challenging Fay law. No more children are to be born to you."

"No!" Myrica pleaded.

The Elder pointed the bottom of her wooden staff toward Myrica, then pounded it on the floor three times. She broke the staff across her knee and threw it into the north corner of the room. "The seed of the Earth Mother shall shrivel and die within you."

Myrica silently watched the Wikkens take her son from the hut. Squirrel bones rattled in the darkness and the smell of hemlock burned her nose.

Myrica wrapped the sleeping changeling in a clean linen cloth and laid him in a moss-lined basket. He sucked on his chubby fist.

"He's a perfect baby." Rubra looked up from her needlework. "He's fat and healthy. He has the long fingers of a smith. He'll make a fine craftsman, even if he is human."

Myrica ignored the remarks. At the hearth, she bundled a stack of oatmeal cakes and packed them into a woven sack with dried mushrooms and deer-milk cheese.

"He will be a welcomed member of the clan," Rubra continued. "Tallowman will be glad to have a healthy child he can apprentice as a goldsmith."

"Tallowman will never see this child." Myrica pulled on her worn suede boots and tied them at the ankle. "I presented empty baskets to your clan broch when my first two children died. I'm not presenting a human this time."

Myrica tied her traveling sack about her waist, along with a water gourd and extra linen for the baby. Around her neck she wore a gold chain of fairy bells and god fingers that had been passed to her from her mother. She made a sling for the infant and tied him next to her breast.

"The broch will gladly accept a human. They understand the reason for the laws and the consequences of not following them," Rubra pleaded.

"Laws. Is that all that concerns you? The Wikkens steal my son, and all you talk about are laws. You don't understand the love of a mother."

"Foolish child! You talk about understanding, but what do you know?" Rubra dropped her sewing. "I lost my only child in a pool of blood in the winter snow. A small faceless beast, with crippled arms and a hollow heart. I cried for days. I cried for my baby, and I cried for myself. And I accepted my loss. I never tried to have another child, for I knew what could come of bad blood."

Myrica was silent for a moment. Then she threw on her cloak and fastened it. "I'm sorry your child died, Rubra," she said finally. "But not all children born the Seventh Year are born with bad blood. My son was not deformed. I want him back."

"Your son was taken for a reason. Please, Myrica, think about the Fay children of the future."

Myrica opened the door. The sun was just starting to lighten the eastern sky beyond the dark umbrella of the forest. "I'm going."

"Stop thinking only of yourself!"

Myrica walked out into the crisp morning.

Myrica knelt amid the tall lilies and pressed the dry leaves against her pointed ear.

"From the darkness give me sound, of voices past on this trodden ground," she chanted in the ancient fairy tongue. She heard the faint whispering of a pixie song from a previous night. She heard the obnoxious snorts of a forest troll. The haunting howl of the black dog echoed in the dark. There were sounds of cool nights and windy days, but no fairies had passed this way.

Myrica shivered and pulled at her cloak. She studied the ground and sniffed. "The trail must be here!" Myrica rubbed her tired eyes. "This is the quickest way to the openlands. What magic did the Wikkens use? There's no sound, no track, no scent."

An ashen moon rose in the eastern sky. Myrica looked in the direction the new elm saplings grew; she chewed a sassafras twig and combed hemlock needles through her hair. There was still no signs of the Wikkens' passing.

The human child cried, as he had done every hour. Myrica slumped on a mossy patch near a rotting oak and pulled the wet baby from the sling. The bells of protection around his neck jingled.

"Shut up, you pig beast." She changed the baby and offered him her aching breast. "I should leave you here for the dogs."

Myrica leaned back, careful not to hold the baby too close. She studied the moon and stars. Ursa, the bear, pointed to the north, and Draco protected the skies. As she watched, Aurora threw her blood-red curtain across the darkness.

Myrica stood up. Still looking at the heavens, she turned in a circle.

"That's it! How stupid could I have been? The sky, that's where the signs are. The Wikkens didn't travel on the ground, they flew along the treetops on bundles of ragwort stems."

Myrica tied the baby sling to the lower branches of a white pine and climbed to its top. She brushed the soft needles against her cheek. The odor of nightshade filled the air. Myrica broke a needle from the tree and rubbed it on her forehead, then turned until she could see the moonlight bending in the air, as if being sucked into a tunnel. This was the fairy passing she was looking for.

The path took them northeast toward a small human village. They crossed cultivated land, ready for spring planting.

Cold iron had cut the brown earth. The smell of the metal made her teeth ache.

When they reached the town, Myrica slipped along the streets, hiding in the shadows. She was careful not to touch the iron gates and crosses that were common on human dwellings, but her head throbbed from their nearness.

Myrica sniffed, hoping to catch the scent of her child, but the sour stench of humans overwhelmed everything. Even the herb-tinged smell of the Wikken was lost. She rounded a corner and was overcome by the scent of cooked beef.

"Flesh-eaters!" She vomited against the side of a building.

The baby stretched against his wrap and cried softly.

"Hush." Myrica rocked the baby and fumbled in her pocket. After a few minutes, she retrieved a forked stick carved with runic inscriptions. She held the stick in both hands and closed her eyes.

"Live oak of the forest, show me my child."

The stick pulled against Myrica's hand, leading her down a dark alley. She walked quietly past a sleeping man with a dog, and crossed the deserted town square. A narrow road lined with small houses stretched northward. Myrica followed it until she reached a stone house with a lamp burning in the window.

"This is it." She removed her traveling pack and put the baby on the ground.

Pressing a clove of garlic against the side of her mouth, Myrica crept to the door of the stone house. The pungent herb burned her cheek. She touched the cold wall with her left hand. A female was whispering inside. She was praying.

"Hail Mary, full of grace, the Lord is with thee . . ."

The human baby whimpered from his cold resting place. His cry roared in Myrica's sensitized ears.

"Quiet!" she snapped. "I need to hear if Cedrus is inside."

"Lord, forgive me," said the female, "I didn't know what to do."

The infant cried out again. Myrica turned from the building and picked up the child. "If you don't shut up, I'm . . ." Myrica turned. The crying was coming from the darkness, on the hillock behind the house.

"Cedrus?"

Myrica ran, the baby still in her arms. She crashed through the rose garden in back of the house. The thorns ripped at her legs and arms, stinging like pixie arrows.

"Cedrus!" Myrica struggled against the blackberry canes, not taking the time to walk "with the briars" the way her grandfather had taught her. A dog barked in the distance. Myrica sucked a scratch on the back of her hand and pushed through the new growth until she reached a rocky ledge at the crest of the hill.

"Cedrus!" she cried, gasping for air. She stumbled around on the boulders, searching the crevices for a sign of her child. The only thing she found was fresh rat dung. She cried out to the gods for help.

The moon rose above the trees and cast its light against the hillside.

"My son."

Myrica spotted a small basket tucked into a green thicket. An embroidered blanket covered the still form beneath. "What have they done to you?"

Salty tears burned her eyes. She laid the human child on the grass. Gently she picked up and caressed her withered baby, running her fingers through his soft brown hair. His small hands were blue and cold.

"How could they leave you here like this?"

Cedrus opened his mouth, but there was no cry. She pushed her breast against his dried lips. He would not eat. She smelled death; that same musky sweet odor she'd smelled in her grandmother's hut, just before she had died.

"Please eat, Cedrus." A tear dripped from her cheek to his. Cedrus closed his dark-brown eyes.

"No! Don't take him from me now! No! Wake up!" She tried to blow life back into his lungs.

"You're the grandson of Tanoak, wizard of the wood." She grabbed some sassafras leaves and rubbed them on his forehead, then held him up toward the east.

A cold wind blew.

Myrica looked at the small limp form in her arms. She fell to her knees, howling a death scream in the language of the wolf.

The human baby cried again.

"You shut up! You're never going home again. I'll leave you here for the wild dogs and the rats, the way they left Cedrus. A curse. I will put a curse on you and your house."

Myrica wrapped her dead son next to her breast and climbed down the hillside. She broke a branch from a hemlock and laid it at the back door of the stone house.

"They will pay for this." She cleared the ground and cut a pentagram in the soil with a forked oak stick.

"Gods of the forest and sky. Gods of the water and earth. I, Myrica, daughter of . . ."

The cries of the human baby echoed in the distance.

"I, Myrica, daughter of Fay and all that is of the forest, call you."

"Hail Mary, full of grace, the Lord is with thee," the female prayed inside.

"Bring my revenge against this house. Bring death to . . ."

"Our father who art in heaven," the woman prayed.

Myrica looked down. She touched her fingers to her dead son's head—What was she doing? Killing another child in revenge? Cursing a mother who lost a child?"

"They left you to die," she whispered. "Those flesh-eating beasts!"

The female inside was crying.

"Bring my revenge . . ." Suddenly Myrica stopped. Was Rubra right? Was she being selfish? Refusing to think of her son's welfare when she kept the Fay-erie from him, had she caused her own son's death?

She brushed the pentagram from the dirt and looked up at the wooden door of the house. Tears blurred her vision as she realized what she must do.

Myrica carefully wrapped her scarf over her ears and hair to disguise her appearance. She knocked lightly on the door.

"Go away. I want no beggars here in the middle of the night."

"Please," Myrica whispered.

"Go away, or I'll call my husband from his sleep."

"Your baby is in the basket." Myrica's voice caught. She paused.

The woman opened the door. She stared, wide-eyed and

unspeaking, a white handkerchief twisted between her fingers.

"Your baby lives!" The words sprang from Myrica like a curse, rasping her throat raw. Tears fell thickly, but could take none of her rage with them. How could these humans leave Cedrus on the hillside to die? Beasts! Myrica wanted to scream. Killer of helpless babies! The words would not come; her throat was closed as tightly as her fist.

Opening her cloak, Myrica exposed the still form of Cedrus. She knew she had cursed her own child in the name of mother's love. His death was not entirely the human's choice. She had kept the Fay-erie from him.

The female gasped and made the sign of the cross against evil. Myrica stopped the door as the woman tried to slam it in her face. She forced the woman to meet her eyes.

"They took my son from me, just as they took your son from you." She grabbed the woman's sleeping gown. "You let my baby die, but the death of your son will not change the mistakes we have both made."

"I'm . . . sorry," the woman stuttered.

The human baby cried again.

Myrica backed away into the darkness. She tarried at the edge of the alleyway only long enough to watch the female retrieve her child, before making her way back to the forest.

About Peter L. Manly and "Dragon Three Two Niner"

One of the misconceptions I've had to fight against most vigorously in a long career as a writer, is that I have no sense of humor. It's true that my funny bone is a little harder to reach than some; I don't, for instance, find most TV sitcoms very funny. But no one in my office who has come in and found me literally rolling on the floor laughing at—say—Dorothy L. Sayers's *Busman's Honeymoon*—the funniest book, without exception, that I ever read, or something like this Peter Manly story, has ever accused me of being inaccessible to something funny. My readers loved this one too; it took first place in the Cauldron vote.

I remember laughing till I cried over this. Granted, this has only happened to me twice with the magazine slush pile; the other story I found equally hysterical was a story called "Falling Apart" by one Larry Hodges, who didn't make it into this volume. Now you know what tickles my funny bone.

Peter Manly says he is an astronomer and physicist by training, who puts bread and peanut butter on the table by being a consultant in aerospace, electro-optics, and instrumentation, supplemented by writing in the nonfiction field about computers and astronomy.

People have asked me over the years why writers have held down such an assortment of funny jobs. Mostly it's because, unless they are among those who can successfully combine routine teaching or office skills with writing, which many of us can't, they are obliged to keep body and soul together by any assortment of work that will pay at least minimum wage, with one important qualification: the writer must be able, at very short notice, to tell the boss to take this job and shove it—which you can't do with something like teaching, where you have to finish out the year, or any career that demands dedication and a commitment of many years.

I've worked telling fortunes at a carnival, selling fashion frocks and kids' clothes door to door, singing in nightclubs and at weddings (a mug's job if there ever was one, though my musical daughter doesn't mind it), teaching junior choir in a Texas church, et cetera, et cetera, et cetera, even cleaning apartments; doing anything where I could cart the kids around under my arm. People used to ask me how I got any writing done with kids around; I always answered that it was easier to park the kids somewhere near the typewriter and let them romp, pausing now and then to make peanut butter sandwiches, than to haul them around somewhere else.

Dragon Three Two Niner

Peter L. Manly

"**D**ark Castle Approach Control, this is Princess Iru-lana aboard dragon November Bravo three two niner requesting landing instructions." Georgine was laboring beneath me, sensing that the long flight was almost over. Her silver-dark wings stretched outward as she caught a slight updraft and made the most of the altitude gain.

I mused that the castle tower operators must be asleep at the switch and was about to call again when they finally answered, "Ah, dragon three two niner, this is Dark Castle. Hold at the outer marker over the Enchanted Forest beacon. We have some traffic to clear."

"Dragon three two niner, holding," I acknowledged, slipping the empathy shell into my tunic and making sure it was secure. Its twin was kept at the castle, and whatever was said into one shell came out the other. It's a neat spell and it works well. The only problem was that I had to have a separate shell for each castle at which I might land. With the recent proliferation of landing fields, one accumulates a rather lumpy collection of shells.

I hated holding over the forest. It was full of downdrafts, probably caused by the constant use of magical energy and arcane forces. Georgine responded to my slight nudges, banking off to the right in one of her perfect turns. She was a good old girl and she really liked to fly. I could see her glancing off to the left at the castle, however, and sensed that she would rather have taken a straight-in approach. I began searching for the beacon, an energized jewel placed on a golden pillar for all dragon flyers to navigate by. Off to my right was a large gray passenger dragon, circling high over the forest, and we flew to a point underneath them. The pillar was there but the jewel was gone, probably taken by the elves again. They'd give it back later, after some concessions and maybe the sacrifice of a virgin, but meanwhile, night flyers would have no beacon. Local politics, ugh!

The downdrafts weren't too bad over the forest, but Georgine had already flown the long distance from the Blue Mist Mountains and I wanted to get her bedded down. She kept looking longingly toward the castle, her large green eyes searching for a rookery which could provide shelter. The Lesser Sun had already set. Its sharp blue cast was now missing from the landscape below. In the slanting rays of the Greater Sun, the scenery took on a soft ruby glow, enhanced by the leaves of the trees preparing for winter. The first snows had fallen in the mountains and I wanted to finish my business at the castle quickly, lest my return trip become a winter ordeal. It shouldn't take too long. All I had to do was find a reasonably competent sorcerer, have him break the counter spell on my older sister's gown, and return home. Any little trinkets I could scare up—a magical amulet or a portable curse—would be pure profit. Maybe I could flirt with one of the King's knights too—but business came first.

The Oracles had predicted that if my older sister, the Greater Princess Katrashkip of Granite Keep, couldn't wear this gown at the Midwinter Ball, then she probably wouldn't wed the prince of the Dark Castle. Without a wedding to cement the uneasy truce among the castles of the Northlands, a terrible war would break out and we would be plunged into a dark age for millennia. The seers were very specific about the point. I, for one, was glad to be a Lesser Princess so I wouldn't have to marry for politics.

Above me, I noticed the passenger dragon turning toward the castle. Georgine watched the larger dragon head for the rookeries and grunted a bit as we kept wheeling over the empty golden pillar. I patted her neck and hugged her tighter with my knees. "Don't worry, old girl. We'll probably be next." She made the humming rumble which indicated she was pleased with me, and I let her drift a bit from the pillar, in order to catch a weak updraft. She played with it for several minutes.

The empathy shell came to life. "Dragon three two niner, come to a heading west by northwest. Maintain altitude."

"Dark Castle, where are you vectoring me?"

"Dragon three two niner, we're sending you out over the ocean for a long approach to runway niner zero left at the castle. You can follow dragon one twelve heavy in."

"Ah, Dark Castle, we're a small flight. Request a straight-in approach to the timber rookery."

"Negative, dragon three two niner, your dragon hasn't been fire suppressed. New Air Transport Safety Regulations prohibit fire-breathing aircraft from utilizing timber facilities. You'll have to land on the old stone parapets."

"Three two niner out." God, but I hate bureaucrats! Georgine wouldn't belch any fire in a rookery. She's much too civilized.

I searched for and found the large passenger dragon descending ahead of me. We turned to line up with it and Georgine strained to catch up. She likes to fly tight formation, but I held her back. We were going to have to allow the larger dragon time to land and clear the apron before we swooped in.

I kept up my altitude over the Troll thickets. The last time I'd gone through their airspace they'd fired off a few arrows at me, and at least one of them had a dragon spell on it. Although they were supposed to be civilized, they were not above plundering booty from airliners which chanced to crash in their territory, and I'd always suspected that they pushed the concept of "chance" to its limits.

As we approached the cliffs of the coast, I knew there would be updrafts. Georgine could sense it, too; I could see the fine tendrils on her snout feeling for the change in wind direction. I was going to ask Approach Control for permission to spiral in the wave of air which climbed the cliffs, but they called me first. "Dragon three two niner, traffic alert at your three o'clock position. Please acknowledge."

I looked off to the right and saw six military dragons flying in formation in two flights of three. They were cruising down the coast, taking advantage of the updrafts from the cliffs. "Dark Castle, this is dragon three two niner, I have them on visual." Their wings were unmoving as they glided in precise, tight groups. It was a pretty sight as they soared over me and then peeled off to the left, one by one. As they came around in wide sweeping left banks, they separated into a line of dragons, following me as I flew out to sea. The passenger dragon ahead of me had started his crosswind turn, and I lengthened my downwind leg to give him more unloading time.

It was a normal approach. The passenger dragon was unloaded quickly and the landing apron cleared. I looked behind and saw the six military dragons strung out behind. "OK, girl, just hit the big D in the white circle and we'll be down for the night. Make it a clean one, we're visitors here." Georgine hummed and straightened her wings, preparing for the final swoop and stall. As we came in over the parapet, she dropped her clawed talons and placed the tips lightly on the lettering of the dragon port. A single beat with her wings and she was down, without even ruffling the banners on the watchtower. It was a perfect landing, and I was proud of her. She folded her dark silver wings and hummed as I patted her back.

Swinging one leg over her thick neck, I urged her head downward so I could slide to the ground. Once down, I called to her, "Come on, girl, give Mamma a kiss." She dipped her large fanged head and I kissed her below the eye, while rubbing the huge tooth which protruded through her lips. She hummed and exhaled a mixture of gas and breath, but she didn't ignite it. As I said, Georgine's a cultured lady.

I still had the reins in my hand, so I led her off the landing ground before the first of the military dragons arrived. The ground crew was approaching and I said, "We'll be here several days. Need a rook for the dragon and a refuel." At their hesitation, I proffered my Wizard's Express credit card—I wouldn't leave the Keep without it. They were satisfied.

* * *

The red Greater Sun was on the horizon as I walked Georgine down the old stone ramps to the dragon rookeries. I could look out over the leaden water and see a storm approaching from the north. The parapet to the ramp supported stone gargoyles of hideous shapes which would effectively hold the ghosts and wraiths of the night at bay.

The rookery was a well-sheltered cave, with bays for individual dragons. Several of the animals were permanently quartered, and one of the females was tending two cute babies. They were barely as tall as I and must have been newborns, although they were already spitting sparks. There were other dragons quartered in the visitor's spaces, it being late in the flying season. We were shown a large dry cove for Georgine, and before the ground attendant left, I said, "Georgine will sleep for an hour or so. Then she'll feed. Let her have two barrels of Dragon Chow and half a barrel of water. I'll come down later and give her a treat. Now, help me get her saddle and pack off. I'll need a bearer to take these to my rooms." Georgine hummed as I bedded her down, and I sat with her until slumber overtook her.

The attendants took my saddle and packs up the ramp, while my guide ushered me to a small door in the cave wall, which I hadn't seen on my previous trips to the Castle. I was unsure of what he was doing until he disappeared upward in a whoosh of scintillating light. I'd heard of elevator spells before, but I'd never used one. Dark Castle was certainly acquiring all of the modern conveniences. I was lifted easily to the main courtyard of the castle.

Getting my bearings, I walked toward the great door of the Royal Arms Hotel. As I approached the gate, I was met by a Grade Two Flunky, who made a medium bow and said, "My Lady, how may I serve you?" He had enough deference not to offend even the highest queen, but not so much that he'd be making a fool of himself if I turned out to be a swineherd.

I stopped, straightened my back, held my head high, and placed one hand on the hilt of my dagger. "I am Irulana, Lesser Princess of Granite Keep, Dragon Rider First Class, and Acolyte to the High Priestess of Imbriana."

He stood his ground. I flashed the credit card and he bubbled over with welcome. "My Lady, please follow me. Have you luggage?"

"It will be brought from the dragon rookery. Have it placed in my room. Gently. I should also like a bath drawn for me immediately and a pig, only half roasted— for my dragon— to be ready in one hour. For now, I shall enter the salon and quench my thirst while the room is being arranged."

He hurried off across the echoing lobby. I headed for the bar. The hotel seemed moderately busy, with travelers and locals. In the dim light of the bar, I could make out the usual bands of soldiers, salesmen, and scalawags. There was one knight present, but he was surrounded by several fat merchants. The jukebox was playing Country. (Isn't that a law in most bars?) The ladies present were not totally decadent, but I felt I shouldn't tarry too long if I hoped to maintain my reputation in the castle. While accepting a tankard from the proprietor, I mused over what my reputation should be. As the younger daughter of a minor nobleman, I was probably unknown in the bigger castle. My older sister Katrashkip carried all of the responsibility of marriage to noblemen for political purposes. Indeed, the object of my mission of Dark Castle was to rid a magic gown of a counterspell, so she could wear it and snag a husband. Imbriana knew she wouldn't catch one without a spell: Katrashkip had buckteeth, a hook nose, and the personality of a wounded viper with cramps. I, on the other hand, was free to dabble in magic, a trade normally forbidden to women. I could also ride dragons—and ride them better than most anybody else. I wore green leather flying pantaloons and a jaunty cap, and I carried a weapon (only a small dagger and it had just the slightest blood spell)—all to the distress of my parents, who wished that somehow I would act more like a princess. As I gazed at the heavy oak beams of the salon, I remembered their attempts to civilize me. The music from the bar reminded me of my failed studies in the gentler arts. First the dance lessons, and then music. When I showed an interest in the veil dances and salty sailor's tunes, they hid my musical instruments, dispatched my instructors to the hinterlands, and started me on classical studies.

They had made me an Acolyte to a High Priestess. I fingered the talisman of my office as I waited in the dim lounge. Imbriana, the Goddess of Domesticity, is a minor deity, but she lent sufficient respectability to my status as a Lesser Princess. The Priestess was also a closet magician and a powerful one. From her I learned both the arcane ways and the practical knowledge of being a young woman. She encouraged my work with the dragons and fueled my interest in spells. She tolerated my dress, and usually my outrageous ideas.

The doorkeeper, accompanied by a footman, interrupted my reverie, and announced that my room was ready. "My Lady, if you will walk this way . . ."

I'd be damned if I'd walk the foppish way he was sliding along, but I would follow his lead. We crossed the lobby and ascended a grand staircase. Someday I would have to make an entrance down such a staircase, just to see what it was like. Perhaps wearing the magic gown . . . naw, not my style.

The footman rushed ahead to open the room door and said, in a nearly breathless voice, "Princess, your luggage has been delivered to your room, and the chambermaids are drawing your bath." He held the door. "After you . . ."

The room was very adequate: comfortable, not too large, with a view of the ocean. The footman stood with his hand out, waiting for a tip. As an Acolyte of a Priestess, I can circumvent a tip by bestowing a magical blessing. I bade him bow down, and said the sacred words. A slight yellow corona passed over his face, and he felt the tingle of a truly unique spell. He thanked me profusely and backed out the door. Should he ever become married, the spell would make him more adept, and at peace with the role of being a subservient homemaker.

Before sliding into a warm bath, I decided to call home and tell them I had arrived safely. I rummaged in my pack and located the empathy shell. As I whistled into the opening of the hand-size pink seashell, my mind envisioned the dark crags of Granite Keep, my home castle. A disgustingly cheerful voice on the other end said, "Hello, the Baron and his staff aren't available right now, but if you'll leave your name . . ."

"Lizzie, is that you?" Lizzie was my rather scatterbrained maid-in-waiting. Being a lesser princess, I wasn't entitled to the best or the brightest of help.

"Irulana?"

"Yes. Can you take a message?"

"Not really, I can't see to write. The candles . . ." She couldn't read or write even in the broad light of both suns.

"Yes, I know. Now try to remember this. I've arrived at Dark Castle safely. I'll see the sorcerer tomorrow. If everything goes well, I should be on my way home in a couple of days. Got it?"

"Well, I'll try to remember."

"OK. I'll call again tomorrow afternoon. Anything going on that I should know about?"

"Well, your sister Katrashkip stormed out of here right after you did."

"Oh, any reason why?"

"Well, the scuttlebutt around the lackeys' quarters is that she thinks you're going to use the gown to enchant the prince yourself. She's flying to Dark Castle to stop you."

"Great! All I need is old Horseface mucking around while I'm making delicate negotiations with a feisty sorcerer."

"Pardon?"

"Oh, nothing, Lizzie. Look, just tell Pops—ah, the Baron—that I've arrived safely and will call tomorrow. OK?"

"OK. Have a nice day."

"Lizzie, how many times have I instructed you not to tell me what kind of day to have?"

"Uh, three?"

"More like three hundred. Good-bye."

I went to the next room, anticipating a long relaxing soak. There were perfumed scents and soaps handy. There was a glass of chilled wine by the tub. There were soft dry robes waiting. Unfortunately, in the center of it all was my elder sister Katrashkip, her bony shoulders and fatty thighs submerged in the tub which I had ordered. One look at me and she threw a bottle of scent, screaming, "You think you can sneak off with my magic gown and capture the heart of the Prince? Well, you've got another thing coming, you little . . . you little . . . you little . . . !"

I calmly closed and lock-spelled the door to the bathroom, and picked up the room's empathy shell. "Front desk? I'd like a different room, please. Yes. Preferably one without a screaming demon in the bathtub. Thank you. I'll return the key on my way down to the dragon rookery. And please have my things moved. Thank you again." I'm going to be really glad when she does marry some poor hapless prince and is out of my way once and for all.

The walk down to the dragon rookery was cool, the sea breeze bringing a salt tang to my nostrils. As I approached Georgine's cove, she rumbled with pleasure. She even stopped eating for a few moments while I rubbed the spot behind her ears which causes her to go limp. After a while, the half-roasted pig arrived; Georgine smelled it long before she saw it. Her humming rumble reverberated throughout the cavern and she sat up, her tail banging against the wall with a solid thumping sound. It was at times like these, after a long and successful journey, that the bond between dragon and rider was cemented.

I sat leaning against one of her large legs as she slowly finished roasting the pig to perfection. Then with my dagger I cut off a token slice and left the rest to her. Since I had missed dinner, I made my token a bit larger than usual, but Georgine, ever the grand hostess, did not begrudge me the extra meat. The leather flagon of wine I had brought added the last touch to a perfect meal.

Soon, Georgine was lying on her bloated stomach, snoring peacefully at about two point eight on the Richter scale. I was becoming drowsy myself, so I quietly stole away and headed for the hotel. After I'd gotten my new room key and was heading toward the stairway, I was confronted by a rather garishly dressed fop with ladies of questionable merit on either arm. He was obviously drunk. He let one of them go and reeled toward me, slurring, "Hey, baby! You wanna grab a little gusto?"

He wrapped his arm around me and placed his hand on a portion of my anatomy normally reserved for sitting. If I'd been able to reach my dagger, he'd have pulled back a bloody stump. As it was, I merely loosened several cartilage joints in his wrist, then returned his hand to a more polite location, saying, "If there's one thing I can't stand, it's gustoes that are . . ." I looked at his midsection " . . . little!" It made my day.

The room was better this time, and the bath was excellent. After a long day traveling, it was comforting to know that Georgine was well bedded down and all I had to do was relax. As I stood on the balcony, wrapped in a long warm robe, I finished the last of the wine and felt at peace. Sleep came swiftly, and the morning slowly.

I was up early, as usual, and checked on Georgine. She was too bloated to fly now, but tomorrow we'd make a short flight for the exercise, and just for the fun of it. I made a note to find somebody else to fly with. Perhaps they would know the good soaring areas locally.

After breakfast, I set out along the narrow passageways above the market to find the old sorcerer. The scents and sounds of foreign traders arose from the stalls and tables of the hawkers, following me through the slim corridors of the ancient guilds. Finally, I reached the crooked door of the sorcerer. I could sense a lock spell on it, so I knocked. There was no answer. I knocked again. The lock spell wavered, then held steady. Somebody or something had moved through the field: probably someone on the other side of the door, looking at me through a spy-hole. I knocked again and waited. Finally, I shouted, "I'm going away to get a good book and something to eat. Then I shall come back, sit on your step, take my meal, and read until I finish the book." There was no answer. "Then I'll get another book and come back."

The spell disappeared and the door creaked open. There were cobwebs across the opening, as if nobody had entered the sorcerer's shop in a long time. The dark room was mostly empty, but the hearth smelled of recent use. On the mantel was an owl. I couldn't tell if it was stuffed or alive, so I watched it for more than a minute until it blinked. Alive, then. I scanned the musty interior, noting the vials and potions lining the walls.

"All right," I said to nobody in particular. "When do I see you?" I waited in silence, the owl watching my every move. Near the window was a tall stool, and I sidled over to it. As I sat down, I called out, "Remember, I am prepared to spend a long, long time waiting."

After another minute, a short balding man came bustling through a doorway from the back and said, "The sorcerer will not be able to see you today. Perhaps tomorrow. Now please . . ." He was motioning to me with his hands, almost as if he were guiding a flock of chickens. "I must ask you to leave. He is a very busy man. An appointment is required. The procedures, you know . . ."

I could feel the power in the funny little man and knew he was the sorcerer. The fact that he did not have an assistant to shoo me out bespoke only his poverty. In an age of increasing technology, magicians and sorcerers were falling on hard times. I reached into my pouch and withdrew a large gold coin. He didn't notice it until I spoke his name: "Fastasertine!" Knowing a sorcerer's true name deprives him of some of his power over you. It was only a quirk of luck that he had, in his younger days, tried to bed a Priestess of Imbriana, and she had, in later days, given the secret to me.

He froze and said, "You guess!" His eyes locked on the gold piece as they would devour a lover.

I smiled and countered, "I know, Fastasertine!" I know who you are, and I know how much you want this gold piece. It would warm you in the winter, lend power to your spells, and ward off the cold fate of age which gnaws at your bones."

The sorcerer licked his lips and asked, "What is it you want?"

"A simple task, really. I have a magic gown. She who wears it is irresistible. Unfortunately, some magician has put a spell on it, rendering it useless. I need the spell removed."

A light beamed in the sorcerer's eye, "Surely you have no need of such a gown, for you are indeed irresistible."

"The gown is not for me. It is for my sister. She wishes to wed the Prince of Dark Castle."

The sorcerer cast his eyes downward and said, "My lady, I am perfectly willing to remove the spell, but first I must warn you. The Prince is not . . . Well, he just hasn't . . . I mean, perhaps he is not the right man for your lovely sister. The prince is, in fact, a weakling, a drunkard and a womanizer. Only last night, some wench in the hotel broke his wrist—and he had two other hussies with him at the time. I was called to mend the bones this morning and the harlots were still with him. I pray that you warn your sister of his ways. Perhaps if you were to meet him yourself . . ."

"We've met. Now break the spell." I was removing the gown from my pack. It was a quite ordinary ball gown, neither too revealing nor too prim. I could, however, feel the power of the enchantment in the garment.

The old man took it. He felt it, sniffed it, closed his eyes and ran his hands over it. "The gown is ancient. Hundreds of queens and princesses have used it to gain power. Others have used and misused its enchantment. Adulteresses have worn it more often than maids. There is much sorrow and misery in the gown, much more than there is happiness. Are you sure that it is wise to break the spell blocking the gown's use?"

"Positive. You haven't met my sister. She needs it."

He chuckled and replied, "Probably not as badly as the poor wench I met at the hotel this morning. The face of a beaver combined with a gargoyle, the chest of a dead man, and the hips of a rhinoceros. Now she could . . ."

"Then you've met her." Nobody else could possibly fit that description.

"Oh my," he chuckled, "the prince would really get what he deserved." He thought for a moment. "But is that fair to your poor sister? Although she may look . . ."

I interrupted him. "I'm not entirely sure, but I believe she had several people killed in order to obtain this gown. Good people. And if she didn't, then I still believe she's capable of it."

"I see. And if I remove the blocking spell, then they will both get what they deserve. May I also suggest a spell of my own as a wedding gift?"

"And what is that?"

"I have one and only one portable spell left. It ensures absolute fidelity in a couple."

"Absolute? How does it do that?"

He gave me a fatherly frown and said, "You don't want to know."

"Oh." My mind raced through several unpleasant methods of ensuring fidelity. All were acceptable. Some were funny. Some were disgustingly funny.

I gestured toward the gown. "Then you can break the spell?"

"Oh, yes. It's a Class Five spell, not too old, say a century and a half. Feels like a couple of rank amateurs have tried to break it recently—put some dents in the spell, but no harm done." He spread the gown out on his workbench, mumbling to himself. Gathering some powders from the glass vials on the nearby shelf, he looked, for a moment, like a man thoroughly happy doing what he does best. "Step aside, there, young lady," he said as he made preparations. "Never know when some fool has put a hidden backfire on one of these. Some people have a strange sense of humor."

Smoothing the gown, pressing the wrinkles out, he said, "Oh, my!"

"A problem?"

"I do believe so."

"Well?"

"The spell was made by a Guild brother of mine. I'm afraid I can't just go off willy-nilly breaking Sorcerer's Guild spells. It wouldn't be ethical!"

"Well, how can you tell who made the spell?"

"It's here in the back of the neck. See the label?"

It took three more gold coins to convince him that guilds weren't what they used to be. As I left the shop with the newly reactivated gown, I considered wearing it for a grand entrance down the staircase at the hotel. Then I mused that the Prince might once again be in the lobby, and shelved the idea.

Back in my room, I called home and reported success in my mission. I'd stay two more days and then fly home on a leisurely southern route. Pops (the Baron) rumbled his approval, and gave me the verbal equivalent of a pat on the top of my head. Why is it that fathers feel they have to pat their daughters on the head? Then again, why is it that I like it so much?

I took the gown to big sister Katrashkip's room to present it to her, but found she had checked out and gone to the dragon rookery. Since I had to check on Georgine anyway, I went to the rookery, thinking my sister had perhaps rented a dragon to fly home. The thought crossed my mind that I might have to rescue my elder Princess, since her skill at flying dragons really stank. She knew it, and any dragon she got on knew it.

Georgine was gone!

There was a letter with my name on it nailed to the gate. It read, "Return my magic gown intact and I won't kill your stupid lizard. It's being kept under a fear cage spell at Bloody Cove. Don't show up without the gown. Katrashkip, Greater Princess of Granite Keep."

My sister does some really dumb things, but most of them don't affect me, so I don't bother to try to beat any sense into her head, as she well deserves. This time, however, she had gone too far. Georgine was a sensitive, gentle friend who trusted even idiots like Katrashkip. I hurried to the rent-a-dragon lot, and endured a sales pitch of high order before I gave the dragon jockey the ultimatum: either shut up and rent me a dragon or point me toward his competitor. The charge card helped, although he pointed out that I was reaching my credit limit rapidly. I'd worry about that tomorrow.

"Dark Castle, this is Rent-A-Wing November one two seven requesting clearance for departure."

"Ah, November one two seven, we don't seem to have a flight plan filed for you."

"Dark Castle, this is a local flight."

"November one two seven, it's still recommended . . ."

"OK, we'll do it your way. Dark Castle control, this is Rent-A-Wing November one two seven declaring an emergency. Dragon theft, suspect at Bloody Cove. Do not, repeat do not, apprehend until dragon is set free. Dragon is under a fear cage spell."

"What are your intentions, November one two seven?"

"Suspect has requested ransom. I intend to apprehend the

suspect and free the dragon. If any military forces land, she'll kill the captured dragon. Understand?"

"Understand, November one two seven. You are cleared. We will scramble a military flight, but will hold off until you give the word." I was airborne without acknowledging his clearance. I could hear him shouting, into another empathy shell, "Air Force Bravo and Charlie, operational scramble— this is not a test! This is not a test! Follow that dragon!"

The blare of the klaxon reached us and spooked my rented dragon. I nudged her and gave her a soothing sound. Usually I try to establish rapport with a dragon before I'm airborne, but there just wasn't time. I nudged her again to bank left and follow the rugged coastline south. The military dragons were forming up behind me.

Bloody Cove wasn't far, just a few minutes' flying time away. As I circled the cove, I could see my precious Georgine cowering under an invisible net. Katrashkip was standing out on the headland, her long stringy hair blowing in the wind, revealing her bald spot.

She shouted something at me as I approached, but I couldn't make it out. I circled once again and landed inland, near the grassy slope which led to Georgine's prison of fear. Katrashkip came running to me, screaming, "You little . . ."

"Back off, big sister! I've got the gown and I'm even going to let you use it. Now what have you done to my dragon?"

"Your stupid lizard is OK. It's only in a fear cage. Now give me the gown!"

"First, I've asked you repeatedly not to refer to Georgine as 'it' or 'stupid lizard.' Georgine is a 'she,' and sometimes I think she has more common sense than you do."

"Well, if you ever hope to fly on 'her' again, you'd better get off that dragon and hand me the gown."

"First you release Georgine."

"First you get off that dragon and show me the gown." We were at a stalemate. "Remember, I can make the cage smaller and drive your pet lizard insane with fear." Round one went to Princess Katrashkip.

I slid off the rented dragon, holding the pack with the gown. "Where did you get that portable cage spell?"

"It's really simple, you just add water. Daddy gave it to me." She was pleased. "He said it might come in handy if I were ever assaulted—you know, by some sex-starved maniac." I mused that anybody sexually interested in Katrashkip would have to be certifiably insane, so I guess it made sense.

"OK. Here's the gown. Now release Georgine."

"Not until I'm on the rented dragon—with the gown."

I smelled a rat, but I had the Air Force backing me up, so I let her get on the dragon. "OK. Now how do you nullify the cage spell?"

She nudged the dragon upward into flight and shouted, "You think I'd tell you, sucker?"

The dragon had made one tentative flap of her wings and was about to make her takeoff thrust when I shouted the secret command which only dragons and a few humans know. She was commanded to land immediately. She faltered, falling on her chest, and dumped Katrashkip in an unglamorous heap on the ground. I ran to my ungrateful big sister and knocked her down with a flying body slam (and Pops said I wouldn't ever learn anything watching professional wrestling).

Katrashkip had had the wind knocked out of her, so I grabbed her in a half nelson. She managed to get a good elbow into my ribs, but I held on, fighting for supremacy, and finally turning my grip into a full nelson. I rolled her over onto her face and spat, "OK, big sister, either you tell me how to release Georgine or you die right here. Right now." I wasn't really going to kill her, but I gave her a knee in the ribs to remind her just how serious I was.

She sobbed and said, "Can't . . . can't breathe!"

I let up on her and she squirmed out of my hold, scrambling free. She had grabbed my dagger and was brandishing it in a rather amateurish manner. Sometimes an amateur can be fairly lethal, but I was well trained in unarmed combat, and simply kicked the dagger from her grasp. I'm proud to say that I did it without damaging the blade. As to Katrashkip's wrist, well, her backhand will never be the same.

She came at me again, fighting the way a girl fights. It's no match for somebody who has trained well. In a few punches it was all over. She was lying on the ground, and I stood over her. "Well?"

"Well what?" She put her hand to her face. Her nose may have been broken, but I thought it was a definite improvement.

"Well, how do you release Georgine?"

"Just whistle. You know how to whistle, don't you?"

I stuck two fingers in my mouth and let loose. Georgine shot into the air and across the sky.

The Air Force boys gave me a lift back to the castle. I convinced them it was all just a big misunderstanding—family squabble and all. No charges pressed.

I found Georgine in the rookery. I had to soothe her for a week before she would fly with me again.

Katrashkip married the Prince of Dark Castle and they lived ever after. Now and then I wander by the castle to show the Air Force boys a trick or two—in the air. Georgine can still outfly those military nags.

And the moral of this tidy little tale? Sometimes you have to damn near kill the Princess just to rescue the dragon.

About Lynne Armstrong-Jones and "The Case of Kestra"

Lynne Armstrong-Jones embodies perfectly one of my major maxims for beginning writers: if you get a rejection slip, don't take it personally; just send me something else.

Many people who could make it in writing give up too quickly; after one or maybe two rejections they go away, God knows where, and I never hear of them again. These are seldom the people to whom I'd like to suggest that they take up knitting afghans if they want a hobby, but the ones I really want to hear from again.

Lynne, who has become one of my more valued contributors—if I see her name on a manuscript, at least I know it'll be worth reading even if I can't print it just now—took this advice to heart. In the pile of manuscripts when I began reading for the magazine were half a dozen stories—and I forget how many I read before she finally sent me something I could use. Since then I don't believe I've printed an anthology without one of her contributions.

And the moral of this story is: never get discouraged; if I reject your story I'm not saying, necessarily, "Go away and take up stamp collecting, never darken my door again," but "I can't use this particular story this week. Try me again, maybe next time when I'm not so overbought or with a better story that I can't bear to turn down."

Charlie Brown of *Locus* made a very good point; one of the worst things that can happen to a small magazine is success; and on at least one level it's true. I get more good stories that I can use. Rejection may not even mean your story is so bad, just that I can't wedge it into an already overbought issue. Now, if I could only get as many subscriptions as I do manuscripts! I sometimes think if all my contributors subscribed, the magazine would be solvent—and they'd be contributing to our survival.

When I first knew Lynne she was expecting her first child; she now has both a son and a daughter. She lives in Canada with her family. Sooner or later, no doubt, I'll run into her at a convention. Until then, I know everything I need to know about her: she can deliver a good story. I think this may have been the first of many stories of hers I printed, though granted most of them were in anthologies rather than in the magazine—and a story that is right for one market seldom fits the other.

The Case of Kestra

Lynne Armstrong-Jones

Quite a while had passed now since the accident. Most of her body had healed, but it would never again be the same.

And she hated it. She detested this new body of hers.

Oh yes, people had told her again and again that she was lucky just to be alive.

Sometimes she wondered if that was true. What good was life when she couldn't walk?

Drew watched her as she sat there looking out of the window. That was all she ever seemed to do anymore.

He sighed. Was it going to be another one of those days? He dreaded even talking to her. When she got into one of her looking-out-of-the-window days, it meant that she was spending her time thinking about everything she couldn't do now.

He remembered only too well the last time that he'd interrupted her window-gazing. She'd gone on for what seemed like hours—forever pointing out all the people who were walking by. Or running, or bike-riding, or anything else she could no longer do.

Drew was at a loss. She wouldn't even paint anymore. Wouldn't read. Nothing but feel sorry for herself.

For once, Drew was wrong. Today she wasn't looking at the people. The hustle and bustle below in the streets was not holding her attention today.

Her mind and eyes were very much on something else.

A small bird hopped happily along the rooftop just beside the bowed window of their little living room. There was a level section extending beneath the eaves. It was in this space that Kestra had once seen the nest, but she hadn't had time then to pay much attention. . . .

She watched as the little bird stretched out its wings and preened.

How wonderful it would be to fly, thought Kestra with a sigh.

"Something else I can't do!" she muttered aloud.

"What? Kestra, honey, did you say something?"

The young woman just shook her head as she watched the bird fly away.

Drew sighed. Was there any way to bring her out of her depression?

After he'd helped Kestra onto the bed for her nap, Drew found his eyes drifting once more to the phone book where it sat in its tray.

Should he do it? He knew that Kestra would be furious.

He grabbed the big book and opened it in front of him on the table.

Let's see—how the hell was it spelled? P . . . p . . . psy . . . psychiatrists. That was it!

He seized the pen from its holder and began to write down numbers.

Kestra's mind had drifted into the comfort of sleep's escape.

She was no longer disabled once she was asleep. Usually she dreamed of how she'd been before the accident—but this time was different.

Kestra soared. Her wings were strong and big. She felt the glory of the sun upon her face and closed her eyes to intensify the sensation. She felt the updraft catch her and push her onward.

She altered the position of her wings, ever so slightly, and felt her incline slow to a steady soaring. She looked downward, grateful to be seeing the trees once more, rather than the dusty rooftops of the small city.

Happily, she floated down, extending her feet toward the branch of the tallest tree.

She steadied herself and then studied her surroundings. The gentle breeze brought with it interesting sounds and smells.

It was beautiful here!

Suddenly, another sound distracted her—

"Kestra! Honey, wake up! It's almost time for supper."

Drew tried to be as gentle as he could, but his voice had risen when she failed to respond.

Her eyes opened. She blinked, confused.

"Is something wrong, honey?" Kestra seemed so disoriented! He pulled her carefully up to a sitting position, mindful of her useless legs.

"Mmm." She was shaking her head, needing to clear it.

She looked around herself, at the furniture, at the enclosed space imposed by the square room—at the man.

She was furious.

"Here! Here—in a room! Damn you—damn you!"

Drew's jaw dropped. He felt anger rising inside of him. He wanted to shove her away and say "good riddance" or something—

But he couldn't. He loved this woman—or, at least, he had loved what she had been.

His eyes were teary. *I've worked so hard,* he thought, *so hard, to try to help you.* . . .

Finally, she turned to look at him. She didn't even notice his tears.

"You brought me back," she said.

His brow puckered as he tried to figure out what she was talking about.

"You brought me back," she repeated, with less animation this time.

Drew licked his lips. "It's almost time for supper" was all that he could think of to say.

Supper? The word instantly brought to mind images of mice being ripped apart by sharp beaks and powerful talons—

She shook her head again . . . somewhere between the mists of what could be and what truly was . . .

Kestra looked into Drew's face. Her gaze was blank.

Drew swallowed. He eased her into her wheelchair, and into the small dining area.

There was something here, she had decided—something important.

She was staring out the window again. But she would have more peace this time, now that Drew had gone to work.

Kestra was trying to summon the bird back. She'd tried whispering "birdie, birdie" until it had dawned on her that that was a bit weird, considering that it couldn't hear her anyway. After she'd stopped saying the words, though, her mind had continued.

It seemed as though only seconds elapsed before the little thing had alighted once more upon the rooftop beside Kestra's window.

She laughed aloud with delight.

Had she fallen asleep? No. She was awake.

Yet, somehow, she was with the bird.

She was the bird.

No. Not that one. A bird of prey. Most definitely a bird of prey.

But it did not matter what kind it was.

The wind caught her and pulled her along—a slow, gradual incline. This time the sun was on her back. She felt beautifully warm and comfortable, happier than she could ever remember being. It was absolutely glorious to feel the different wind currents as they caught her wings, lifting and lowering her.

It was an incredible experience to dive downward, watching the trees and bushes on the ground come closer, closer, while the air rushed by her face.

Once she lit upon a low-hanging branch in a field of long grasses, and a few bushes. Fascinated, she watched the little creatures going about their business. From time to time, one of them would sense her presence and scurry away as quickly as its tiny feet would carry it. Her eyes were upon it until the end of its tail disappeared down its little burrow.

She tightened her grasp upon the branch as the gentle breeze set it to swaying.

Kestra lifted her face into the slight draft and closed her eyes, deeply content. . . .

The noise was like a thunderclap, but sharper, and more painful to the ears.

The blast came again—too powerful to ignore.

Kestra felt her world collapsing around her—desperately she clung to her little branch, to her gentle breeze, to her warm sunshine, to her feathers and wings.

But the blast came again. She felt as if she was being ripped apart—

"Kestra!"

The sound filled the room.

Kestra's eyes opened. Strange images whirled before her—

Where was she? Had the wind blown her far away?

No. That wasn't it.

This was a strange place. Somehow, that horrible noise had brought her here.

But why? She had the feeling that she should remember . . .

"Kestra!"

She became aware of the pressure on her shoulders. Someone was shaking her.

Her lips moved.

"Drew." Her voice was a hoarse whisper.

The man sighed. Then he leaned forward and embraced her. He was trembling.

"Kestra," he moaned. "Kestra."

"I will not see a psychiatrist! I am not disabled in the head, too!"

Drew took a deep breath. "Kestra. I won't let you use that

tactic with me anymore. I'm sorry you're crippled, I really am. But you've got to face reality. You've got to go on with your life!"

She had turned the chair so that she was looking out of the window.

The man walked over and turned her toward the inside of the little apartment.

Kestra's eyes were like ice as Drew knelt in front of her.

"No escape this time. I want you to hear me through."

She said nothing as he took her hand in his.

"Kestra, I care about you. I want you to be happy. I want you to get help." He spoke more quickly as she turned her face away, trying to avoid him. "Listen—I felt as if I was really losing you this time. It was as if you were somewhere else! Please, Kestra! Have some concern for my feelings."

Frustrated by the lack of response, he rose and walked back toward the kitchen.

I've had enough of this, he thought. Maybe I've been too nice to her.

"I've made up my mind," he said, still facing the spice rack. "I'm going to take you to see Dr. Simpson, and that's that."

His firmness made him feel a bit better. But when he turned to her, he could see that she was already gone.

She had never flown this high before! The updraft was incredible! Up and up and up farther still, her wings pushing hard to give her more speed—

Rain droplets caressed her, refreshing her.

She had thought that she could never run out of energy, but she knew that she'd gone as high as she could—this time.

Gradually, she stretched out her wings at her side, leveling off, decreasing her speed. The fine mist dampened her feathers, but she didn't mind, even though she knew that she would need to alight somewhere and let them dry.

The sun had come out once more, and so she sat upon her favorite branch, watching other birds, and forest creatures, as she enjoyed the comforting warmth which emanated from the now-golden sky.

She was hungry after her flight. Her sharp eyes scanned the greenery of the forest floor, alert for any movement.

She sat motionless, secure in the knowledge that her brown feathers made her virtually invisible in the thick, shadowy leaves.

Only her golden eyes were active.

Then quickly she was in motion. Her entire body moved at once: every feather, every tendon, every element of her being, together in its quest.

She extended her talons. Then the mouse was in her steely grasp.

With a cry of victory, she sought the updraft and flew easily to the uppermost branches of the pine. She held the little morsel against the branch, while she tore its flesh with her curved beak.

The meat was delicious.

Kestra had been musing over how much easier it was now. Sometimes slipping into her bird persona was more natural than rolling her wheelchair from window to window.

She had noticed, too, that different birds had been returning to her window ledge more and more frequently.

What a strange little bird this was. It didn't quite resemble any other bird she'd ever seen. She'd even tried to find it in a reference book, but had had no luck.

"What are you, little one?" How very weird, she thought, regarding it closely. It looks like some sort of small hawk, but it's not.

Kestra sighed, fascinated, and smiled as she focused her thoughts and prepared to send her spirit inside the creature. This time, though, she focused even more of her energy into escaping from her prison—

And then, as usual, she had become the bird—but this time, something was different!

Somehow, no matter what had happened before, she had always suspected, deep inside, that it was only occurring in her mind.

This time, it felt real, more natural . . . scarier . . .

She looked through the screen, at the inside of her apartment—at herself.

This can't be happening! She looked closely at the human body, which sat looking at her, a smile on its lips. She swallowed hard.

When I open my eyes, I'll be back in my apartment.

But she wasn't!

Kestra realized that she had moved away from the ledge. She looked below and was fascinated to see how the street, with its cars and people, appeared from this angle.

She moved her wings, noticing how real everything was this time. She flew toward the sun, feeling the wind streaming past her—so beautiful, so wonderful.

She soared and dove and climbed again, loving the feeling of strength and freedom . . . how awful even to think of what it was like before.

A strange cry filled the air. She turned to see the hawk, gliding gracefully, not far from her. He came alongside her for a moment—then dove away, into the trees.

Without hesitation, Kestra turned to follow—then heard another cry, which sounded as if it came from far away. She found herself slowing to a hover, as though held by some invisible force.

She paused for a moment, unsure, then moved again in the direction of the strange cry. It was a mournful sound, almost a lament.

Kestra glided back to the city, mesmerized by the sorrowful keening. Hovering at the window, she saw him . . .

Tears trickled steadily from his eyes as he called the woman's name.

Kestra opened her beak and called to him, urgently. He looked up, confused. He looked at the unresponsive woman, and back to the bird.

Kestra called to him again, willing him, begging him. She closed her eyes, and concentrated all of her energy . . .

When she soared toward the forest, she saw him. Yellow eyes met hers, and she felt a strange yet familiar tingle down her spine.

Kestra called, and his response was immediate. She led

Drew toward the taller trees, her mind filled with images of stick-gathering and nest-building. She could almost feel the warm roundness of the eggs beneath her. The joyous excitement captivated them both.

About Lawrence Watt-Evans and "The Palace of al-Tir al-Abtan"

Lawrence Watt-Evans had—at the time of this story—a novel in print, and when this story appeared he had dropped out of college to concentrate on his writing, while his wife retained her job at IBM. He was unwilling to give his advice to young writers when asked—rare for writers, who are usually, words being their business, ready to give all sorts of unsolicited advice to anybody at the drop of a subordinate clause. When convinced that we meant it—our slant has always been almost as much to writers as to readers—he suggested that a beginning writer "write novels; first because they are easier to sell—" which is certainly true, the market for short stories being very tight. Second, he says, in a novel a few flaws won't show; not the case with a short-short." And this from the winner of a Hugo for a short story! That may be why he won it; in a very short story, every word counts, while in a novel you can waste a few.

The Palace of al-Tir al-Abtan

Lawrence Watt-Evans

This is a tale of the wizard al-Tir al-Abtan, when he dwelt in the ancient city of Tahrir, on the shore of the southern sea.

The Palace of al-Tir al-Abtan stood, of the wizard's choice, in the poorest quarter of Tahrir. To reach it, a determined traveler would find himself required to pass through alleys that were little more than tunnels through crumbling piles of brick, and down streets that were no more than mud-filled gaps between one decrepit tenement and the next. The Most Profound Tir, the great magician of the age, had raised his palace here to avoid the petty intrigues of lesser wizards, and the maddening importunities of nobles and kings upon his time and talent. He did not care directly to refuse the lords of the earth admission to his palace, for that would mean constant harassment by those seeking exceptions or an end to the ban; but instead, he put the palace where no self-respecting nobleman would dare approach it, and where those who did approach it could be freely dealt with.

The Most Profound Tir made it impossible for any save himself to find a gate in the outer wall of his residence. Whether the gate was concealed somehow, or moved about, or did not actually exist at all was a matter of much debate among the people of Tahrir. Certainly, when he chose to enter or leave, a gate appeared, but no one else could ever find it again afterward, or remember just where it had been.

Thus did the wizard guard his privacy, and for fully a century his palace remained inviolate, while he grew in necromantic prowess, and those about him lived and died; and in all those years that passed without touching his citadel, no man or woman other than al-Tir al-Abtan saw the inside of the marble walls that separated the palace grounds from the remainder of the city. Even when the magician himself was away about the world, the palace was said to be guarded by a demon, or ghoul, that none saw but all feared. It was said, also, that other creatures, equally terrible, patrolled the gardens.

As tales grow in the telling, it was soon rumored that Tir used djinni and afrits as his household slaves, and his palace was shunned as an unholy and fearsome place, even when unrest came upon the city.

And unrest did come, for it happened that, many years after al-Tir al-Abtan completed the construction of his vast edifice, a foolish and evil man ascended the throne as Sultan of Tahrir, one Selim ibn Jafar. This sultan so oppressed his people that those who could, fled the city, leaving behind only the poor and wretched, who knew that they would be no more welcome elsewhere.

Thus, while the magician's palace remained untouched, the condition of the city about it grew ever worse. The loathsome stench of poverty spread across the city, as beggars, thieves, whores, and cutthroats played an ever-larger role in the life of Tahrir.

The city became as a stinking swamp about the foot of the Sultan's throne, and like a rising tide about a seaside rock the decay closed in, as more and more of the wealthy fled the city, allowing their homes to be overrun by the starving beggars and bloody-handed thieves. The rot came ever nearer to the Sultan's Palace, as if to surround it as it already surrounded Tir's palace.

The Sultan Selim ibn Jafar was not totally insensible to this situation, and in the fourth year of his reign he could no longer stand the idea of his home being lost amid filth and poverty. He did not see that his own actions were the cause, but rather cursed Allah, in his folly, for sending this blight upon his city. He declared open war upon his own people, accusing them of treason in their failure to maintain his city despite the burdens he placed upon them and the mistreatment and injustice he perpetrated. His men were sent out with torches, instructed to burn the tenements and brothels to the ground; but most of these soldiers simply disappeared forever in the maze of streets, either through desertion or because the unhappy citizens had ambushed them and cut their throats. The fires that began were short-lived and ineffective.

The only outcome was the incitement for the populace, and it was then that the Sultanate of Tahrir ended, as the sultan's subjects stormed the palace, and tore it stone from stone, and treated all those within its walls in barbarous fashion, leaving none whole enough to be recognized.

When the Sultan's corpse lay sprawled upon the floor of his own throne room, and his head adorned a spike on his own gate, the beggar-king who had led the mob and usurped the throne looked about himself and was well pleased with what he saw. His ragged followers had slaughtered every noble and man of wealth left in the city, staining the floors of the remaining great houses with their blood; he was absolute ruler of everything in Tahrir.

Everything, that is, except the palace of al-Tir al-Abtan.

That, the beggar King saw, would not do. He did not intend to let anyone remain who might interfere with his rule.

He knew that the palace was the work of a mighty magician, and he did not care to face such a foe himself. Instead, the new overlord of Tahrir determined to send a single expert thief into the Palace, to see whether the enchanter, whom no one had seen in years, still lived.

Chosen for this task was a lad of twenty, whose name was Abu al-Din; this name was known throughout much of the city as the most promising housebreaker of the time. He was a bold and brash fellow, and when news of his selection reached him he proudly accepted the commission as his due. The King summoned him to the royal presence, and charged him as follows:

"You will enter the palace of the wizard al-Tir al-Abtan,

by surmounting the wall that guards it, since there is no gate to be found. You will explore the grounds, taking careful note of all traps, pitfalls, and sentinels; you will enter the palace, and learn as best you can its plan and arrangement, once again taking note of all safeguards. Should you be spotted by any resident, slay him; should you find the necromancer, alive or dead, bring back his head. Do you understand?"

Abu al-Din nodded and said, "I understand, and I obey." He bowed low, with perhaps a touch of mockery in his action, and then took himself quickly home to his little attic to prepare.

Perhaps thirty enthusiastic fellow citizens followed him, calling advice and encouragement, and waited outside his window to see if he would actually do as he had promised, and enter the demon's lair.

Abu ignored them. He ate a fine meal, but not a heavy one, while he considered what to bring.

He knew nothing of what he would face, and therefore could not prepare for any specific dangers. Since all other magicians of degree had departed Tahrir, he could not obtain any magic to aid him.

At last he decided to equip himself as he would for any ordinary housebreaking, and trust in luck and the will of Allah to see him through.

He wore a robe with a stout quilted front that would turn a light blow. He wrapped a long, strong rope about his waist, and tied its end to a heavy iron hook that he hung on his left shoulder. He bore a good, long dagger on his belt. Nothing else.

He was followed through the streets by a small crowd of well-wishers, but when he came at last to the avenue that ran along the palace wall, when he faced that black marble barrier, he was suddenly alone. His entourage had faded into the shadowy alleys, terrified of the legendary power of the archimage beyond.

Whistling loudly, to show any watchers he knew were there his lack of fear, Abu flung his hook, trailing rope, over the wall; on the second toss, the barbed iron hook caught and held.

He clambered quickly up the line. At the top of the wall he turned and waved briefly and bravely to his unseen audience; then he turned and looked down at the palace grounds.

He saw nothing. Though the sun was bright overhead, it was as if he peered into a deep, dark cave.

Puzzled, he gathered up the rope and peered into the gloom, trying to make out any detail at all.

He could not. The blackness was impenetrable.

Cautiously, he freed his hook from its lodgment on the wall's inner edge and then lowered it slowly down into the dark.

After a moment's descent he heard it strike ground with a muffled thump; as he handed down more rope the line grew slack.

Something, he knew, was down there, something that seemed to support the iron hook without difficulty.

A shiver of apprehension ran through him, and he glanced back out at the surrounding streets.

He saw no one, but he knew that he was being watched. He would not, he swore silently to himself, show himself a coward so quickly as this!

He pulled up the hook, secured it solidly to the wall's outer edge, and then with a prayer and a gulp of air lowered himself down into the blackness.

His feet and legs vanished, yet he felt no different. Then his body was gone. And finally, as his head fell below the top of the wall, he was engulfed in darkness—but only for an instant, and then he was below the blackness and able to see a fine grassy sward just below him, no more than a man's height away, surrounded by flowering bushes.

He looked up, and saw the blue sky and bright sun, and he smiled.

"A conjuror's trick, no more!" he told himself quietly. He quickly pulled himself back up onto the wall, freed the hook, and then, gathering up the ropes once more, he dropped down inside. To the watchers in the alleys, he was gone, and did not return, and gradually, as the sun descended the western sky, they grew bored and drifted away.

Inside the wall, Abu landed catlike, crouched and ready for anything—or so he thought to himself.

When he saw his surroundings, however, his alert eyes glazed slightly. He was in a garden, a garden like none he had ever imagined.

Raised in the streets, he had rarely seen any gardens save those scraggly patches of vegetables and herbs in back lots and on rooftops that some of the frugal citizens of Tahrir cultivated. Now he faced a garden like no other anywhere; even the late Court Gardener to Selim ibn Jafar would have been amazed. Blossoms were piled high on every side, a profusion, a myriad of flowers, all vividly colored, varied in size from tiny pinpricks of gold and scarlet to vast parasols of azure and white with petals each as broad as a man's height. All about the thief, save only behind him where the black marble wall stood, were flowers; it seemed as though he had landed in the only clear spot to be found, and that was only a tiny patch of grass scarce big enough for him to stand upon.

He marveled that he had somehow not seen this fantastic beauty when he clambered down his rope, and could only guess that it somehow connected with the wizard's illusory darkness.

After a few moments, with a shake of his head Abu recovered his senses. He was not to be put off by a bunch of flowers! He stepped forward, and his leg brushed a nearby blossom, a yard-wide whorl of purple and black; and as though released from long bondage, there burst forth all about him the perfume of the flowers, like all the incense of all the world's mosques and temples in one place, pouring out on all sides. He was breathing in thick clouds of scent, such sweet scent as cannot be described. He could not catch his breath, for the perfume so filled him that his lungs could not take in air. In desperation, he drew his blade, flinging his arm out as far as he could and slashed at the mockingly beautiful blossoms. Then he was spinning, and the world went dark.

He came to later, he never knew how much later, and found himself lying on the sward, green and smooth, untroubled by the flowers. He could still smell their perfume, but was no longer overpowered by it. Looking up from where he lay he could see no blossoms nor leaves.

He stood up warily. Before him, twisted hideously, the purple-and-sable flower that he had first touched lay on the grass. Its thorny stem was slashed through where his dagger had cut it, and from the slash flowed fresh red blood.

The lower portion of the stem did not end in a rooted stalk, but in a narrow green body with a whiplike tail, four short legs, and scaly feet, like those of a great lizard.

Shuddering, he wiped his blade on the lawn and looked about him.

Behind him was the marble wall; to either side was empty grass, and the dreadful gardens stood beyond. Abu realized that even these strange and magical flowers are delicate things. The death of one had frightened away the other plants.

He was sure he had nothing more to fear from the gardens if he kept his wits about him. He looked on to the next obstacle.

Ahead of him was another wall, a dozen paces away across the green, not the wall of the palace but another line of defense, this one only a little taller than his head, and surely no higher than his reach. It appeared to be made of ivory, though he could make out little detail from where he stood. The sun was very low in the west, and already the day's light was fading.

He looked down at the plant-creature he had slain, and kicked at the dead thing, wondering if perhaps he should dispose of it; a sharp pain in his foot informed him that a needlelike thorn as long as his index finger had passed right through his leather boots into his flesh. Upon pulling his foot away he saw that behind the petals the entire upper part of the plant was a ghastly mass of dull-green thorns, all razor sharp and strong as steel.

After removing his boot, bandaging the wound as best he could with a strip torn from the hem of his robe, and slipping the boot back carefully so as not to dislodge the cloth, he limped across the grass to the ivory barrier.

Beyond this inner wall he could see the glistening crystal and stone of the palace itself, its tiled domes flashing and bright in the slanting sunlight.

The ivory wall proved not to be completely solid; there

were small openings between the carved figures. A curious feature was the nature of the carvings themselves, for each was a different variety of serpent; Abu saw among them vipers, adders, cobras, and a thousand others. Some were such as are not known any longer among men.

That was nothing to Abu. Undaunted by the fearsome appearance of the wall, and seeing that the openings made excellent handholds, he leapt up to climb it; but scarce had he left the ground when he felt the ivory writhe beneath his hands. He almost began to drop back, but then thought better of it, and instead, with all his strength, he vaulted over, to land rolling upon a stone-paved terrace. Behind him, the carved serpents hissed, twisting venomously about each other; for one terrible instant he thought they were preparing to follow him. At last, though, they stilled, and were again only lifeless ivory.

Trembling, Abu lay upon the flags; then, slowly, he got again to his feet, wincing as he put pressure on his wounded foot.

He was on a broad, paved terrace, bounded on one side by the ivory barricade, on two sides by decorative pools and fountains, and on the last by the palace that was his goal. The palace wall was blank, however; there were no doors, no windows, no opening of any sort. High above colored tiles adorned the roof edge, but otherwise the wall was sheer and flat and featureless. Abu saw no hope of gaining entry there. Instead, he turned to his right and limped to the little stone-rimmed ponds that edged the terrace.

He saw hundreds of good-sized pools, scattered as irregularly as the stars in the heavens for as far as he could see, each with a fountain in its center, and paths of translucent golden bricks, like amber, wound between them. Each pool was lit from beneath by some means the thief could not fathom, and each glowed a different hue. Abu watched the fountains dance and play in the gathering dusk; they were, like the flowers, much more beautiful than anything in his previous experience. He wondered if they, too, held some hidden menace; their gentle hissing began to seem somehow ominous to him. Still, he had to go on, for he had a task to perform, and did not care to go back over the ivory serpents into the gardens of the poisonous lizard-legged flowers. He could do nothing with the blank walls of the palace; an attempt to scale them, even if successful, might do no good, since he had no reason to believe that there were openings in the roof. He could see no end to the expanse of fountains; it seemed to continue forever. He had already noticed that the grounds inside the wall seemed to be much more extensive than the length of the wall, as seen from outside, could contain, but after all, this palace had been raised by magic, and he had already seen, coming over the wall, that its master was not above the use of illusions. Surely, the water garden did not, in truth, go on forever. If he walked steadily in one direction he would surely come to an end, in time. With a shrug, he set out along one of the walks.

He strolled easily along, his dagger loose in its sheath; his wounded foot hurt only a little, as he learned how to walk smoothly without putting his weight on the injured area. The fountains whispered on every side as he walked, and their light drew his gaze. He wound on among them, listening to their liquid voices, imagining that they were murmuring secrets to one another; he even thought, absurdly, that he could catch their words. Yes, he thought, there was a word, most certainly, a very clear word: "death." A soft chill ran through him, but he still listened, and again he heard the words of the spilling fountains. "Death," they said, "death," and "sleep." Sleep—yes, he thought, he had come far, he wanted to sleep . . .

He caught himself suddenly as a sharp pain ran up his leg; the thorn-wound has slammed into the low rim of one of the pools, and the sudden jolt brought him back to alertness. He looked about, wildly asking himself what he was doing. He had, he saw, been about, to fall headlong into a great silver-blue pool of light, where a towering spray of vivid wine-colored light danced madly. The sussuration of the fountains had mesmerized him; had he woken a moment later, it might have been too late, as he would have been well into the enchanted liquid that filled the pool.

He had no idea just what the liquid might do, and a powerful urge to dip his hand in it, perhaps to taste it, came over him, but he fought it off. That, he told himself forcefully, was the fountains' spell, making a final try for his mind and soul. He stepped back, well clear of the enticing, luminous water.

Shaking his head to clear it of the mistiness left from his trance, he looked about him. It abruptly occurred to him that he had no idea how long or far he had wandered among the fountains while enthralled; he could see nothing that gave him a clue. Far to the right, between the flashing columns of liquid, he glimpsed carven ivory; and far to the left, he saw the polished stone and tile of the palace. Behind him, though, the fountains seemed to go on forever; and before him was the same.

Seeing no point in continuing farther through the forest of pools, and perhaps risking fresh ensorcellment, he turned left and made his way toward the citadel itself, with the intention of scaling it. At least from the roof he might be able to see some way in.

As he walked, he realized he no longer heard mysterious whispers in the sound of the water; it seemed that by breaking his trance he had lost forever the influence of that soft, soft murmur.

The renewed pain in his foot, he thought, might also help. His limp was back, worse than ever despite his best efforts.

A few minutes' hobbling walk brought him to a narrow plaza between the watergarden and the palace, and to his astonishment he found himself before a pair of great gem-encrusted golden doors. He paused to stare up at them, dumbfounded; from a single step back, the portal had been invisible, the palace wall blank.

Another illusion, of course—but which, he asked himself was real? Was the blank wall an illusion, or were these doors?

Well, he answered himself boldly, there's one easy way to find out.

He crossed the polished red marble of the plaza and mounted three steps to the portal.

There, however, he had to halt, for he saw no latch or handle; not so much as a knocker marred the expanse of glittering gold, studded irregularly with rubies and sapphires. For that matter, he realized he could see no hinges; there were simply two huge golden panels, set flush in the stone wall, with only hairline cracks marking their edges.

He stepped back down to study the situation, but could see no solution. Returning to the top step, he pushed with all his strength against the metal, but there was no give or play whatsoever; he could not budge it. He then tried to get a grip on the projecting gems, to pull the door open, which likewise had no effect. At last, disgusted, all caution lost, in frustration he cried out an oath.

The doors trembled expectantly.

He froze. Nothing more happened. Hesitantly, he said, "Allah?" The doors quivered.

Cursing himself for not trying the obvious means for opening enchanted portals, described in any number of old tales, he cried out, "Open, door of al-Tir al-Abtan, in the name of Allah, the great, the merciful!"

Slowly and majestically, the golden portals swung inward, revealing a vast reception hall walled with jade, a vaulted ceiling almost out of sight above him, and a floor of green marble. It was bare of all furnishings, and all but empty; the only thing in all that great chamber was al-Tir al-Abtan's guardian.

Abu had his dagger out in a twinkling, upon seeing the dark, twisted form of the demon; it was indeed a ghoul, a loathsome twisted creature, a travesty of human shape with gray skin and long, greasy ropes of black hair. Fangs jutted up from its lower jaw; its eyes had no iris or pupil, but glowed a fiery yellow. Across one side of its face an oozing, leprous growth clung. The demon was naked, and grotesquely male. Although no taller than Abu al-Din, it must have weighed twice what he did, for it was as thick around as a barrel. It was armed with two-inch claws on every finger.

The thief could see the monster clearly, for a soft light emanated from the jade walls. Rather than be caught outside, he sprang inside and attacked first.

The ghoul fought like a mad dog, snarling and tearing at Abu without thought, its only aim to hurt and weaken its opponent. Abu, on the other hand, concentrated on dodging, only occasionally thrusting at the creature with his knife. He realized quickly that his blade could not pierce the thick hide of the demon; but still he kept stabbing at it, hoping against all evidence that it had some vulnerable spot.

Only when the blade snapped off did he recognize how badly he had erred. His only other equipment being his rope, he struggled to bring that into play; at last, he managed to break free for a moment and dash across the chamber. When the ghoul came after him it met a hard-flung iron hook, which, as Abu had hoped and aimed for, took him in the eye.

The eerie golden orb burst with a blinding flash; the thief was staggered. An instant later the demon's roar of pain and hatred brought Abu back to full alertness, and taking quick advantage of his opponent's shock, Abu proceeded to swing the deadly hook into the other blazing eye. The flash was expected this time, and he recovered immediately from its effects.

The demon roared again, horribly, sat still in the center of the chamber; then, in a burst of motion, he sprang at his tormenter. Abu dodged to the side, and the ghoul followed; blind as it now was, it could still track him by sound.

Although he had improved his chances, Abu realized he was still facing a formidable enemy; he fled desperately, hampered by his injured foot and a dozen gashes from the demon's claws, trying to keep out of reach of the maddened monster.

As he fled he continued to swing the iron hook at the ghoul, annoying it, but failing to wound it, until at last it grabbed the rope out of his hands, tearing the skin from his palms. The rope coiled and whipped about as he released it, and to the surprise of both combatants, it wrapped itself about the demon. Abu saw his chance; and snatching up the loose end, he began to run around the room, winding the cord about his assailant until the creature was unable to move.

By the time the blinded monster had freed itself, Abu was out of range of even a demon's sensitive ears.

Now, at last, the thief was loose in the palace, free to roam; prowling like a cat, he made his way through endless corridors and countless chambers, losing himself hopelessly in the maze of rooms.

He saw wonders like none he had dreamed of before. He saw peacocks that sang sweet songs, and glistening fish that swam in the air. He saw books written in blood, and scrolls of human skin. He saw fountains that burned, and found a fire that cooled his wounds; strange fragrances filled the air, and stranger sounds and musics. It seemed to him that he wandered for days among the magician's playthings.

And then, at last, he came upon the magician.

This was in a tower room, far above the body of the palace. The walls were polished crystal, yet black as death, and the stairs that he climbed to reach the chamber were lit from within, yet seemed as opaque as coal.

It was at the top of these stairs that he entered the wizard's laboratory, cluttered with ghastly talismans and dusty books. Amid the clutter stood a tall, thin old man—very tall, with white hair that flowed to his waist, and a silvery beard almost as long. He wore an absolutely plain black robe that shimmered eerily, and he was bent over one of the larger and dustier of the tomes.

Remembering the King's instructions, and seeing his intended victim thus absorbed, Abu crept up behind him, the heavy hilt of his broken dagger in his hand.

All strength abruptly ebbed from his limbs, and he collapsed helplessly, to lie unmoving on the floor.

The wizard finished reading the page, closed the book, and put it atop a pile nearby; then came and stood looking down at the paralyzed thief.

"You have disturbed me," the Most Profound Tir said. "This is not to be permitted. Further, I see in your eyes that all of Tahrir now wishes me ill, and that others will be sent after you. I will not have it." The dry, ancient voice seemed to fill everything, although Abu knew it wasn't really very loud. He tried to speak, but could not.

"What will I do with you, you ask?" Al-Tir al-Abtan stroked his beard. "I don't know. You do bear examination, having gotten this far into my palace, don't you? But I'm too busy to bother with you just now; you'll have to wait."

He waved a hand, and Abu felt himself lifted by unseen hands. Then he was dropped roughly into a small trunk, and the lid fell closed.

It was a very small trunk, and very cramped, but Abu al-Din had nothing to say about the accommodations, or anything else. He could not move, could not speak, and soon realized that he was not even breathing anymore—yet still he lived.

He waited, unwillingly, for al-Tir al-Abtan to find the time to deal with him.

Within a matter of hours, he felt certain that even death could be no worse than continued imprisonment.

As he lay there, events went on without him.

Outside the palace, in the city of Tahrir, Abu al-Din had been given up as lost, and as the Most Profound Tir had said, another was to be sent; but then, word came to the beggar King of strange stirring of the sea at the docks. Curious, he put off other matters to investigate and made his way to the waterfront, so that he was the first man in all Tahrir to be engulfed by the first great wave that washed over the city. In quick succession, a dozen immense waves broke across the stinking mass of Tahrir, washing it into the sea. The land itself sank, and by the time peace had returned to the churning ocean the city of Tahrir was utterly gone, lost forever, save for a single building, the Palace of al-Tir al-Abtan, which through all the tempest and flood remained untouched, as though a great glass wall encircled it. And when the seas stilled, the palace stood alone on a sheer-sided island, half beneath waves that broke harmlessly against that same invisible barrier, while inside, al-Tir al-Abtan worked on, paying scant attention to his handiwork. In his many long years of life and study he had gained knowledge and power of an incomprehensible order; the destruction of Tahrir had been no more to him than squashing a bug.

Thus did the Island of al-Tir al-Abtan come into being, and thus it remained, for many, many years, until at last, one quiet night, al-Tir al-Abtan went away and took his palace with him. Now the seas wash lightly over the island when the tides are high, and gulls perch there calmly when the waves withdraw. All of Tahrir is long dead—save for Abu al-Din, who is still in that trunk, waiting for al-Tir al-Abtan to remember him.

About Mercedes Lackey and "Nightside"

Mercedes Lackey is one of the writers I regard uniquely as my own, even though our first professional encounter took an inauspicious form. Misty, known to me only as a young folksinger at that time (I have a soft spot in my heart, or maybe that should be my head, for young musicians—my own daughter being one), had come to visit us in Berkeley; and, rather diffidently, handed me two stories for *Sword and Sorceress*. I took them without much hope, because my least favorite task is to return a manuscript from a close friend— and I feared being faced with it not once but twice, since I really did have my lineup for the volume pretty well established. So I sat down dutifully to read them and, after a while, my secretary Lisa and Misty, in another room, heard me yell, "Damn you, Misty!"

While Misty cringed, Lisa hastily explained to her that this meant I wanted both stories and I would have to rearrange my whole lineup! Such a nuisance!

Since then, needless to say, I've never even contemplated an anthology without a contribution from Misty; but by the time I started the magazine, Misty had had so much success with her own books that she never got to do a story for the magazine till the sixth issue, when she produced this one, which took second place in the Cauldron vote. There's another Diana Tregarde story in issue 10, and we're trying to get her to do one for the cover story for issue 23 (Spring 1994).

Since then, it goes without saying that whenever she has time to do a story for us we accept with pleasure. And you should hunt up her *Heralds of Valdemar* series; or perhaps the other Diana Tregarde books, or any of her other books; by now an embarrassment of riches.

This story, as far as I've been able to tell, marks the earliest appearance of her famous character, urban witch Diana Tregarde, and her friendly-vampire boyfriend, Andre. Stories of urban magic, except for my own, Dion Fortune's, and Diana Paxson's, didn't usually thrill me; now I read them avidly, always hoping for something as good as this. It goes without saying that I don't often find it.

Nightside

Mercedes Lackey

It was early spring, but the wind held no hint of verdancy, not even the promise of it—it was chill and odorless, and there were ghosts of dead leaves skittering before it. A few of them jittered into the pool of weak yellow light cast by an aging streetlamp—a converted gaslight that was a relic of the previous century. It was old and tired, its pea-green paint flaking away; as weary as this neighborhood, which was older still. Across the street loomed an ancient church, whose congregation had dwindled over the years to a handful of little old women and men who appeared, like scrawny blackbirds, every Sunday and then scattered back to the shabby houses that stood to either side until Sunday should come again. On the side of the street that the lamp tried (and failed) to illuminate was the cemetery.

Like the neighborhood, it was very old—fifty years shy of being classified as "Colonial." There were few empty gravesites now, and most of those belonged to the same little old ladies and men that had lived and would die here. It was protected from vandals by a thorny hedge as well as a ten-foot wrought-iron fence. Within its confines, as seen through the leafless branches of the hedge, granite cenotaphs and enormous Victorian monuments bulked shapelessly against the bare sliver of a waning moon.

The church across the street was dark and silent; the houses up and down the block showed few lights, if any. There was no reason for anyone of this neighborhood to be out in the night.

So the young woman waiting beneath the lamppost seemed that much more out of place.

Nor could she be considered a typical resident of this neighborhood by any stretch of the imagination—for one thing, she was young; perhaps in her mid-twenties, but no more. Her clothing was neat but casual, too casual for anyone visiting an elderly relative. She wore dark, knee-high boots, old, soft jeans tucked into their tops, and a thin windbreaker open at the front to show a leotard beneath. Her attire was far too light to be any real protection against the bite of the wind, yet she seemed unaware of the cold. Her hair was long, down to her waist, and straight—in the uncertain light of the lamp it was an indeterminate shadow, and it fell down her back like a waterfall. Her eyes were large and oddly slanted, not Oriental; catlike, rather. Even the way she held herself was feline: poised, expectant—a graceful tension like a dancer's or a hunting predator's. She was not watching for something—no, her eyes were unfocused with concentration. She was listening.

A soft whistle, barely audible, carried down the street on the chill wind. The tune was of a piece with the neighborhood—old and timeworn.

Many of the residents would have smiled in recollection to hear "Lili Marlene" again.

The tension left the girl as she swung around the lamppost by one hand to face the direction of the whistle. She waved, and a welcoming smile warmed her eyes.

The whistler stepped into the edge of the circle of light. He, too, was dusky of eye and hair—and heartbreakingly handsome. He wore only dark jeans and a black turtleneck, no coat at all—but like the young woman, he didn't seem to notice the cold. There was an impish glint in his eyes as he finished the tune with a flourish.

"A flair for the dramatic, Diana, *ma cherie*?" he said mockingly. "Would that you were here for the same purpose as the lovely Lili! Alas, I fear my luck cannot be so good. . . ."

She laughed. His eyes warmed at the throaty chuckle. "Andre," she chided, "don't you ever think of anything else?"

"Am I not a son of the City of Light? I must uphold her reputation, *mais non*?"

The young woman raised an ironic brow. He shrugged. "Ah, well—since it is you who seek me, I fear I must be all business. A pity. Well, what lures you to my side of this unseasonable night? What horror has Mademoiselle Tregarde unearthed this time?"

Diana Tregarde sobered instantly, the laughter fleeing her eyes. "I'm afraid you picked the right word this time, Andre. It is a horror. The trouble is, I don't know what kind."

"Say on. I wait in breathless anticipation." His expression was mocking as he leaned against the lamppost, and he feigned a yawn.

Diana scowled at him and her eyes darkened with anger. He raised an eyebrow of his own. "If this weren't so serious," she threatened, "I'd be tempted to pop you one—Andre, people are dying out there. There's a 'Ripper' loose in New York."

He shrugged, and shifted restlessly from one foot to the other. "So? This is new? Tell me when there is not! That sort of criminal is as common to the city as a rat. Let your police earn their salaries and capture him."

Her expression hardened. She folded her arms tightly across the thin nylon of her windbreaker; her lips tightened a little. "Use your head, Andre! If this were an ordinary slasher-killer, would I be involved?"

He examined his fingernails with care. "And what is it that makes it extraordinary, eh?"

"The victims had no souls."

"I was not aware," he replied dryly, "that the dead possessed such things anymore."

She growled under her breath and tossed her head impatiently, and the wind caught her hair and whipped it across her throat. "You are deliberately being difficult! I have half a mind—"

It finally seemed to penetrate the young man's mind that she was truly angry—and truly frightened, though she was doing her best to conceal the fact; his expression became contrite.

"Forgive me, *cherie*. I am being recalcitrant."

"You're being a pain in the neck," she replied acidly. "Would I have come to you if I weren't already out of my depth?"

"Well—" he admitted. "No. But—this business of souls, *cherie*. How can you determine such a thing? I find it most difficult to believe."

She shivered, and her eyes went brooding. "So did I. Trust me, my friend, I know what I'm talking about. There isn't a shred of doubt in my mind. There are at least six victims who no longer exist in any fashion anymore."

The young man finally evidenced alarm. "But—how?" he said, bewildered. "How is such a thing possible?"

She shook her head violently, clenching her hands on the arms of her jacket as if by doing so she could protect herself from an unseen—but not unfelt—danger. "I don't know, I don't know! It seems incredible even now—I keep thinking that it's a nightmare, but—Andre, it's real, it's not my imagination—" Her voice rose a little with each word, and Andre's sharp eyes rested for a moment on her trembling hands.

"Eh bien," he sighed, "I believe you. So there is something about that devours souls—and mutilates bodies as well, since you mentioned a 'Ripper' persona?"

She nodded.

"Was the devouring before or after the mutilation?"

"Before, I think—it's not easy to judge." She shivered in a way that had nothing to do with the cold.

"And you came into this how?"

"Whatever it is, it took the friend of a friend; I—happened to be there to see the body afterwards, and I knew immediately there was something wrong. When I unshielded and used the Sight—"

"Bad." He made it a statement.

"Worse. I—I can't describe what it felt like. There were still residual emotions, things left behind when—" Her jaw clenched. "Then when I started checking further I found out about the other five victims—that what I had discovered was no fluke. Andre, whatever it is, it has to be stopped." She laughed again, but this time there was no humor in it. "After all, you could say stopping it is in my job description."

He nodded soberly. "And so you became involved. Well enough, if you must hunt this thing, so must I." He became all business. "Tell me of the history. When, and where, and who does it take?"

She bit her lip. "'Where'—there's no pattern. 'Who' seems to be mostly a matter of opportunity; the only clue is that the victims were always out on the street and entirely alone, there were no witnesses whatsoever, so the thing needs total privacy and apparently can't strike where it will. And 'when'—is moon-dark."

"Bad." He shook his head. "I have no clue at the moment. The *loup garou* I can recognize, and others, but I know nothing that hunts beneath the dark moon."

She grimaced. "You think I do? That's why I need your help; you're sensitive enough to feel something out of the ordinary, and you can watch and hunt undetected. I can't. And I'm not sure I want to go trolling for this thing alone—without knowing what it is. I could end up as a late-night snack for it. But if that's what I have to do, I will."

Anger blazed up in his face as if from a cold fire. "You go hunting alone for this creature over my dead body!"

"That's a little redundant, isn't it?" Her smile was weak but genuine.

"Pah!" He dismissed her attempt at humor with a wave of his hand. "Tomorrow is the first night of moon-dark; I shall go a-hunting. Do you remain at home, else I shall be most wroth with you. I know where to find you, should I learn anything of note."

"You ought to—" Diana began, but she spoke to the empty air.

The next night was warmer, and Diana had gone to bed with her windows open to drive out some of the stale odors the long winter had left in her apartment. Not that the air of New York City was exactly fresh—but it was better than what the heating system kept recycling through the building. She didn't particularly like leaving her defenses open while she slept, but the lingering memory of Katy Rourk's fish wafting through the halls as she came in from shopping had decided her. Better exhaust fumes than burned haddock.

She hadn't had an easy time falling asleep; and, when she finally managed to do so, tossed restlessly, her dreams uneasy and readily broken—

—as by the sound of someone in the room.

Before the intruder crossed even half the distance between the window and her bed, she was wide awake, and moving. She threw herself out of bed, somersaulted across her bedroom, and wound up crouched beside the door, one hand on the light switch, the other holding a polished dagger she'd taken from beneath her pillow.

As the lights came on, she saw Andre standing in the center of the bedroom, blinking in surprise wearing a sheepish grin.

Relief made her knees go weak. "Andre, you idiot!" She tried to control her tone, but her voice was shrill and cracked a little. "You could have been killed!"

He spread his hands wide in a placating gesture. "Now, Diana—"

"'Now Diana' my eye!" she growled. "Even you would have a hard time getting around with a severed spine!" She stood up slowly, shaking from head to toe with released tension.

"I didn't wish to wake you," he said, crestfallen.

She closed her eyes and took several long, deep, calming breaths; focusing on a mantra, moving herself back into stillness until she knew she would be able to reply without screaming at him.

"Don't," she said carefully, "Ever. Do. That. Again." She punctuated the last word by driving the dagger she held into the door frame.

"*Certainement, ma petite,*" he replied, his eyes widening a little as he began to calculate how fast she'd moved. "The next time I come in your window when you sleep, I shall blow a trumpet first."

"You'd be a lot safer. I'd be a lot happier," she said crossly, pulling the dagger loose with a twist of her wrist. She palmed the light switch and dimmed the lamps down to where they would be comfortable to his light-sensitive eyes, then crossed the room, the plush brown carpet warm and soft under her bare feet. She put the silver-plated dagger back under her pillow. Then with a sigh she folded her long legs beneath her to sit on her rumpled bed. This was the first time Andre had ever caught her asleep, and she was irritated far beyond what her disturbed dreams warranted. She was somewhat obsessed with her privacy and with keeping her night boundaries unbreached—she and Andre were off-and-on lovers, but she'd never let him stay any length of time.

He approached the antique wooden bed slowly. "*Cherie,* this was no idle visit—"

"I should bloody well hope not!" she interrupted, trying to soothe her jangled nerves by combing the tangles out of her hair with her fingers.

"—I have seen your killer."

She froze.

"It is nothing I have ever seen or heard of before."

She clenched her hands on the strand of hair they held, ignoring the pull. "Go on—"

"It—no, he— I could not detect until he made his first kill tonight. I found him then, found him just before he took his hunting-shape, or I would never had discovered him at all; for when he is in that shape there is nothing about him that I could sense that marked him as different. So ordinary—a man, I think, and like many others—not young, not old; not fat, not thin. So unremarkable as to be invisible. I followed him—he was so normal I found it difficult to believe what my own eyes had seen a moment before; then, not ten minutes later, he found yet another victim and—fed again."

He closed his eyes, his face thoughtful. "As I said, I have never seen or heard of his like, yet—yet there was something familiar about him. I cannot even tell you what it was, and yet it was familiar."

"You said you saw him attack—how, Andre?" She leaned forward, her face tight with urgency as the bed creaked a little beneath her.

"The second quarry was—the—is it 'bag lady' you say?" At her nod he continued. "He smiled at her—just smiled, that was all. She froze like a frightened rabbit. Then he—changed—into dark, dark smoke; only smoke, nothing more. The smoke enveloped the old woman until I could see her no longer. Then—he fed. I—I can understand your feelings now, *cherie*. It was—nothing to the eye, but—what I felt within—"

"Now you see," she said gravely.

"*Mais oui,* and you have no more argument from me. This thing is abomination, and must be ended."

"The question is—" She grimaced.

"How? I have given some thought to this. One cannot fight smoke. But in his hunting form—I think perhaps he is vulnerable to physical measures. As you say, even I would have difficulty in dealing with a severed spine or crushed brain. I think maybe it would be the same for him. Have you the courage to play the wounded bird, *ma petite*?" He sat beside her on the edge of the bed and regarded her with solemn and worried eyes.

She considered that for a moment. "Play bait while you wait for him to move in? It sounds like the best plan for me—it wouldn't be the first time I've done that, and I'm not exactly helpless, you know," she replied, twisting a strand of hair around her fingers.

"I think you have finally proven that to me tonight!" There was a hint of laughter in his eyes again, as well as chagrin. "I shall never again make the mistake of thinking you to be a fragile flower. *Bien.* Is tomorrow night too soon for you?"

"Tonight wouldn't be too soon," she stated flatly.

"Except that he has already gone to lair, having fed twice." He took one of her hands, freeing it from the lock of hair she had twisted about it. "No, we rest—I know where he is to be found, and tomorrow night we face him at full strength." Abruptly he grinned, "*Cherie,* I have read one of your books—"

She winced, and closed her eyes in a grimace. "Oh Lord— I was afraid you'd ferret out one of my pseudonyms. You're as bad as the Elephant's Child when it comes to 'satiable curiosity."

"It was hardly difficult to guess the author when she used one of my favorite expressions for the title—and described me so very intimately not three pages from the beginning."

Her expression was woeful. "Oh no! Not that one!"

He shook an admonishing finger at her. "I do not think it kind, to make me the villain, and all because I told you I spent a good deal of the Regency in London."

"But—but—Andre, these things follow formulas; I didn't really have a choice—anybody French in a Regency romance has to be either an expatriate aristocrat or a villain—" She bit her lip and looked pleadingly at him. "—I needed a villain and I didn't have a clue—I was in the middle of that phony medium thing and I had a deadline—and—" Her words thinned down to a whisper. "—to tell you the truth, I didn't think you'd ever find out. You—you aren't angry, are you?"

He lifted the hair away from her shoulder, cupped his hand beneath her chin, and moved close beside her. "I think I may possibly be induced to forgive you—"

The near-chuckle in his voice told her she hadn't offended him. Reassured by that, she looked up at him, slyly. "Oh?"

"You could—" He slid her gown off her shoulder a little, and ran an inquisitive finger from the tip of her shoulder blade to just behind her ear. "—write another, and let me play the hero—"

"Have you any—suggestions?" she replied, finding it difficult to reply when his mouth followed where his finger had been.

"In that 'Burning Passions' series, perhaps?"

She pushed him away, laughing. "Andre, you can't be serious!"

"Never more." He pulled her back. "Think of how enjoyable the research would be—"

She grabbed his hand again before it could resume its explorations. "Aren't we supposed to be resting?"

He stopped for a moment, and his face and eyes were deadly serious. "*Cherie,* we must face this thing at strength. You need to sleep—and to relax. Can you think of any better way to relax—"

"No," she admitted.

"Well, then?"

She briefly contemplated getting up long enough to take care of the lights—then decided a little waste of energy was worth it, and extinguished them with a thought. "C'mere, you—let's do some research."

He laughed deep in his throat as they reached for one another.

She woke late the next morning—so late that in a half hour it would have been afternoon—and lay quietly for a long, contented moment before wriggling out of the tumble of bedclothes and Andre. No fear of waking him—he wouldn't rouse until the sun went down. She arranged him a bit more comfortably and tucked him in, thinking that he looked absurdly young with his hair all rumpled and those long, dark lashes lying against his cheek—he looked much better this morning, now that she was in a position to pay attention. Last night he'd been pretty pale and hungry-thin. She shook her head over him. Someday his gallantry was going to get him into trouble. "Idiot—" she whispered, touching his forehead, "—all you ever have to do is ask—"

But there were other things to take care of—and to think about. A fight to get ready for, and she had a premonition it wasn't going to be an easy one.

So she showered and changed into a leotard, and took herself into her barren studio at the back of the apartment to run through her katas three times—once slow, twice at full speed—and then into some Tai Chi exercises to rebalance everything. She followed that with a half hour of meditation, then cast a circle and charged herself with all of the Power she thought she could safely carry.

Without knowing what she was to face, it was all she could do, really—that, and have a really good dinner.

She showered and changed again into a bright-red sweat-suit and was just finishing that dinner when the sun set and Andre strolled into the white-painted kitchen, shirtless, and blinking sleepily.

She gulped the last bite of her liver and waggled her fingers at him. "If you want a shower, you'd better get a fast one—I want to get in place before he comes out for the night."

He sighed happily over the prospect of a hot shower. "The perfect way to start one's—day. *Petite,* you may have difficulty in dislodging me now that you have let me stay overnight—"

She showed her teeth. "Don't count your chickens, kiddo. I can be very nasty!"

"*Ma petite*—I—" He suddenly sobered, and looked at her with haunted eyes.

She saw his expression and abruptly stopped teasing. "Andre—please don't say it—I can't give you any better answer now than I could when you first asked—"

He sighed again, less happily. "Then I will say no more, because you wish it—but—what of this notion—would you permit me to stay with you? No more than that. I could be of some use to you, I think, and I would take nothing from you that you did not offer first. I do not like it that you are so much alone. It did not matter when we first met, but you are collecting powerful enemies, *cherie.*"

"I—" She wouldn't look at him, but only at her hands, clenched white-knuckled on the table.

"Unless there are others—" he prompted hesitantly.

"No—no, there isn't anyone but you." She sat in silence for a moment, then glanced back up at him with one eyebrow lifted sardonically. "You do rather spoil a girl for anyone else's attentions."

He was genuinely startled. *"Mille pardons, cherie,"* he stuttered, "I—I did not know—"

She managed a feeble chuckle. "Oh, Andre, you idiot—I like being spoiled! I don't get many things that are just for me—" she sighed, then gave in to his pleading eyes. "All right, then, move in if you want—"

"It is what you want that concerns me."

"I want," she said very softly. "Just—the commitment—don't ask for it. I've got responsibilities as well as Power, you know that; I—can't see how to balance them with what you offered before—"

"Enough," he silenced her with a wave of his hand. "The words are unsaid, we will speak of this no more unless you wish it. I seek the embrace of warm water—"

She turned her mind to the dangers ahead, resolutely pushing the dangers he represented into the back of her mind. "And I will go bail the car out of the garage."

He waited until he was belted in on the passenger's side of the car to comment on her outfit. "I did not know you planned to race him, Diana," he said with a quirk of one corner of his mouth.

"Urban camouflage," she replied, dodging two taxis and a kamikaze panel truck. "Joggers are everywhere, and they run at night a lot in deserted neighborhoods. Cops won't wonder about me or try to stop me, and our boy won't be surprised to see me alone. One of his other victims was out running. His boyfriend thought he'd had a heart attack. Poor thing. He wasn't one of us, so I didn't enlighten him. There are some things it's better the survivors don't know."

"Oui. Drive left here, *cherie."*

The traffic thinned down to a trickle, then to nothing. There are odd little islands in New York at night; places as deserted as the loneliest country road. The area where Andre directed her was one such; by day it was small warehouses, one-floor factories, an odd store or two. None of them had enough business to warrant running second or third shifts, and the neighborhood had not been gentrified yet; no one actually lived here. There were a handful of night watchmen, perhaps, but most of these places depended on locks, burglar alarms, and dogs that were released at night to keep out intruders.

"There—" Andre pointed at a building that appeared to be home to several small factories. "He took the smoke-form and went to roost in the elevator control house at the top. That is why I did not advise going against him by day."

"Is he there now?" Diana peered up through the glare of sodium-vapor lights but couldn't make out the top of the building.

Andre closed his eyes, a frown of concentration creasing his forehead. "No," he said after a moment. "I think he has gone hunting."

She repressed a shiver. "Then it's time to play bait."

Diana found a parking space marked dimly with the legend "President"—she thought it unlikely it would be wanted within the next few hours. It was deep in the shadow of the building Andre had pointed out, and her car was dead black; with any luck, cops coming by wouldn't even notice it was there and start to wonder.

She hopped out, locking her door behind her, looking now exactly like the lone jogger she was pretending to be, and set off at an easy pace. She did not look back.

If absolutely necessary, she knew she'd be able to keep this up for hours. She decided to take all the north-south streets first, then weave back along the east-west. Before the first hour was up she was wishing she'd dared bring a "walk-thing"—every street was like every other street: black brick walls broken by dusty, barred windows and metal doors, alleys with only the occasional Dumpster visible, refuse blowing along the gutters. She was bored; her nervousness had worn off, and she was lonely. She ran from light to darkness, from darkness to light, and saw and heard nothing but the occasional rat.

Then he struck, just when she was beginning to get a little careless. Careless enough not to see him arrive.

One moment there was nothing, the next, he was before her, waiting halfway down the block. She knew it was him—he was exactly as Andre had described him, a nondescript man in a dark windbreaker and slacks. He was tall—taller than she by several inches. His appearance nearly startled her into stopping—then she remembered that she was supposed to be an innocent jogger and resumed her steady trot.

She knew he meant her to see him, he was standing directly beneath the streetlight and right in the middle of the sidewalk. She would have to swerve out of her path to avoid him.

She started to do just that, ignoring him as any real jogger would have—when he raised his head and smiled at her.

She was stopped dead in her tracks by the purest terror she had ever felt in her life. She froze, as all of his other victims must have—unable to think, unable to cry out, unable to run. Her legs had gone numb, and nothing existed for her but that terrible smile and those hard, black eyes that had no bottom—

Then the smile vanished, and the eyes flinched away. Diana could move again, and staggered back against the brick wall of the building behind her, her breath coming in harsh gasps, the brick rough and comforting in its reality beneath her hands.

"Diana?" It was Andre's voice behind her.

"I'm—all right—" she said, not at all sure that she really was. Andre strode silently past her, face grim and purposeful. The man seemed to sense his purpose, and smiled again—

But Andre never faltered for even the barest moment.

The smile wavered and faded; the man fell back a step or two, surprised that his weapon had failed him—

Then he scowled, and pulled something out of the sleeve of his windbreaker; and to Diana's surprise, charged straight for Andre, his sneakered feet scuffing on the cement—

And something suddenly blurring about his right hand. As it connected with Andre's upraised arm, Diana realized what it was—almost too late.

"Andre—he has nunchuks—they're wood," she cried out urgently as Andre grunted in unexpected pain. "He can kill you with them! Get out of here!"

Andre needed no second warning. In the blink of an eye, he was gone.

Leaving Diana to face the creature alone.

She dropped into guard-stance as he regarded her thoughtfully, still making no sound, not even of heavy breathing. In a moment he seemed to make up his mind, and came at her.

At least he didn't smile again in that terrible way—perhaps the weapon was only effective once.

She hoped fervently he wouldn't try again—as an empath, she was doubly vulnerable to a weapon forged of fear.

They circled each other warily, like two cats preparing to fight. Then Diana thought she saw an opening—and took it.

And quickly came to the conclusion that she was overmatched, as he sent her tumbling with a badly bruised shin. The next few moments reinforced that conclusion—he continued scatheless while she picked up injury after painful injury.

She was a brown belt in karate—but he was a black belt in kung fu, and the contest was a pathetically uneven match. She knew before very long that he was toying with her—and while he still swung the wooden nunchuks, Andre did not dare move in close enough to help.

She realized (as fear dried her mouth, she grew more and more winded, and she searched frantically for a means of escape) that she was as good as dead.

If only she could get those damn 'chuks away from him!

And as she ducked and stumbled against the curb, narrowly avoiding his strike, an idea came to her. He knew from her moves—as she knew from his—that she was no amateur. He would never expect an amateur's move from her—something truly stupid and suicidal—

So the next time he swung at her, she stood her ground. As the 'chuks came at her she took one step forward, smashing his nose with the heel of her right hand and lifting her left to intercept the flying batons.

As it connected with her left hand with a sickening crunch, she whirled and folded her entire body around hand and weapon, and went limp, carrying it away from him.

She collapsed in a heap at his feet, hand afire with pain, eyes blurring, and waited for either death or salvation.

And salvation in the form of Andre rose behind her attacker. With one *savate* kick he broke the man's back; Diana could hear it crack like a twig—and, before her assailant could collapse, a second double-handed blow sent him crashing into the brick wall, head crushed like an eggshell.

Diana struggled to her feet and watched for some arcane transformation.

Nothing.

She staggered to the corpse, her face flat and expressionless—a sign she was suppressing pain and shock with implacable iron will. Andre began to move forward as if to stop her, then backed off again.

She bent slightly, just enough to touch the shoulder of the body with her good hand—and released the Power.

Andre pulled her back to safety as the corpse exploded into flame, burning as if it had been soaked in oil. She watched the flames for one moment, wooden-faced, then abruptly collapsed.

Andre caught her easily before she could hurt herself further, lifting her in his arms as if she weighed no more than a kitten. *"Ma pauvre petite,"* he murmured, heading back toward the car at a swift but silent run. "It is the hospital for you, I think—"

"Saint—Francis—" she gasped, every step jarring her hand and bringing tears of pain to her eyes. "One of us—is on the night staff—Dr. Crane—"

"Bien," he replied. "Now be silent—"

"But—how are you—"

"In your car, foolish one."

"But—"

"I can drive."

"But—"

"And I have a license. Now, will you be silent?"

"How?" she said, disobeying him.

"Night school," he replied succinctly, reaching the car, putting her briefly on her feet to unlock the passenger-side door, then lifting her into it. "You are not the only one who knows of urban camouflage."

This time she did not reply—because she had fainted from pain.

The emergency room was empty—for which Andre was very grateful. His invocation of Dr. Crane brought a thin, bearded young man around to the tiny examining cubicle in record time.

"Godalmighty! What did you tangle with, a bus?" he exclaimed when stripping her sweatsuit jacket and pants revealed that there was little of Diana that was not battered and black-and-blue.

Andre wrinkled his nose at the acrid antiseptic odors around them, and replied shortly. "No, your 'Ripper.'"

The startled gaze the doctor fastened on him revealed that Andre had scored. "Who—won?"

"We did. I do not think he will prey upon anyone again."

The doctor's eyes closed briefly; Andre read prayerful thankfulness on his face as he sighed with relief. Then he returned to business. "You must be Andre, right? Anything I can supply?"

Andre laughed at the hesitation in his voice. "Fear not, your blood supply is quite safe, and I am unharmed. It is Diana who needs you."

The relief on the doctor's face made Andre laugh again.

Dr. Crane ignored him. "Right," he said, turning to the work he knew best.

She was light-headed and groggy with the Demerol Dr. Crane had given her as Andre deftly tucked her into her bed; she'd dozed all the way home in the car.

"I just wish I knew what that thing was—" she said inconsequentially, as he arranged her arm in its Fiberglass cast a little more comfortably. "—I won't be happy until I know—"

"Then you are about to be happy, *cherie,* for I have had the brainstorm—" Andre ducked into the living room and emerged with a dusty leather-bound book. "Remember I said there was something familiar about it? Now I think I know what it was." He consulted the index and turned pages rapidly—found the place he sought, and read for a few moments. "As I thought—listen. 'The *gaki*—also known as the Japanese vampire—also takes its nourishment only from the living. There are many kinds of *gaki*, extracting their sustenance from a wide variety of sources. The most harmless are the 'perfume' and 'music' *gaki*—and they are by far the most common. Far deadlier are those that require blood, flesh—or souls.'"

"Souls?"

"Just so. 'To feed, or when at rest, they take their normal form of a dense cloud of dark smoke. At other times, like the *kitsune*, they take on the form of a human being. Unlike the *kitsune*, however, there is no way to distinguish them in this form from any other human. In the smoke form, they are invulnerable—in human form, however, they can be killed; but to destroy them permanently, the body must be burned—preferably in conjunction with or solely by Power.' I said there was something familiar about it—it seems to have been a kind of distant cousin." Andre's mouth smiled, but his eyes reflected only a long-abiding bitterness.

"There is no way you have any relationship with that—thing!" she said forcefully. "It had no more honor, heart, or soul than a rabid beast!"

"I—I thank you, *cherie*," he said slowly, the warmth returning to his eyes. "There are not many who would think as you do."

"Their own closed-minded stupidity."

"To change the subject—what was it made you burn it as you did? I would have abandoned it. It seemed dead enough."

"I don't know—it just seemed the thing to do." She yawned. "Sometimes my instincts just work . . . right . . ."

Suddenly her eyes seemed too leaden to keep open.

She fought against exhaustion and the drug, trying to keep both at bay without success. Sleep claimed her for its own.

He watched her for the rest of the night, until the lethargy of his own limbs told him dawn was near. He had already decided not to share her bed, lest any movement on his part cause her pain—instead, he made up a pallet on the floor beside her.

He stood over her broodingly while he in his turn fought slumber, and touched her face gently. "Well—" he whispered, holding off torpor far deeper and heavier than hers could ever be—while she was mortal. "You are not aware to hear, so I may say what I will and you cannot forbid. Dream; sleep and dream—I shall see you safe—my only love."

And he took his place beside her, to lie motionless until night should come again.

About Jacqueline Lichtenberg and "Aventura"

Jacqueline and I go back a long way, before either of us was a well-known writer, when I was author only of a few little-known Ace Doubles, and she was still a writer of good but illegal Star Trek fiction. It was I who told her in no uncertain terms that it was definitely time to stop playing around with fanzines and Star Trek and start writing in her own series—which at that time was the Sime-Gen universe. The result was her wonderful Sime-Gen novel *Unto Zeor Forever*. For my taste it is still the best of her books; I go back and reread it every few years.

Jacqueline has two daughters, who were when I first knew her still in diapers; one of her earliest letters was headed "thoughts while changing a diaper." It was not a good time in my career; I was stuck on Staten Island, and my friendship with Jacqueline was one of the few good things coming out of that time.

Jacqueline and I have drifted away from one another over the last several years; we've both been too busy for much letter writing. But I was very glad to get from her this story, 'Aventura'; it's a delightfully whimsical idea that maybe only she could have pulled off; beginning with a sorceress whose job is to enchant bread dough to rise, and going from there to a magical sword—quite unlike any other magical sword. This story took third place in the Cauldron vote, after Misty Lackey's "Nightside."

Aventura

Jacqueline Lichtenberg

I was enchanting the raisin bread when the boss called me to the phone. I worked in a commercial bakery then. I'd been promoted to raisin bread and jelly donuts because I could preserve the raisins' plumpness and the dough's yeasty freshness for two weeks on the store shelves. I could do a hundred forty-four jelly donuts at once, and keep the jelly hot and the icing just right for eight days.

The job paid poorly, and there was no future in it. At twenty-four, I was already a top bakery enchanter. But I expected to quit at the end of the month to get married. So when the boss called me to the phone, I thought it was the wedding caterer.

"Miss Tira Nau?" asked a voice.

"Yes."

"This is Forbes, of Forbes, Gibbon and Reilly, attorneys for the Prosper Nau Estate. We'd like you to come down to our office on a matter concerning your uncle's will."

My father's older brother, Prosper, had died a year ago. He'd split with my father long before my father, who scorned magical education, was killed when a fireworks plant lost control of a fire elemental. A cousin had told me Prosper, a Certified Public Wizard, had died never knowing his brother was dead because he'd warded himself against hearing his brother's name.

"Where are you located?" I asked.

He told me. It would take an hour to get there on the public bus. "I can make it at five tomorrow."

"Fine. I'll wait for you." He gave me directions.

I scribbled them down, and said I'd be there.

The attorney's offices were typical of any wizard-class business—sedate, staid navy-blue and silver carpets and drapes, with snow-cloud-gray plush furniture. The blond receptionist showed me into a huge office where Forbes sat behind a desk bigger than my apartment's living room.

The desk was hand-chipped obsidian, of course, and utterly bare except for a gleaming white Paraphernalia Case about five feet by two feet. Behind the case sat the wizard, wearing his peaked cap and long black robe, as if he were in court.

"Please be seated, Miss Nau. These proceedings are being recorded for the court records."

I swallowed my nerves, perched on the edge of the visitor's chair, and pretended he didn't intimidate me. How could they hold me liable for Uncle Prosper's debts?

He told me my uncle's will dispersed his considerable wealth to various charities for underprivileged magicians, but specified that this one item should go to his wayward but talented brother, who refused to practice the craft.

Then he shoved the white case toward me. "Since you are your father's only heir, this now belongs to you."

Not without trepidation, I opened it.

Inside was a sword shaped from translucent quartz flecked with gold. The guard and pommel were jeweled, and carved, and the whole thing glowed with power. It was a magical Implement such as only the most accomplished could use, and only the most affluent could afford.

Hesitantly, I picked it up. The charge tingled along my arms and made my hair stand on end. I could enchant the entire bakery's produce for the day with this! "Oh, I don't— this couldn't—I couldn't—there must be some mistake!"

"No, indeed. Hold the sword vertically."

I did, feeling it resist being turned; then it leaped from my hands to hover before me. A small area cleared in the blade, and suddenly I was looking at my uncle's face.

"Greetings, Gil. As you receive this small bequest, please believe that I wish you only happiness. This sword is called Aventura. Perhaps it will bring you freedom. Blessings he . . ." The eyes squinted, as if trying to make out something blurry. ". . . on you and your progeny."

The picture flickered out. I suppressed a shiver as I said to the wizard, "I can't—"

"Well, you needn't use it. You can store it and bequeath it to your children." He closed the Case. "You did say you were busy, so I won't detain—"

"Doesn't the Case come with it?"

"Oh, no—that belongs to the firm. But Paraphernalia Cases can be purchased—"

"I know," I replied, standing up, *for twice my annual salary!* The sword bobbed to my shoulder height, still glowing with that luminous charge. Perhaps I could use it in my hall as a coat tree? "Is there an owner's manual?"

"No, this is all we received. It's quite old. The original papers have long since disintegrated. You can look it up in any good reference. Or—as any quality item of the sort, it will be glad to instruct you."

"I see." I didn't. "Well, thank you, Mr. Forbes."

Out on the street, I felt self-conscious with the quartz sword following at my shoulder. People who owned such things had their own limousines. I had to take a crowded bus.

I tried to ignore the stares Aventura collected as I dropped coins into the slot. The bus pulled away from the curb. People standing in the aisle stared and made way to let me through. A seat was vacated near the back door, and I swooped into it, trapping the sword next to the window.

It was a long ride across town. We passed through the university section. The bus emptied, and students piled on. The sword attracted only mild curiosity here.

Finally, one woman student asked, "May I sit here, Professor?"

Professor? "Oh, uh, certainly." Who else but a professor could look so seedy and own such an Implement?

Politely, the student asked, "It's an Attitudinal, isn't it? Finnish manufacture?"

"Um." I was embarrassed at how little I knew.

"Will you be teaching with it next semester?" At my confusion, she apologized. "I'm interested in Attitudinals. I'm majoring in Social Work."

"I see," I replied. My own education included only two years of Enchanter's Trade School.

"I'm in organic chemistry, actually. Reaction Arrestment specialist."

As we talked, new notions awakened in the back of my mind. By the time she got off, I could see myself married, raising kids, and working for a Wizardship. I wondered where I'd get the money. Aventura wasn't the sort of thing one could sell. Um, I'd have to master it before I could pass it on to another owner who wasn't my child.

My fiancé, Rogero, was waiting when I arrived at the jewelry store where we were to pick up our wedding rings. We'd chosen them on an auspicious day a month ago, and they'd been sent out to the Monogramming Sorcerer. Rogero had ordered mine set to record permanently how I looked the moment he put the ring on my finger; and he'd paid extra to have an anti-loss spell put on it.

He looked dapper in his neat, black suit and ever-clean patent shoes. He carried a businessman's Paraphernalia Case made of dark-purple leather, with a woven shoulder strap. And he was wearing the hat I'd bought him for his birthday. I felt twice as dowdy as I walked up to him, still in my bakery whites, with my old cloth coat thrown over.

He turned. "I thought you'd never— What's that?"

He eyed the sword bobbing at my shoulder. I told him, adding, "An hour ago, I'd no idea what to do with it. Now, I'm thinking I'll go back to school and learn to use it."

He shook his head, saying, "Well, come on, let's get the rings before the store closes."

It was early autumn, and already getting dark. We inspected the rings, and signed for them, as the jeweler admired Aventura and tried to sell us a more expensive wedding band set. Hiding exasperation, Rogero put him off.

Out on the street, he fumed, "You've got to get rid of that thing."

That had been my goal since I first saw it. But when Rogero made it an edict, I rebelled. "Why? It could be useful. It got me a seat on the bus!"

"Tira, it's going to be nothing but trouble." He walked around it, inspecting it, as passersby gave it a wide berth. "How do you turn it off?"

"I don't know. It didn't come with a manual. I'll have to do some research."

"Where will you get the time! I'm not having that—that thing—on our honeymoon!"

"Now wait a minute!" His attitude made me angry. Aventura bobbed faster and began to glow more brightly.

Rogero sighed, gesturing placatingly. "It's all right, Tira. I've got connections. I'll find out how to turn it off for you. Then we can pack it away and forget it. Come on." He turned toward the subway.

"Where are we?" I started, hanging back. Aventura made a menacing twang at Rogero.

He stopped in the middle of the sidewalk, exasperated. "I had this evening all planned to be one of the happiest memories of our lives. Tira, we've got celebrating to do—I've been promoted!"

"Then you got the Infant's Clothing Department?" It was a plum of a job for a fireproofing charmer because of the cost of manufacturer's liability insurance; it was a responsible, well-paid, management position.

He took my shoulders, glaring at Aventura. "No! I'm now Managing Charmer of the Commercial Textile department. The Chief Sorcerer took me aside and told me I could've had the post anytime these last two years, but they wanted a stable, married man. So it's all your doing, and I'm going to take you out on the town!"

I squealed with delight, and kissed him. "What a piece of luck. Now we can afford university courses!"

"Anything you want, Tira—anything." He pulled me toward the subway. But as we flowed down the stairs with the rest of the crowd, he muttered, "I just don't think you're going to have time, though."

Since I'd be quitting my job, I didn't see what I'd have except time, but I didn't argue; no point spoiling his mood.

He took me home, and I dressed in my best. As we left my apartment, the sword insisted on following. I tried standing on the threshold and slamming the door before the sword could squeeze through after me, but it danced and slithered through. Once I caught it between the door and the jamb, but it resisted being crushed and popped out after me, flickering brightly, as if proud of itself.

Rogero and I tried all the spells we could think of to turn it off, which was a lot, since he had two years more school than I. "It's no good," he admitted at last. "We'll miss the show if we don't get going. Just ignore it."

"Can you?" Aventura seemed to intimidate him.

"Certainly," he said, and kissed me.

I thereupon forgot everything, and followed happily.

As always, he was as good as his word. Aventura hovered behind my aisle seat at the play (to which Rogero had been given tickets), stationed itself behind my chair at the restaurant, and bobbed rhythmically when we danced.

He acknowledged it only when people from his firm came up to congratulate him, and inquired about it. "My fiancée inherited it," he'd say, and steer the conversation away.

At midnight, I yawned, and said, "It's getting late, and I have to be at work early in the morning."

"I hadn't thought! I'm sorry, Tira." He called for the check.

As we collected our coats, one of his bosses came in, congratulated him, and was introduced to me. As we were leaving, Rogero said, "This is why you've got to quit that job. I can't afford to leave now. To get beyond lower management without a Sorcerer's Certificate, I've got to make all the right contacts. I don't have to be at work until noon."

In the cab, I fell into a strange mood. I'd always had such deliriously happy times with Rogero—parties at rich friends' houses, restaurants, and theaters—places I couldn't afford. We always met exciting, important people who made me feel wonderful. Tonight had been even better because Rogero was a center of attention. But I didn't feel good about it.

I was annoyed, peeved, and rebellious. I suddenly couldn't see spending the rest of my life as Rogero's smiling and witty decoration. I'd be no more to him, after a few years, than Aventura—an accoutrement that should be turned off when convenient. Suddenly, I wanted to be important.

I kissed him goodnight, but my heart wasn't in it.

I lay awake, my nice dark bedroom glowing with the sword's light. The darn thing even followed me into the bathroom!

In the morning, I couldn't get the sword to stay home. I tried explaining to it, calling it by name, and even asking it for instructions on how to get it to stay home. But it still dogged my steps. I tried slamming the door on it again, and almost broke my wrist. Finally, I ran for the bus and just made it to work on time.

I was so tired from the late night, I didn't even notice the swirling mutter of comments following me across the floor to my station. I climbed up to survey the conveyor belt. The first rank of raisin breads was still ten minutes away.

Wishing I'd had time for another cup of coffee, I tooled up and got ready to cast my freshness enchantment, wondering how I'd muddle through the day. I didn't want to get fired before I quit—I might need the recommendation someday. So I pulled myself together and began to raise my cone of power. I was so fuzzy-minded, this would take all my energy.

The ranks of loaves arrived, and I enchanted. I picked up the familiar rhythm and began to feel jaunty. I could do this in my sleep. Surely I could get a Charmer Degree.

I prepared to shift to jelly donuts, when coffee-break time came and the boss called me to his office. He had a tray of unrisen, unbaked raisin loaves on his desk.

Eyeing Aventura, he asked, "Would you mind explaining just what is going on around here?"

I started to tell him about the lawyer, and how Rogero and I had tried to turn the sword off.

"I didn't mean the sword, Miss Nau. I meant this!"

"That's raisin bread."

"No, that's dough."

"Well—give it time," I suggested lamely.

"Miss Nau, this bread rose and was baked this morning. It passed your station at nine-fifteen—and entered the wrapping plant in this condition! You did this, Miss Nau. Eighteen hundred loaves that cannot be baked—according to our lab analysis—for another two weeks, because of your ultra-freshness spell!"

He'd become more livid as he spoke, and I felt the old shiver of intimidation start. Something snapped inside me. "Well, then," I quipped, "sell it as bake-at-home!"

"I don't have to take lip from a 'chanter! You're fired, Miss Nau, effective this minute! Pick up your pay and leave—and take that with you!" He gestured to the sword.

Aventura spat sparks at him, very much as I wished I could. I turned and stalked out of the office and across the floor, without speaking to any of my friends. I picked up my pay, and as I cleaned out my locker, Myra, who 'chanted the hot buttered toast, came over.

"What happened, Tira?" She eyed the sword.

"Got fired." I refused to cry. Myra wanted to console me, invite me over to dinner. I explained about the sword, and said, "I've got a million things to do. I'll call you."

I walked to the bus stop, berating myself. I knew better than to snap at a manager during a richly deserved reprimand! But maybe one 'chanter in a hundred could have done what I did—even if it wasn't the job I was hired for. Maybe I'd snapped at the boss because I'd been feeling important, like the people Rogero knew. But I wasn't really that good, only a little better than I'd been yesterday. Yet—no, I'd have known if the sword had amplified my enchantment. I'd done it all myself.

Still, I'd never have done it without the sword. Rogero was right: I had to turn it off before it made chaos of my life.

I got off the bus at the university and bought a campus library card.

After an hour of fruitless labor, I asked for help. It took three librarians another hour to locate the history of Aventura. With copies of those pages and a stack of books, I found a nook among some lawn statuary where I could sit in the afternoon sun, sheltered from the wind, and read.

Aventura was easily a thousand years old, but the books only traced it back to the Magical Renaissance. I'd been right, one had to master it to pass it on.

As an "Attitudinal," it operated on the psyche, not the physical world. It didn't add power to the magician's work, but helped the magician tap his own. Uncle Prosper's words suddenly made sense: he'd willed Aventura to my father to induce my father to change his attitude about magic. Now, it seemed to be changing mine. And the only way I could make it stop was by mastering it.

I'd never done well in school. I'd almost flunked out of Enchanter's Trade School. But perhaps I hadn't done well because I didn't think enough of myself. I mused on this until shadows crept over my toes; then I strode over to the administration building and picked up some catalogs.

I caught an express bus home in time to meet Rogero. He was going to help me sort my junk and pack what I needed off to his apartment, which was much larger than mine.

When I arrived, he was pacing back and forth in front of my door. Dressed in his immaculate blue suit and white shirt, with navy shoes and hat, he carried a large bundle (probably work clothes), and his Paraphernalia Case was bulging.

I came toward him brimming over with good news, and started to babble out all I'd discovered.

He cut me off. "Where've you been? I've been waiting for half an hour!" I could hear how offended he was.

My head was full of muzzy plans for unlocking my latent talents. I'd even daydreamed of becoming a professor. But I leashed back my temper, offering my armload of reference books. "At the university. Research."

"You took off from work?"

I confessed I'd been fired for cause.

"Fired? Insubordination?"

"Rogero, he had a right to fire me. There are thousands who could replace me." Tears sprang to my eyes. I'd never been fired before, and I felt humiliated.

I sniffed, holding my breath against the urge to sob. Rogero put an arm around me, his whole attitude melting into protectiveness. Strangely, I felt it was as if he'd always expected me to fail, and it was his prerogative to comfort me when that happened—like a child. Just as my father always had. Was this why I've never felt my own power? I've soaked up my father's attitude toward me, fulfilling his unconscious expectations?

"There, now, feel better?" he asked, taking the key from my hand and opening the door. As we went on in, dumping our things in the living room, he said, "While you start dinner, I'll see what we can do about this sword. We'll have it whipped in an hour or so."

I went cold all over. He wasn't even looking to see what I'd brought home. He would rely on his friends, and his contacts, and his knowledge, as if mine didn't exist.

True, I didn't move in the kind of exalted circles he did. He could probably find out from a wizard friend what I'd be charged a bundle for in an office consultation—and he could use what he found out. But—I paused in the kitchen door. "Rogero, you know Aventura is my sword, and I don't think anyone else is going to be able to affect it."

"I'll call you when I need you."

He's going to call me when he needs me. If that didn't summarize our entire relationship. He did things, and called me when he needed me. When he didn't need me, I should be put away in a closet. I don't know why I hadn't seen it before. It was as plain as my nose reflected in Aventura's blade.

He started to spread a symbol cloth on the floor, consulting a diagram drawn on a napkin.

"That seems awfully elaborate, just to find the off-spell for an Implement," I observed.

"How many swords like this have you seen turned off?"

"Probably as many as you have!"

Exasperated, he said, "Look, I know what I'm doing. Leonardo explained it to me, step by step."

"So explain it to me."

"You wouldn't understand."

"Try me."

"Tira, we don't have all night."

"I just wanted to make sure it wouldn't get damaged."

"Now, how could you think I'd do anything like that? That's a valuable antique, and it will add a certain—elegance—displayed in our living room."

"Our living room," I repeated. Always before, those words had lit in me a warm wriggling of anticipation and happiness; but, suddenly, I heard what he, himself, didn't know he was saying. It was his living room, and I was his, and my sword was his, and we'd both be displayed there. "My Implement will add a touch of elegance to your living room."

He put one hand on a hip and cocked his head aside. "What has gotten into you? All last night, and now this. That sword is ruining your attitude."

"Ruining my— Suppose I like my new attitude?"

He said, softly, as if speaking to an excitable mental patient, "That could be the sword talking, not you. Now, just be calm awhile, and we'll have it turned off and put away. And then you'll be your old self."

"Suppose I don't want to be my old self? Suppose I want to turn Aventura back on again?"

"Tira, neither of us has the training to wield it. It's already got us fighting. It's best to be laid aside."

"Who are you to decide what's 'best,' and without even consulting me!"

"Your fiancé, that's who. In just a few days, we'll be married. With this new promotion, I'll be able to move you into a lovely house. And with you by my side, there's no limit to where I can go in the company. They're already talking about sending me to the West Coast."

My whole vision of married life crashed around my ears. "I can't go to the coast if I'm in the middle of college here!" My voice was loud enough now for the neighbors to hear, but I didn't care.

"It doesn't matter. There are schools out west." He kept his voice down, but the effort made him growl.

It was clear he didn't think any more of my chances in school than my father had. No, I didn't have the strength to fight that every day and night. "Maybe we better get this straight right now. I decide what's to be done with and to Aventura. I decide what school I'm going to, and what I'm going to major in, when I'm going to move, and where I'm moving to. If it's not convenient, you can adjust to it. Maybe you'll have to go to the coast for a year or two without me—"

"Tira, you're out of your mind! There's no point my going anywhere without you! Who would entertain for me? How would I get ahead? What would people think?"

"That I have a career of my own?" There was an edge to my voice. "And who's going to entertain for me? How am I going to get ahead?"

He frowned, as if suddenly hearing me for the first time. "Are you telling me you don't want to marry me?"

I heard myself for the first time. Choking back disgraceful tears, I said, "No, but I don't want to marry anyone who doesn't know I exist."

"What an awful thing to say!" Now he was yelling, deeply offended. "I've spent hours today taking care of your problems. You're practically all I've thought about for months and months now. Everything I do is for you!"

"Which makes me some kind of burden!" That's how Dad always thought of me—a chore, a burden.

"Is that why you want to go back to school? So you don't need me to do things for you?"

I snapped, without thinking, "That'd scare you, wouldn't it? Well, I've decided I'm going to get my Wizardry Degree, and if you don't like it, there's the door!"

He stood dumbfounded for a moment. "You think it'll be that easy?" He gathered up his cloth, saying, "Well, it's not, Tira. You're making a big mistake. You'll never even pass the entry exams. And now you've been fired," he added, ramming his hat on his head, "you'll never get another decent 'chanter's job. You'll live the rest of your life on public assistance. Mark my words. Good-bye!"

The door slammed with total finality, and I crumpled into a heap and sobbed my heart out. It was only afterward that I realized Aventura hadn't spat sparks at him. It just hung in the air, barely glowing—letting me fight my own battle.

The landlord had already rented my apartment to an elderly gentleman. I couldn't get it back. So I went apartment and job shopping near campus. Bus fare ate into my small savings, and what I could get from selling the ring I'd bought for Rogero. I wondered how I was going to survive.

Nights I lay awake, hungry because I was chintzing on meals—besides, I could afford to lose a few pounds—and alternately wishing Rogero would call and make up, and exulting in my fortitude in not calling him. I wanted to be established before he called, or I knew I'd fall weakly into his arms and let him turn Aventura off. And I'd hate myself for the rest of my life.

I began to talk to that sword, telling it my troubles as if it could understand why I couldn't face any of my friends from the bakery until I was settled. Rogero's parents had a secretary who'd do the work of calling the wedding off. None of the guests were mine, anyway.

I made myself read the university library books, even when I didn't understand a word in five. I answered every ad for a part-time job in my field, and even some outside it. I filed with every agency, and went to dozens of interviews, glibly reciting the explanation of the wizard class, dull quartz sword bobbing beside me. Twice I was promised a job and then turned down—after they'd had time to check my references. I began to wonder if I should cheat and not mention the bakery, because they'd blackballed me.

The day before I was to be evicted, I went to campus to return the books. Afterward, I crawled into the nook of the lawn sculpture where I'd first gotten the idea I could go back to school. Less than three weeks ago, I'd had a good home waiting, a solid husband, and a bright, open future. Now I was all but a vagrant without a place to sleep for the night.

But the sunset was gorgeous. The cricket song was balm to the nerves. The grass was soft and sensuous beneath my bare feet. The rough, hard granite sculpture was warm from the sun, and eased my aching back better than a heating pad. The buildings around me seemed the very definition of beauty, as they blended with the natural setting. Students strolled or bicycled or jogged about; anxious, listless, worried, or joyful, each was uniquely alive.

The world hadn't changed; I had. Suddenly, my heart was bursting with tearful gratitude that I was finally allowed to know this hidden beauty. I sat spellbound for nearly an hour, until the exquisite pain of that knowledge abated. I knew I was happy. I'd never been happy before. Better that all trace of that former life be gone.

At last, it began to get chilly. I thought of beds, breakfast, toilets. Soon the campus would be closed, the students off to their apartments or dorms.

I pulled myself to my feet, and noticed Aventura's dull light in the growing shadow. It had never so much as sparkled since the night I threw Rogero out. It seemed to have turned its back on me. I stood up, almost nose to pommel with it, and said, "Uncle Prosper, you sent me freedom and happiness—but being jobless and homeless is no blessing!" I hardly recognized my own voice. It was an octave too low, and sounded like a wizard's. "Aventura, I will not allow you to master me."

"Yes, Mistress. How may I serve?"

Stunned, trembling, for this was the first response the sword had ever made, I continued in that same tone. "Help me find a place to live, and a job."

"This way, please, Mistress."

I followed, glad Aventura didn't sound like Prosper, or my father. The sword vibrated, glowing brightly. It sounded a C natural, then tilted and picked up speed, as if homing on a beacon. I felt ridiculous, panting along behind a very conspicuous sword, calling, "Not so fast! I'm coming."

It twanged again, but went faster. It led me through tunnels of greenery, up stairs set in hillsides, across a wide glade, under some ancient trees, and to the edge of campus, where the buildings were more than a century old.

There, on the steps of a three-story brown-shingle building half smothered in old ivy, I found a young woman in flowered shorts and a scanty top, crying softly and desperately into her cupped hands. It was the woman I'd met on the bus. "Aventura," I hissed, still trying to catch my breath, "I meant paying work, not counseling distraught students."

The sword didn't answer. It had gone dull again, bobbing serenely behind me. I started to fade back into the shrubbery. Whatever her problem, I had no time or resource to help her. But that desolate sound grabbed my heart. Maybe the old me could have walked away pretending to mind my own business when I was really just intimidated by a problem bigger than I was. The new me was so sure I could help that it would be a crime to turn away.

Reluctantly, I presented myself at the bottom of the steps. She looked up, recognized the sword, and exclaimed, embarrassed, "Professor!"

"I'm no professor," I confessed. I sat down beside her, and said, "But I've done some crying in my life. Want to trade tales of woe?"

"Mine's about a man."

"Mine, too."

"Are all men like that?"

"Not any more than all women are like us."

She told me how the guy she'd been living with had pulled out, taking her things and leaving a big rent bill, a whopping disillusionment, and a broken heart that would never mend. She ended, blowing her nose into a wad of tissues, "If I can stop crying long enough, I'm going to see if they can help." She indicated the building behind us.

I read the sign. "Campus Women's Counseling Center. What do you suppose they can do? What you need is a better-paying job, not a psychologist."

"Or a new roommate. They keep a roommate-wanted list—what's the matter?"

"What would you think of taking in me and my sword?"

"What?"

"I told you, I'm not a visiting professor." I sketched my story briefly. "So you see, if I can find work—"

She was eager to have me—or maybe Aventura. "They keep a jobs list inside, too—let's go!"

The place stank of dampness and disinfectant, stale coffee, and, even this late, it rang with the sounds of phones and busy people calling to each other. Hallways led in three directions, and behind an abandoned secretary's desk heaped with papers, a stairway led upward. Bulletin boards were layers deep in old notices. The floors were tilted this way and that, as if the building had been jacked up many times, and there was a stain on the thin carpet where water had leaked through the roof.

"Come look at this—" my new friend called, then laughed. "I don't even know your name!"

"Tira Nau. Yours?"

"Nadine Shellman. Look, here's a whole kitchen outfit for sale. Norm took everything I had when he—"

"I've got tons of housekeeping stuff—I need a job."

"Which one of you said that?" came a deep voice.

I jumped with a start, as if caught at something naughty. "I did," I admitted. Suddenly, I was intimidated, driven back to being that same, ultimate failure of a person I'd been all my life.

The woman was tall, overweight, gray-haired, not very crisply groomed, but imposing in her manner. She questioned me, shotgun style. "What sort of job?"

I listed my qualifications.

"Three years in a bakery? You a student here?"

"Not yet. I'm going to enroll next semester." I tried to hold my head high and sound as if I meant it, but my voice squeaked, and I could hear, see, and feel all the ways I'd ever projected failure to everyone I spoke to.

She quirked an eyebrow toward the sword, as if wondering what I was doing with such a powerful thing.

Slowly, it came to me that I had gotten Aventura to call me Mistress—which was more than Rogero would ever have tried for. "I've come here," I said, my voice dropping into the wizard's tone, "to master this sword. But I'm already a top freshness enchanter. I'd be valuable in the cafeteria, setting food to stay hot or cold, or preventing overcooking."

"Those jobs are usually reserved for students."

It was a cold put-off, the sort of thing that once would have made me slink away with my head between my shoulders, wondering where I'd gotten the nerve to apply in the first place. But not now.

"As they should be," I replied. "And I'm going to be a student, as soon as registration opens." I had no money, but perhaps I'd get a scholarship, or a loan. I met the woman's eyes, confident in my own powers.

She turned and shouted to someone in another room, "Forget it, Madge. The job's filled." And to me, she said, "You start tomorrow at five-thirty, preparing breakfast in the main cafeteria. I come on at six, and you'd better be there, and working. I run the place, and I don't stand for any nonsense. Come on, I'll show you around."

I had a new boss, tougher than any I'd ever worked for; but I had a new toughness myself. By the time she checks my references, I'll have proven myself invaluable.

About Jo Clayton and "Change"

This story contains one of the most fascinating aliens I've ever encountered. I found the Ouloud, in Jo's story, quite different from any of the other imaginary beasties whose line stretches from the Medea in the pre-Iliad Greek sagas, though these are really science fiction in the tradition of A. E. Van Vogt's *Voyage of the Space Beagle*.

Jo herself is a friendly and forthright lady whose work is intriguing and always just a little subtler than you expect; this was her first story for the magazine, and it took second place in the Cauldron vote. Her story "Arakney's Web," in issue 18, proved so popular that while I'm in general not much of a one for series, I'm holding one or two more Arakney stories.

At least, being a thoroughgoing professional, Jo went about it the right way, selling me the first one as an independent story, and when I liked it, producing a sequel. All the series I've ever printed started like that; but I've lost track of the amateurs who write me hard-sell letters about their unwritten series. They ought to save their time and postage, and try it the way Jo did . . . sell me one good story first. But they so seldom do.

Change

Jo Clayton

1

In the hollow the Ouloud had dug into the lake shore's hardened mud, damp dripped slowly from fine root hairs feathering the irregular ceiling, droplets crawling down the roots, clinging for a last moment to the blunt tips, dropping finally into the emptiness below with sometimes sharp tings if they fell into the deepening puddle, sometimes hard rattles as they hit the dead husk of the hibernating Ouloud. The tap-slap-ting continued uninterrupted as the pool around the husk rose higher and higher until at last the drops no longer fell on husk or mud, fell only on water.

A sharp crack jarred through the plinks.

A line of blue-white light shimmered in the muddy water.

The husk moved, lay still, moved again in short sharp jerks, lay still again, again jolted about as the crack widened.

The cold light strengthened in the hollow, winking back from silicate crystals in the dirt and shining through the agitated water onto the pale roots.

Her back and buttocks out, the Ouloud rested again, then with one convulsive heave, she kicked free of the husk and straightened her cramped limbs. Her eyes were sealed shut, dark smudges behind translucent lids. Her head was studded with hundreds of small nodules, the tight-coiled threads inside writhing and pressing against skin still too soft and thick for them to burst through. Skeleton and pulsing organs and the Daughter Within were dim shadows in fleshlike milk glass lit by her self-generated radiance.

Like a great worm she wriggled up the slippery mud to the highest point of the hollow and began scratching blindly at the plug of packed earth that sealed her in. At first her hands scrabbled over the cold soil without effect, then her fingers broadened and grew harder until they were deep gouges that bit into the plug and tore away great gouts of earth.

When she burst from the hollow, she crouched on the steep slope of the lake shore, blind head turning slowly from side to side, shape-shifting hands groping clumsily at the night air until she lost the sense of where she was and tumbled in an awkward sprawl into the water.

Passively she accepted the embrace of the snowmelt, sinking until she floated a dozen feet below the surface; she let the currents nudge her where they would until she came to rest against a rocky islet near the lake's outlet where a creek tumbled downslope over a spray of boulders.

The sky began to gray, a red line spread along the eastern horizon.

The slow process of waking went on; the Ouloud's skin hardening and thinning, her metabolism speeding up.

When sunlight touched her face, she stirred, opened her eyes, her ice-gray irids darkening to the color of wetted stone. Webs spread between lengthening fingers. Gills opened on neck and chest. She breathed her first breath and began swimming, aimlessly at first, then she became aware of hunger. She snatched a fish, tore it into small bits, held them in her toothless mouth while her digestive juices liquefied them.

The day continued to brighten. She stopped swimming and floated upright in the center of the lake, her head a dozen feet below the surface, waiting with plantlike patience for the moment of ripeness.

When the sun was directly overhead, shimmering down to her through the clear cold water, her cilia burst from their nodules, springing out from her head like dandelion fluff.

The tendrils tasted the lake water, fluttered wildly.

Change. Danger. She tasted again. Poisons. Yes. Metals. Yes. Burning her cilia, oozing into her body. Other substances. Unhealthy. Disorienting.

She raged about the ragged oval, trilling her fury, her outrage. Her lake and its contiguous land especially, but also every inch of the Island, from the peak of her Mountain to the seashore, this was her Place, an extension of herself. Its violation was a knife in her flesh, but rage alone was futile, there was no healing in anger, so she calmed herself and let the water settle around her.

Hanging motionless again, she searched into the layer upon layer of memory passed from Ouloud to Ouloud since the first of their line ripened into awareness, searched for croons that she could weave together to exorcise the poisons and destroy the poisoners and give her back her peace. Shadows crept across the water as she considered and discarded.

When she found what she sought, she abandoned memory for the moment and kicked toward the surface, her body altering as her head broke water, gill slits closing, air sacs thickening into lungs.

NOISE. Shrieks of hurting metal, thumpings and roarings, rattles and squeals, SOUNDS that hammered at her, louder than storms, terrible, punishing SOUNDS. With their echoes bouncing back at her from her loved Mountain, they were all around her, everywhere, she couldn't tell where they were coming from. She shuddered and cowered in the water unable to think or move, battered almost shapeless by the NOISE.

Slowly, painfully, her cilia coiled tight against her head, she reduced her hearing, circumscribed it until the pummeling was bearable and she could string thought to thought once more.

Eyes refocused for longsight, she turned in the water and scanned the Lakeshore, beginning at the outlet and the creek, turning slowly, seeing only trees and a few birds, turning to face her Mountain. Oo-loo! There was a hole in the mountainside, with debris piled carelessly around it. Coming out of the hole there were two lines of metal set on heavy baulks of wood half buried in gravel. A wooden flume ran beside them, filled with water from a spring higher on the Mountain—she knew that as clearly as if that flume carried fluids from her body. A line of carts with metal wheels came worming out the hole, pulled by a team of ponies, a Talking Beast riding the first cart with a long whip in his hand that he flicked now and then at the ponies' tails. The carts went clacking along the rails until they vanished into the trees. She turned through another quarter arc, saw smoke rising, saw the ridgepole and the upper part of a shingled roof, the rest of the THING invisible behind more trees. The wind was blowing snatches of that smoke toward the Lake. She could smell the poisons in it. Rage seized her again, shook her until her head ached and the Daughter Within stirred dangerously.

A new fear chilled her. No. This is not the time. Not yet. She wrapped her arms about her body and sang a quieting croon at the dark worm inside her. One day the Daughter Within would truly wake and eat herself free and a new Ouloud would swim these waters, walk this land. But not now. No.

She frowned at the smoke, considering the order of her acts. The Lake first. The lake MUST be cleansed. That would be hard. It would mean waiting and resting before she undertook the second act. No matter. The Lake first. Then the THING that poisoned the Lake. Then the Beasts who built the THING. When the Island was clean again, she could rest and consider the Daughter and what the stirring meant.

She drew power into herself and began singing the new-made croon that shaped and ordered it.

Waterspouts like spinning tops grew from the surface of the Lake, sucking up the tainted water and spitting it out purified in a light continual rain, the muck that poisoned it left isolated in thickening collars near the rim. The watercones swayed and twisted on their tiny bases as the pollutants continued to accumulate, wobbling more and more wildly as the Ouloud strained to hold them up, her cilia whipping in a white cloud above her head. Her croon grew more intense, louder, until the sound filled the lake valley and came murmuring back to her, weaving in and out of the Thing-sounds.

When the burning in her cilia was gone, she wove a new trill into the croon, a trill that hooked into a high wind and drew it down across the spouts. Another trill. The stain-collars turned to dust and the wind snatched them away, taking the poisons out over the ocean, away and away from HER Land.

Her throat raw, her eyes burning, the Ouloud loosed the spouts and drifted into sleep, letting the lake currents take her until she lodged against the rocky islet, her body cradled by the cold water, her sleep so deep she knew nothing for many hours, missing completely the excited shouts from the smelter workers and their haphazard search of the lake and lakeshore.

2

As if she hit at Toja and Moriawha and the rest of the Whaka-ekinriks infesting House and Island—and Issian and Tarag and Cunnothat and every muc that shamed the name Huanin with the way they sucked up to the conquerors—Tassin knelt on a piece of sacking and stabbed the trowel again and again into the dark, crumbly soil, loosening the earth about the bubble roses with a controlled ferocity that sent the tight pink buds swaying on their curved stems. If Old Moriawha found her out here working the earth like a farm girl, the hag would yell her into the House and scold her until a beating would be a welcome change, but if she stayed inside another minute with the rest of Toja's whores, she'd be clawing the walls or killing someone, probably Issian, that fluttering bitch. Fitha Spog, you'd think she'd have a proper value for herself, lovely as she is. Like Mama said, lovely is as lovely does. And that being so, I'm a hag as well.

She straightened her spine, grunting with the effort, scraped the back of her hand across her forehead, ignoring the crumbs of dirt that dropped from the trowel onto her bulging middle. Ah-weh ah-weh, who am I to call them names for doing what they have to. It's their pride in it I spit on. Me. Toja's whore. She stuck the trowel into the earth beside her knee and began tweaking out chinchea weedlings whose small trefoils dyed her fingers green and raised a minty smell that bit sharply through the sweeter scent of the bubble buds. The odors brought back the times when she was free and young and exploding with the springtime. Before. She wrenched a trefoil loose and flung it away. Before. It was an ugly word. Ugly and filled with pain. Before. Yes. Before the Whaka-ekinriks came in their hideous metal steamboats. Before the Rik Taua Apekoura came with his Ka-eera and took the Island away from Clan Huanin. Before his son-heir Toja Apekojira caught her carrying water from the spring and carried her off instead. Before she was heavy with his cursed brat. She'd shed it even now, given half a chance, and take her licks from the Mother's Wrathrod for disdaining Life.

Half a chance? No chance. Old Moriawha, she did the divination and swore it was a boy. The only one he'd got with all his whores and his kinrik wife Namiwi, a knife-blade bitch that one was, addicted to lacha and barren in the bargain.

Moriawha. Fitha Spog, I loathe that one. Old witch, kinrik witch, doting on her fosterling boy, wanting what he wanted and ready to do anything to see he got it. But she was right, curse the hag with boils and itches. A woman of the Huanin knew what her child was as soon as the child knew.

He'd think she was trying to rid herself of her burden if he caught her out here now, so close to the herb garden. Fool man, there was nothing there that would do the job, she'd thought of that ages ago and given it up. The evil creature would beat her on the feet, ah yes he would, and it would be a week at least before she could hobble about without weeping at the pain. And she'd bite her lip till it bled before she'd weep in front of Issian or any of that pack.

She moved across to the tubers, began pinching back shoots and clearing away the weeds. A pair of warbler daymoths fluttered past overhead, looping and fluting through a vigorous, noisy courting. The chimer in the corner thrust its puzzle crown above the outwall and trapped late-afternoon sunrays in yellow-green crystals that sang loudly enough to cut through the noise of the shearing sheds down past the U-bend where the creek met the river. The sun was hot on her back and neck, a pleasant heat, the moist dark earth was cool

and accepting under her. She forgot her servitude, forgot her
resentments, forgot the dangers of lingering out here, forgot
the boredom waiting inside the house, felt once again a part
of earth and everything. . . .

A SOUND came down the mountain, an eerie rising and
falling that stood the hairs up along her spine.

Tassin shivered. The Ouloud was awake at last and SHE
was raging. The smelter. Anyone with a grain of sense would
know SHE'd hate it.

The last Ahraddin to Speak the Ouloud died thirty years
before, during the Invasion, but the Awashin Sagolar took
her role and told the Rik not to build the smelter up there. If
you have a need for water, build your contrivance on the
River, he said. SHE doesn't go there often, he said. You'll
taint HER lake, he said. SHE'll wake and destroy us all in
her anger, he said. And that was true, true it was. And true,
too, that Toja would not hear him.

Tassin got heavily to her feet, shook out her skirt, hid the
trowel behind the loose brick beside the kitchen door.

Toja never listens to what he doesn't want to hear. The
Awashin tried and all he got for it was his tongue ripped out.
Poor man, ah the poor man. That won't work with HER, you
bastard son of a bastard line. HER you'll hear, oh yes. She
looked at her hands. They were stained with earth and green
ooze. Ah-weh ah-weh, I'd better get inside.

Moriawha caught her going up the back stairs. "And
where have you been?"

Though it gave her gas to do it, Tassin bowed her head
and bent her knees in a sketch of a curtsy. "In the garden, listening to the songs of the Mountain, Tikan Moriawha."

"You should be resting."

"Respectfully, Tikan Moriawha, it is you keeping me from
my bath and bed."

The old woman scowled at her, Tassin could see her wrinkled hands itching to slap. "When the boy is born, we'll see,
we'll see."

"A ra, Tikan Moriawha," Tassin said politely and brushed
past her.

The bath she'd ordered was waiting, the water tepid, the

scent gone stale a bit, but she sank neck deep into the infusion and lay there floating, feeling the warmth creep into her and erode away a moiety of her fears.

She sniffed at her hands before she washed them, smelling the earth again, drawing a bit of strength from it, clearing the dither from her mind. Ah-weh ah-weh, well I know what I should do, but how I'll do it, that's another thing altogether.

She was afraid again and cold, more than the cooling of the water could be blamed for. She turned the tap and let the hot water come splashing in. Give them this, the Whaka-ekinriks were good for something. Running water hot and cold and lamps that didn't smoke and choke you and inside toilets and steam irons that didn't burn you and what you were pressing and mirrors you could actually see your face in and books, oh the grand books that Toja had, books she never saw him open except once, late at night when she couldn't sleep and wanted something to pass the hours until dawn.

Except for the books, that was an evil evil room; she hated it. Like his father before him, Toja kept his trophies there, rounds of skin cut off the chests of the Huanin men he'd killed in battle and in chase, the part where the totem signs and the name cartouches were tattooed. She'd made the mistake once of telling him how gloriously her lover had pleasured her and how much he disgusted her. That was the night he showed her the round from Tonn's chest, smooth and supple, a long time tanned. He watched her vomit and scream and pull out chunks of hair. He sat there holding the round of skin and watched her cry until she'd wrung all the tears from her body. He sat there silent, without moving all the time of her grief. Then he walked away and left her. She never saw that skin again; it wasn't with the others when she looked.

Issian kicked at the door. "You asleep in there, you long-faced ewe? Have some consideration, will you?" She kept on yammering and punctuating her yammer with more kicks and a bang or two.

"Shut up, gasti," Tassin yelled back. Groaning at the effort, she caught hold of the towel rail and lifted her clumsy body from the water. She hobbled to the door, banged her fist on it. "You don't stop your blathering, I'll set my fist to your blue blue eye and you won't be seeing a thing but black for the next seven days."

In the ensuing silence Tassin toweled herself as dry as she could. Having wrapped a quilted robe about herself and tied the belt, she lifted the latch, straight-armed the door open, and marched out; her belly going before her, Toja's get that Issian wouldn't have the nerve to lay a hand on.

An hour after midnight, a workbag hanging on her shoulder, Tassin slipped from her room. She listened a moment, grinned as she heard Moriawha snoring, stretched out on the pallet dragged across the door. Bad dreams and bellyaches and knowing that your bones are sore for nothing, hag, I'm using the headwife's exit.

Keeping close to the wall, she ghosted to Namiwi's door, took a butter knife out of the bag, and pushed back the tongue of the lock. When she had the door open, she dug out the wad of bread that she'd stuck in there to keep the tongue from going all the way in when Namiwi turned the key, tossed the bread aside and walked into the sitting room. She listened a moment at the bedroom door, heard what she expected to hear. All the livelong day Namiwi had been acid as a just-budded grape, temperish from need. Now she was muttering and giggling, making the bed creak as she thrashed about. Chewing lacha and not about to care if the world went red and turned to dust.

Tassin crossed to the door into the hall and swung up the bar, eased the door open a crack, and looked along the hallway. There was no guard out there. She reevaluated the sounds in Namiwi's bedroom and grinned again. The gander's getting sauced tonight and all the luck in the world to the cook. She still thought Namiwi was a bitch on wheels, but there was a touch of fellow feeling in her as she slipped through the dark, silent halls and crept into the kitchen. By smell and by feel she found bread and cheese and stuffed them into the workbag, then fumbled her way to the door that led from the kitchen into the stables.

She groped across the stable, unbarred and pushed open the door to the outside, and let the light of the full moon come flooding in. There wasn't much likelihood she'd be interrupted. Taseachan, the stableman, was snoring in the loft and fumes of sourflon came dropping down to mix with hay and horse.

Nose twitching, rubbing sneezes back, she saddled and bridled one of the gentler geldings, hauled herself into the saddle, and clattered out to find the smelter road. It was a long road and a hard one and she had hours before her to regret this, but all the regrets in the world wouldn't change what had to be.

3

It was early morning when the Ouloud woke, a crisp clear morning with a vigorous breeze that ruffled the surface of the lake and set glitters dancing through the water. She looped and tumbled about the lake in a dance of celebration that woke echoes in the liquids of her body until they fizzed through her in joyous effervescence. Hungry, she caught three fish and ate them in her slow way, continuing to announce her contentment with bits of wordless song between dissolving bites.

Then she put her joy away. Time to prepare the second act.

She floated upright in the middle of the lake and thought.

It was a strong THING. Stone and mortar, black iron and iron's tougher cousin. Unmasking it would take a very strong croon and a long one—and drain away her strength.

She searched memory once more, a croon for metal things, some way to erase that monster roaring in her Valley. A croon for building, yes, it could be twisted thus and thus and turned toward unbuilding. A croon for shielding, yes ah yes, turn it thus and thus and thread it in the other. Yes. Undo the THING, undo the disease that made the THING, the Talking Beasts, the Toolmakers. Clean the island of them all. Let them rot and feed the beasts and the plants, instead of feeding on them. YES!

She thought some more. Yes. Let them feed ME. She had to be strong and fish wouldn't do it. She needed blood.

The Ouloud sat beneath the flume and watched poison gush into the lake, watched the gush die to a trickle, then a few drops. Subduing her fury, she fluted a summoning croon, calling one of the Beast workers swarming at the THING, called him to come to her, come, come.

He came from the trees, fighting her with every step, trying to escape the iron hold of the croon and to scream for aid from others of his kind. She blocked that easily. They were tougher than the other beasts, but they had no croons to protect them, no skill at Shaping except with their hands and that was weak, so weak.

He was afraid; the sharpness of that fear gave a dark pungency to the rich meaty smell that rolled off him.

She leaned forward eagerly, tongue altering to hollow needle. Humming with pleasure, she pressed her lips against his neck, pierced the blood channel beneath the tough resilient skin, and drank. As the link between them intensified, she pulsed to the beat of his heart. She drained him, rested a moment with her lips against his cooling skin, then withdrew her tongue and let the husk fall away.

"Ouloud."

The Ouloud looked lazily at the female Beast who'd come without being summoned. She was sated for the moment; she didn't want nor need more blood. Then she stiffened. There was something about this one, like a perfume remembered from long ago. Something . . ."Ou-loo," she cooed. She held up a hand, the fingers changing to claws, dark and hard as horn, one forefinger left pale and straight; she pointed at the ground, waggled her finger impatiently. There was time now while the blood worked in her, readied her for the Unmasking. Time to taste for that perfume, to summon that memory.

4

Tassin.

The Rik Toja Apekojira looked down at the rumpled bed and the pile of needlework dumped in the middle of it; the early sun slanted in through the small window and touched to life a half-finished warbler moth. He reached down, touched it; the threads were silky soft.

Tassin. The word was a wound in him.

Namiwi stood with her head thrown back, temper in the arch of her nostrils, the line of her mouth; her eyes were red from the lacha weed and her hands trembled. "The door was locked," she said. "I was asleep. The whore slithered out some other way. Your kurekure, she was snoring so loud, a herd could walk over her."

"Find her." Tassin. He bled inside. He would not let her see it.

Moriawha bent over the basin, chanted at the oil-filmed water.

The film shivered, swirled, then smoothed out and a pale image formed. Tassin rode up a red-dirt road on a weary gray gelding, weary herself. On one side of her, the creeks, on the other, the twin rails of that tram that brought ingots down from the smelter to the steel mill he'd built on the coast.

"Who is she going to?" Tassin. "Show him to me."

Moriawha blew across the basin, chanted again.

When the film cleared, Toja cursed. It wasn't a man but a Thing. Tassin.

Taseachan lay on his face in the dust and straw.

The Rik Toja Apekojira took the shotgun and shotbag from the Kapen. Tassin. "He was careless and tried to cover himself." He broke the shotgun, plugged in two shells. "Kill him and bring me the roan. Kapen Atoatan, I want four from the Ka-eera following me. Five minutes." He ignored the sounds of the strangling Huanin, swung into the saddle, and sent the roan clattering out of the stable. Tassin.

5

Tassin kicked her feet from the stirrups, clutched at the saddle horn, and let herself tilt sideways until she fell off, wrenching her hands from the leather but not before she broke the worst of the fall.

The croon touched her again, cool, impersonal. It wasn't calling her, it was just there. She used it like a guide rope and walked along the lakeshore until she saw the flume and the Ouloud sitting under it.

Shimmering in a sunlit halo of drips from the flume, the Ouloud's body was slender and delicate. Long white cilia fine as spun glass quivered about her thin, high-cheeked face. Stone-colored eyes stared at her.

"I came to tell you . . ."

"Ou-looo." The Ouloud pressed her fingers across her lips, then pointed at the ground again.

"Fitha Spog." Tassin lowered herself awkwardly to her knees, eased her legs around, and got herself seated. "Ouloud."

The Ouloud's crinkled round mouth pursed tighter, she began to hum.

"No!" Tassin held up a hand, palm out. "No. I came to tell you, it isn't us. It isn't the Huanin who did this. Leave us alone."

The Ouloud looked from the body crumpled by her feet to Tassin. She shrugged as if to say it's all the same.

Tassin clenched her fists, her temper up. "The Huanin belong to the land as much as you, Ouloud cun-na. You can kill me for saying it, but then you'll kill me tomorrow if not today and what's a day more or less?"

"Oo-lou," the Ouloud sang. "Greet you, Talking Beast. Come here, give me blood."

Tassin gasped. "Ah-weh ah-weh, I will not," she said forcefully. "Walk to my own funeral, you're saying? It's kicking and yelling I plan to go, not meek as a mewling ewe lamb. I could be lying in a warm bed now, with whores fetching my tea and an ugly big man kissing my toes. Instead I wore my tailbone down till my neck sits on my rump, coming up here to argue my life from you."

"Ou-lou," the Ouloud sang. "Come here, Beast, give me blood."

"Beast I am not. I am Huanin. I am Tassin. Give me my name."

"Ou-Lou," the Ouloud cooed. She stretched out her hands. "Come here, Tas-sin. Give me blood, Ahradda, take healing from me," She trilled her laughter. "For your tailbone."

Tassin stared at her, astonished. Ahradda. SHE names me Ahradda. Ah-weh ah-weh, that's for thinking about another day. "So it's a trade you're offering. That's a different thing altogether." She squared her shoulders, brushed her hands together, and took a short step toward the Ouloud. Still reluctant, but driven by a combination of curiosity and desperation, she rested her palms on the Ouloud's waiting hands.

Warm flesh touched cool, exciting Tassin to her heart's core, stirring her in ways no lover ever had, not even Tonn at the height of her passion for him.

6

Cool flesh touched warm, exciting the Ouloud in ways she had forgot as the years slid past since the last Ahradda had come to her; the hunger grew in her for the sharing, and she forgot the THING roaring and banging up the slope from her.

She touched Tassin's hair; the soft strands clung to her fingers, curled about them. She shivered with pleasure. She slid questing fingers along Tassin's neck, the flesh so soft, so firm, so warm and full of life. She gentled the nervous Ahradda with a low and unintrusive croon, kept the soft touch moving until she felt Tassin sag against her.

She bent closer, touched her lips to the neck. Her tongue changed, hardened, curling over to make the hollow needle that channeled the blood into her throat.

The Ahradda murmured drowsily as the Ouloud pierced the artery at the side of the neck. Her eager delight passed through the link, waking an answering pleasure in Tassin which returned along the link with the rich red alien blood, the feedback lifting them both into a spiraling climb toward a shared explosion of joy.

Reluctantly the Ouloud pulled her head away. "Ooo-louuu Ahhhraaadda," she sang. "Now you, now you."

Tassin blinked, still half dazed. "What?"

"Drink of me." The Ouloud lifted a hand filled with opalescent gel drawn from glands in her wrist. "Oo-lou," she sang.

Tassin bent until her lips touched the gel. She began licking it up, her tongue moving faster and faster, caressing the Ouloud's cool flesh.

When the gel was gone, Tassin lifted her head, smiled lazily, then stretched and groaned with pleasure. She got to her feet, marveling at how easily she lifted her bulky body, at how thoroughly her exhaustion had been banished. "A wonder and a joy, you are you are, a blessing, Cun-nah." She smiled, a broad three-corner thing that warmed the Ouloud head to foot. Then she winced as another chain of cars came down from the mine, squealing and knocking together, rumbling as they off-loaded their rock into the crushers.

The Ouloud got to her feet, took the Ahradda's hand, drew Tassin tight against her. "Ooo-lou," she sang. "Sing with me, Ahradda, it is time . . ."

She began a high whining croon that tore from her throat and made her cilia jerk and shudder. Behind her the water came roaring against the rocks, great waves twice her height racing in successive lines across the lake. Air whirled about them in a vortex that whipped violently through the trees and lifted sand and debris in a rising tide that blanked out everything around them. The air in the whorl's eye hummed and thickened. The stone shifted under their feet, alive and unstable.

With a last howl torn from her straining throat, the Ouloud loosed the Unmasking she had shaped.

And the mine and the miners in it were not.

And the iron cars were not.

And the rails and ties were not.

And the crusher shuddered and screamed and was not.

And the smelter cracked and broke into dust and even the dust was not.

The air hung motionless. The trees stood motionless. Branches arched, leaves caught in mid-flutter. The lake water was frozen in serried peaks. The earth waited. . . .

The Ouloud felt the moment burst within her, darkness splintering into light, the light shrinking to a vibrating dot.

The trees shivered and groaned, the lake fell in on itself and came finally to its usual soft lap-lapping, the earth rumbled and shifted as it settled back to its heavy sleep.

7

Toja rode from under the trees, the roan lathered and stumbling. He pulled him up, sat there staring at the Ouloud and Tassin.

Tassin blinked from her daze. For a moment she was both Huanin and Ouloud and didn't understand who or what he was. Then she knew he was Toja come for her. He shifted. Come for her with a shotgun in his hands.

She pulled free from the Ouloud. "Go," she cried, "get away. He'll kill you."

"Ah-raaa-ou-lou?"

She started to push the Ouloud into the water, but she was too late.

The shotgun coughed; the Ouloud's head came apart.

Tassin screamed and fainted, falling across Ouloud's body, crushing it to a smear on the stone.

8

She woke in her own bed with Moriawha glowering down at her. "What did you think you were doing, kow?"

Tassin turned her head away. She remembered the Ouloud and felt a great emptiness, a grief that nothing would assuage.

Moriawha slapped her, leaving a red print on her face. "You don't turn away from me, whore. And you're not getting out of this bed alone until the boy is born. You hear me?"

Tassin looked past her and said nothing.

Moriawha lifted her hand, then shrugged. "You don't matter," she said. "Nothing you do matters anymore. You're for the strangler's noose when you've done your job. The Tuakais alone know how you'd contrive to corrupt the boy if you were allowed to live and give him suck. Even your milk would poison him.

"There's a guard outside the door," Moriawha went on. "He'll stop you if you try to leave. There's a chamber pot under the bed; use it when you need to. We'll feed you well and treat you tenderly, no fear, it's the boy we're tending. Well?"

Tassin looked past her and said nothing.

Moriawha scowled, shook her head, and left.

One day passed, then another.

Late in the third night, when the full moon shone silvergilt through her window, painting an image of the new iron grating across the coverlet on her bed, Tassin felt a croon grow within her, a song without words, tiny, silent, vibrating inside her bones.

At first she didn't understand.

She listened.

Then she knew.

It was the Daughter Within. Forced prematurely from the Ouloud, it had crept inside her body, nestled against Toja's son.

It was growing in her, feeding on Toja's son, taking his place.

She smiled into the dark, content.

Toja aimed for the Ouloud and killed his son instead.

She lay quiet awhile, savoring the irony, listening to the Song of the Daughter Within.

Then she began planning her escape.

About Phyllis Ann Karr and "The Truth About the Lady of the Lake

Phyllis Ann Karr is another writer known to me and my readers from the early days of *Sword and Sorceress*, where she starred with the paired characters of a sorceress (Frostflower), and a swordsman (Thorn), who, like Misty Lackey's characters Tarma and Kethry, meet various adventures in various universes. Here they stray into a world that seems to be that of King Arthur. Of course, I'm deluged with Arthurian stories; I seldom print them, though recently I succumbed to a marvelous story about King Arthur's horse, of all things! But every story I print on a hackneyed theme is definitely different; this definitely is not the usual Arthur story. Why would I have bothered with "just another" Arthurian story?

But I liked this one—and if I get another one this good, I'll probably print it. That's a safe enough offer; stories like this don't come along very often; in fact, not nearly often enough. Although every time I make an exception to what I say I want, I get a flood of incompetent stories on the same theme; every week I get ninety dragon stories, and only one in a thousand is any darn good.

The Truth about the
Lady of the Lake

Phyllis Ann Karr

"**B**ut what am I going to do with it?" Frostflower eyed the sword that the Monarch of Cockaigne had insisted on giving her because, in the Land of Cockaigne, "all women of worship went armed."

Thorn and Frostflower had set out to travel light this time, leaving Dathru's cumbersome and no-longer-needed book at home with Dowl, the dog, in Windslope Retreat; and now the sorceress was re-encumbered. "Thorn," she asked, "you are sure that you don't want it?"

"A big, clumsy cowkiller like that?" The swordsman shook her head. "Slicer's more than good enough for me. Of course, all those gems in the hilt and sheath are nice. . . . No, let's find someplace where it'll bring a high price. Shouldn't be too hard, now that you can control Dathru's Circle."

The sorceress held the talisman and they reviewed worlds until they found another where warriors dressed up in metal. Anyway, Thorn assumed that the figure lying on a tranquil lakeshore was a warrior taking a nap, with a friend sitting beside to keep watch on their boat. The friend was a whitebeard in a long black robe that looked pretty much like Frost's except for the big silver symbols all over it.

Frostflower smiled. "Another warrior and sorcerer team." The two women went through.

No sooner had they stepped out onto the lakeshore than the whitebeard shouted, "Strange powers, avaunt!" and flung up his right arm, pointing his staff at them. A crack of light burst out of it and knocked Frostflower into the middle of the lake. The metal-covered warrior snored on.

"Hey!" said Thorn.

Whitebeard smirked. "I allow no unknown sorcery near my little king. You, it seems, are no sorceress, else would you have been borne into yon water as well."

Thorn aimed a blow at the bogbait, but it bounced off as if the air had hardened around him. So she clanged the flat of Slicer's blade down hard on the sleeping warrior's metal headpiece.

The warrior sat up, still ringing, and opened the mask beneath the cap of the headpiece, revealing a brown-bearded male face. "Zounds?" he cried, fumbling for his sword.

Thorn was sorry she'd wasted time on him. She knew her friend could stay under quite a while by slowing time for her body—if that power worked in this world—but if she tried to hang onto that heavy Cockaigne sword and sheath, too . . .

"Keep your eye on your demon-addled sorcerer," she told the metalpants. "I'm borrowing your boat." She turned toward it.

"Accursed miscreant, turn again!" The words were scarcely audible over the clanking of metal, but the flat of a blade against the side of Thorn's leg was plain enough.

She whirled back. Metalpants had heaved himself to his feet and was waving his sword at her.

She really didn't have the time. She brought Slicer across with a double-arm smack that she hoped would knock the other warrior's weapon out of his hand. There was a ringing crack as her blade broke his in half. Badly tempered iron.

"Behold!" cried Whitebeard. For half a heartbeat, Thorn thought he was beholding the broken sword. His finger, however, was pointing beyond them to the lake. Turning again, Thorn stared.

Frostflower's arm was holding the Cockaigne sword in its

gem-crusted sheath above the surface of the water, the jewels glistening in the sunshine.

"A marvel!" cried Metalpants.

"A token," declared Whitebeard.

"A signal," said Thorn, and strode toward the boat.

She heard Whitebeard say, "Nay, sire, let not that one take it first," and then, with clanks and jangles, Metalpants ran past, surprisingly fast on his feet, strong-arming Thorn out of the way and jumping into the boat.

"Hey!" she shouted, splashing after him. But the boat was already moving, without oars. It slipped out of her reach and skimmed straight for the arm holding the sword.

Thorn glanced back and saw Whitebeard smirking as he wiggled his hands, obviously using sorcery to control the boat. Maybe she'd have to put *him* out of action first. Dripping water from the knee down, she charged back up the shore and—

"Behold!" he repeated triumphantly as she was reaching out to knock him down.

She turned to behold. Metalpants was lifting sword and sheath from Frostflower's hand, holding his prize aloft as reverently as if the burden was a baby. Sounds of almost priestly chanting filled the air from nowhere—more sorcery, of course—as the boat swung around and came back to shore.

Frost poked her head above the surface and watched, grinning mischievously, as Metalpants clanked back up the beach to Whitebeard and the pair of them began marveling at the Cockaigne treasure. "An arm clothed in white samite, mystic, wonderful," the old man was murmuring persuasively, ignoring the blackness of Frostflower's sleeve with as much determination as he ignored her face, now that it had appeared.

Thorn shrugged and waded out to her friend, finding the water so shallow that Frost was quietly kneeling on the bottom. "With the sorceries they seem to have here," she remarked, "I'm surprised the sword can hold their interest as it's doing."

"Yes, well, jewels that big always dazzle people. Besides, they're scramblebrains."

"I'm afraid we won't be able to get a very high price for it now," the sorceress apologized.

"That isn't worrying me. I just want to get out of here before they go crazy again."

Frostflower pulled out Dathru's Circle and the friends stepped through into a saner world without even wading ashore.

About Diana L. Paxson and "The Dancer of Chimaera"

Diana and I go back a long way, too; back to when Diana was an as-yet-little-published writer of a few short stories. She had written a story I liked tremendously; and I told her that if I got a chance to do a non-Darkover anthology, I'd take it right away. Later that year, Don Wollheim gave me a chance to edit *Greyhaven,* and the first thing I did was to call Diana and ask her if the story had sold yet. It was still available—what *were* my fellow editors thinking of?—and it was the first story I bought. My faith in Diana has been justified—all of her work since then has been superb. After half a dozen or so of the Westria novels, she began making a name for herself with historicals; the splendid *White Raven* gave a new look at the Tristram-and-Yseult story, and she has just published a new look at the Siegfried and Brunhilde legend. She collaborated with me on my book *The Forest House*, though the publishers thought it would sell better with my name alone. At this writing it is out in England, but not here till April 1994. We have already contracted for a big historical sequel.

This story is probably the nearest to science fiction ever to appear in the pages of my magazine; to me it has a flavor of a story by C. L. Moore, and hence I couldn't resist it. Nor can I resist the temptation to share it with you.

The Dancer of Chimaera

Diana L. Paxson

They called her Mariposa, and she danced in a tavern on Chimaera Station. She was scarcely a woman yet, but she was female enough for the men who did their drinking at the High Orbit. They were Space Forcers on shore leave mostly, or techs from the defense project that was the main reason the Station was there. In the evenings they drank, and watched Mariposa, and tried to forget the war.

Johnny Yaleran wavered in the doorway. The heat of the tavern reminded him of the generator room of the *Glinka*, though the sour smell of spilled beer and the mixed reeks of tobacco and weed were richer than the high ozone air he'd been breathing since he left home. He bent forward, peering through the gloom.

A bunch of big techs from the repair docks heading for the door were enough to make up his mind for him. They drew him in their wake toward the bar. Even then he might have retreated, but there was an empty place, and he slid into it, trying to look as if he belonged there. Beyond the bar was a small bare stage and a musician's stand. But the synthetor's lights were dead and canned music strove unsuccessfully with the patrons' din.

The man in the stained coveralls on the next perch slurped noisily at his drink and set it down, turning to the thin fellow beside him.

"Well, I say we've nothin' to worry about—" Johnny heard him snort. "The Shifters will never get this far, and if they do, we'll implode 'em." He drank again and wiped his mouth with a beefy hand.

"Think so? They've taken the Iberian system, and Lutece, Lord knows how. The project's a prime target . . ." The thin man stopped, looking at Johnny.

There was a loud cough and Johnny flushed, realizing that the barman was waiting, order disk in hand. There was a list on the wall before him, and Johnny chose at random.

". . . one double Red, straight," the barman repeated, punching the order and waiting impassively while Johnny fumbled in his pouch for his credit chip.

"Thank you," Johnny said. The man smiled automatically and went off.

"You new here?" the big man asked, and Johnny nodded. "Thought so—" He grinned suddenly and extended a hand. "I'm Hank Mendos, 'Ponics Tech, and this here's my buddy Duprey."

Johnny introduced himself, and the thin man beside Mendos nodded.

"*Glinka,* you say? She hasn't seen combat yet, has she?"

"Neither have I," Johnny confessed. "I signed on when she was commissioned on Soyuz."

The barman set a glass of crimson liquid before him. Johnny picked it up, aware of their eyes upon him, but the fluid slid easily down his throat. As he took a second sip, the first exploded in his belly. Their expressions had warned him, but he was still gasping a few moments later when the nova inside him began to die down. Carefully, he drank again.

Duprey smiled with approval—or perhaps it was amusement.

"I wish you luck. Of course, the Shifters' weapons are no match for ours—not their physical weapons, anyhow—" He leaned forward, lowering his voice so that Johnny had to strain to hear. "I'm in Communications, and I've heard the log of the *Tonnerre*."

Johnny stared, remembering the hulk whose orbit they had crossed on their way in. Duprey went on.

"They had picked up a bunch of refugees, and they were all having a concert to cheer them up, see, when it began. There's not much on the disc—just ramblings about the music, and then the sound of the explosion when they hit the asteroid." Duprey sighed.

"What was the music like?" Johnny asked.

"There was no music on the discs," said Duprey. "No music at all—"

"You think one of them refugees was a Shifter?" said Mendos.

"Must have been . . . they must have forgotten to run the test when they took them on."

Johnny shivered, but Mendos was looking past him to the stage. "Well, now, I guess it's time for the show!" He grinned.

The lights of the synthetor were beginning to glow. The operator, only one in a place like this, hunched over the control board, adjusting the dials. Beside him a sleepy-eyed drummer stroked the plastic of his drumhead. From the signs outside, Johnny gathered they were very proud of having a real drum.

The noise diminished slightly and the synthetor chimed once, projecting a pink glow onto the stage. A fat man in a stained purple tunic waved his arms for silence.

"And now—we bring you the star of the Galaxy—La Mariposa!"

The light intensified from pink to purple, then back to red as the drummer took up a slow beat. Johnny leaned forward as the screen shimmered and a girl slipped through it onto the stage.

"She ain't much," said Mendos, "but it don't seem anyone else wants to come out here so close to the war, and she's kinda cute, after all."

For a moment the girl hesitated, flinching as all the male eyes focused upon her face. The drum boomed again and she stepped forward, stretching out her arms so that the flashers on her cloak glittered red. The synthetor began to burble out a tune and she waved her arms aimlessly, swaying back and forth in time to the music.

"You've left me all alone, what can I do? There's no one in the galaxy like you . . ." she sang in a thin sweet voice, still swaying. Johnny recognized the song. It had been popular just before he left home.

The lights changed from red to yellow, to green and blue, while the predictable words trudged on. ". . . unless you give me all your love I'll die!" She let her arms drop to her sides.

"Come on, honey, take it off—that's a girl!" came a shout from the back of the room. The drum rolled demandingly.

The girl stretched her colored lips in a smile and her hands moved to the fastenings at the neck of her cloak. Slowly she undid them. The cloth slithered to the floor and she kicked it aside. Her skinny body was covered mainly by body film, red on one side, silver on the other, with interlocking spirals where the two colors joined.

Johnny took an involuntary swallow of his drink. They didn't have anything like this on Soyuz.

Mariposa walked around the stage, throwing her hips sharply from side to side so that the orfa feathers on her girdle fluttered, hipbones alternately defined under the colored skin. Her little breasts bobbled and the tiny stars glued to them winked at Johnny as she turned.

The barman was asking if he wanted another drink. Johnny pulled out his credit slip without taking his eyes from the stage. The drummer had stepped up the beat. The dancer began to stamp and fling her arms about concluding with a backbend that threw all her ribs into relief.

The music slowed. Johnny took his new drink, swallowed part of it, and set the bulb down. The girl straightened and struck a stylized pose. Johnny noted with strange clarity that some of her hair had escaped from its topknot and clung damply to her neck. She made a vague gesture with her slender hands and quavered out another verse of her song.

"Poor kid—she don't hardly know what it's all about, does she?" said Mendos. "Now I remember the girls on Bagatelle—you ever go to Madam Sue's, Duprey? There was one bitty there who had breasts like . . ." He searched for words and gave up with a lush movement of his hands.

Duprey shook his head, sighing. "No . . . but I knew a little girl on Sianna once. She had hair like black silk that reached to her knees . . ." He broke off, staring into shadow, remembering.

Johnny scarcely heard them. He was watching Mariposa.

Johnny reached out for the girl's hand as they began to walk. Their footsteps echoed on the permacrete of the pedway, almost deserted at this hour. They turned a corner and the pink blaze of the High Orbit's entrance was hidden. Mariposa breathed deeply.

"Thank you for coming with me, Johnny."

He squeezed her hand, still too astonished at the privilege to reply. For the past month, he had been off-duty two nights a week, and he had spent every one of them at the High Orbit, watching Mariposa dance. It had taken a week for him to get up the courage to speak to her, two weeks more before she would let him buy her a drink when the show was done. And tonight she had asked him if he would like to walk her home.

He knew that Mendos and Duprey thought his passion funny, knew that not a man on the Station would have hurt Mariposa, but he could not help feeling the way he had when he stood watch over the generators of the *Glinka* alone for the first time. He breathed a little faster and pressed her hand again.

"It is good to be quiet at last," she said. "I wish I could see the stars."

They looked up at the anonymous dusk of the Station's dome.

"I'd like to show them to you," he said. "In deep space the sky's pure carbon black, and the stars burn steady and bright as glowflies." He paused, trying to find words for the glory. "Could you see the stars from your home planet?"

"I—don't know," she replied. "I remember being on ships, and on other Stations under domes, but I think I must have left home when I was very young. . . . I don't remember it at all."

Johnny felt an immediate protective surge and drew her arm within his. "When the war is over I'll show you all the worlds. There are fields of multicolored grasses at home. You run through them and the wind cools your face with the scent of flowers."

"It would be good to run free and see the sky," she said wistfully. "Since you've been here, have you been outside?"

"No," he replied. "I've seen pictures. It doesn't look like a bad world—a little hot maybe. Too bad there's not enough oxygen in the air for men to breathe."

"I think they mean to terraform it, after the war."

"Well, that can't be long now," he said confidently. "It's been going badly lately, I know—the Shifters are in the next system now. But the Project is almost complete. Duprey says the Mindshield they've installed will stop the psychbending the Shifters have been using to get through. Soon all our ships will have it too."

She stopped, facing him. Johnny realized with a shock that they had reached the end of the residence complex where the few nonmilitary personnel on the Station lived. He paused in front of the entry, fighting a shiver of impending loss.

"Are you cold?" she asked softly.

"Cold? No—"

"You sure? You don't look well. Do you want to come up with me? I can fix you some stimo . . ."

He stared at her.

"It's not much of a place, I guess—" she went on. "Not on what the bar pays me. But I brew stimo as well as any autosnacky!"

"Oh! Of course—sure, Mariposa, I'd be honored to come in!"

She was right. It was not much of a place—a room about as big as his cubby on the *Glinka*, with walls the original noglare green and fold-down furniture. There was one window. Only a poster advertising Mariposa stuck to the wall and some clothing thrown over a chair marked it as her room. Johnny looked about him, his gaze sliding quickly past the curtain that gave nominal privacy to the bedcorner, and came to rest on the girl. She smiled and turned to pull down the kitchen controls.

He lifted the clothes from the chair and sat down, searching for something to say. "Mariposa, do you like it here?" he got out at last. "I mean, are the people nice to you?"

"Oh yes—a Station isn't the prettiest place in the universe, but everyone's polite."

He looked at her thin shoulders and the defenseless line of her back.

"*All* the men?" he asked, his voice hoarse suddenly.

"Why would they bother me?" she said quietly, stirring the brew.

"But you're—a *dancer*—" The words burst out of him.

"And that's *all* I am," she flared. "Look at me. I'm not much temptation even on stage with all my fittings on, and without them—" She thrust the bulb into his hands and started to turn away.

He held it without drinking, looking at her. "Mariposa, I think you're beautiful . . ."

Something flickered behind her eyes. "I'm not . . . Johnny, you mustn't say that!"

"But lots of men—" he began, and then, when she began to shake her head, felt the betraying blush begin and fade and didn't care. "You mean that no one—that you haven't ever—"

She hugged herself, swaying. Johnny got up and stepped toward her, realized that he was still holding the stimo bulb, and set it down.

"Mariposa," he said. "I'm sorry, I didn't mean . . ." She didn't seem to have heard him. Moving with an urgency beyond his analysis, he took her in his arms.

She stood rigid in his embrace, still shaking. But she relaxed suddenly when his mouth touched hers. It was a long kiss, if a little clumsy, and when he released her at last, her eyes had gone unfocused and huge in her pale face.

"What is it?" she asked tonelessly. "What is happening— Oh, Johnny," she cried, seeing him at last. "Let me go! I love you—please go!"

He held her, dismay warring with an exaltation that burned upward from his belly to his brain. She had said, "I love you . . ."

The girl quivered suddenly, then sighed. Her eyes were

glittering; she watched him with a look he had never seen before. Alarm pulsed along his nerves, but even as he started to release her, she gripped his arms and pulled his head down to hers. His body jerked as their lips touched once more.

Mariposa held him now. Her body was hard, her scent sharp and sweet. He wondered vaguely how she had gotten a perfume like the flowers of the faranelle trees at home. Then he stopped thinking at all.

Their clothing was stripped off and they stumbled toward the bed. The current was passing through him more violently now, but he could not break away. As they struggled on the bed, his flesh was melded to hers and their bodies convulsed as one. But it was Mariposa who screamed as in a flash of ecstasy his body went beyond his control entirely and he was consumed.

Above their heads, the little window brightened as the terrible light of Chimaera's dawn filtered through the Dome.

The light in the window had flared and faded once more to dusk when Mariposa rose. Her hair had come undone. She shook it back over her shoulders and then stretched lazily, arching her body in content. She stepped over to the fresher, rotated luxuriously under its needling spray. After a few moments she stepped out, slipped past the motionless body on the bed, and began, with full, sensuous strokes, to brush out her hair.

It was not until she had finished dressing and had picked up her cloak to go out that she glanced at the figure on the bed, a last faint sadness momentarily humanizing her face.

"Have you seen Johnny tonight?" Duprey gestured toward the empty scat beside Mendos as he sat down.

"No, but he'll be here—he never misses Mariposa's show."

"It's getting late . . ."

Mendos, who was on his third drink already, shook his head. "Don't worry, maybe he's backstage with her now. . . ."

Both men laughed, and Duprey ordered a drink.

"That's right, Duprey—drink up! You can afford to, now the Shield's up!"

Duprey grunted and picked up the bulb, glaring at a technician who had started to take the empty chair.

The manager got up to make his announcement, and the noise level sank to its usual dull roar. The synthetor warbled out the introductory theme. There was a shadow behind the screen.

"Well, here's Mariposa—" said Mendos. "Musta been in a hurry—no color on her face. Wonder if she's got her costume on." He snickered happily.

Mariposa stepped over to the musicians, her robe flowing around her. As she spoke to them, the music faded and for a moment, the drumbeat faltered. The manager glared, but in a few beats they had recovered, and the drum boomed, commanding all eyes to the stage. The synthetor sang out a series of high notes, monotonous and pure. The drum pounded again and Mariposa whirled, cloak flaring around her like a red nebula. Then, with a flash, it was off.

Mariposa danced.

Her pale body was washed by the changing lights. Her eyes glittered. Her slender feet stamped out an echo to the rhythm of the drum.

"What's come over the girl? Never saw her move that way—" Mendos blinked as if he were having trouble focusing.

Mariposa swayed with the music, her movements sending adrenaline sparking through the bodies of those who watched her, the flutter of her fingers compelling their attention. She circled in front of the musicians; the synthetor faded and she began to sing.

"I am the sweet surge of the tide . . . I can release the love inside—" was what Duprey heard, and his bulb rolled unheeded from his hand. *"Follow me, follow, out from the shallows, into the depths of the sea . . ."*

Mendos leaned forward, clutching at the edge of the bar.

"I am the scent that stirs the night, I offer measureless delights! Follow me, follow, all here is hollow, and in me ecstasy!"

The drum beat faster now. Mariposa leaped down from the stage and moved among the men. Each one felt the touch of her fingers on his heart, heard her singing to him alone, and they circled her like new-formed planets around a sun.

"Sima . . ." breathed Duprey, stumbling toward her.

"No—it's Honey, my own Honey—lookit those bulbs, just like I told you!" Mendos cried.

Mariposa drifted toward the door, singing. She sang the men out into the street and toward the main pedway. The synthetor whispered to silence, but the drummer slipped the strap over his head and continued to play, and his beat pulsed through the artificial air. Mariposa's singing rode that pulse to echo from the walls of the buildings and reflect from the ceiling of the Dome.

The Station was not very large. It was not long before the strange procession had circled it, and wherever it passed, men came to their doors, and when they had opened, they saw Mariposa dance, and heard her sing, and when they had seen and heard, they followed her.

They came at last to the door that led Outside.

"I am your dream and your desire . . .
I am the burning of love's fire . . .
Follow me, follow, out of the window,
    and we shall be free!
I feed your hunger, I bring you home—
No more to wander, no more to roam . . .
Follow me, follow, into tomorrow,
    oh, follow me . . ."

It took a few moments for the man who knew how to work the handles to make his way through the crowd to the door, and a little longer for another, who had set the pattern of switches that would make them release, to reach the controls. But Mariposa sang.

She danced need for her into their blood, she sang her image into their brains. She was golden-haired with breasts like Perelan honey melons . . . she was doll-slim, veiled by silken black hair . . . or tall and redheaded . . . dark-skinned with eyes like coals . . . petite . . . luscious . . . every man's desire.

The door swung open, and one by one they went through.

Their eyes focused on the dancer before them; they heard her song. They pursued her even as they fell on the burning sand Outside, clutching at throats that choked on the air that was only a little wrong for men. They embraced her image as they died.

The little window in Mariposa's room grew bright as day rose on Chimaera once more. It gilded that scattered clothing and the ruined bed, and illuminated the face of the man who lay there, still set in the smile of one who had been possessed by his desire.

Mariposa quietly closed the door and walked back through the empty ways until she reached Station Control. She passed through its corridors, ignoring the banks of machines with their futilely flashing lights, until she came at last to the one machine that mattered and touched its controls to impotence. Then she moved onward to the viewroom where she could see the Shifter ships drifting silently down.

They called her Mariposa, and she had danced for the men of Chimaera, but she was not a woman . . . she was not a woman at all.

About Elisabeth Waters and
"The Lesser Twin"

Elisabeth Waters is my cousin and has been my live-in secretary/office manager/computer programmer/etc. for sixteen years now. Her "job description" here defies analysis, but seems to boil down to making order out of the chaos of my life, which can be very chaotic indeed. She is a superb short-story writer (this story took second place in the Cauldron vote out of the thirty-nine stories in issue 9). Although she is prone from time to time to throw herself down in a tantrum, declaring that she doesn't want to be a writer at all, she is one of the better writers of short stories I know. Her first novel, *Changing Fate*, will be published by DAW Books in April 1994, which means it should be available when this anthology is published. When you read it, tell me if I'm not right in saying she's a superb writer.

Although she declared from the beginning that she wanted nothing to do with the magazine, my relative inability to cope with prosaic matters has forced her to have a great deal to do with it—which she does as superbly as she does everything else. Our first issue featured one of her better short stories—the illustration for which, as ill luck would have it, happened to be the only time I ever encountered an art plagiarist in the fifty years of my career. Fortunately her other contributions to us have had better luck. She is currently applying to law school at the University of California; but she's done so well handling my complicated legal affairs without a law degree that I hope her legal career turns out to be purely recreational.

The Lesser Twin

Elisabeth Waters

Kiara was just coming upstairs to wash the hall floor when she heard her sister start screaming. For an instant she froze, standing there with the bucket of water in her hand. The wizard Tarnor's instruction, as relayed by Karina, had been clear: they would be working in his temple all afternoon and were not to be disturbed for anything.

As if I *want* to disturb them, Kiara had thought in disgust. She and Karina were twins, and they loved each other, but they were not at all alike. Karina was the elder and the beautiful one, with pale clear skin and glossy black hair that fell to her hips, while Kiara had skin that turned into a splotchy mass of freckles the minute the sun hit it and an unruly mass of very curly red-orange hair. She'd given up on both skin and hair long ago, so her complexion was now almost uniformly brown and her hair, as short as she could persuade Karina to chop it off, stuck out in random directions. The twins also differed in their approach to life: Karina flitted effortlessly from enthusiasm to enthusiasm (and from man to man), while Kiara followed quietly in her wake, picking up the pieces and trying to lend a bit of stability to their vagrant existence.

She'd be glad when Karina got over this craziness. Tarnor had met Karina eight months ago, when she was living with a wealthy and generous merchant, a middle-aged widower with two small sons. Kiara had lived with them and helped look after the children, and she still missed them. But Karina had been getting restless and had been easy prey for Tarnor's offer to make her his priestess and a great sorceress. So they had moved into Tarnor's tower; Karina to share his bed and study and Kiara to run the place and feed them at the irregular intervals at which they surfaced. From the variety of different tastes showing in the decor of the place, Kiara suspected that they were only the last in a long series of "priestesses." Fortunately Tarnor didn't seem to notice her much, which was fine with her—Karina could have him, whyever she wanted him.

But she was *not* going to stand by and see her sister hurt if there was anything she could do to prevent it, and there was both terror and pain in those screams. She hurried down the short stone corridor which separated the temple from the living quarters, shoved open the heavy wooden door with her shoulder, and pushed her way in. A sword, which had apparently been leaning against the door, clattered at her feet, but she stepped over it without seeing it, her attention focused on her sister.

Karina had good reason to be screaming; she appeared to be holding a ball of flame, unable to release it. As Kiara watched in horror, a clump of Karina's hair, tossed about by her struggles, brushed across her hands and flared up as well. Kiara stepped forward and swung the bucket she held; the water arced neatly across the space between them and drenched Karina from eyebrows to knees. The flames went out instantly, with a horrible sizzling noise, which was almost drowned out by Tarnor's yelling in her ear as he grabbed her shoulders from behind.

"You stupid slut! How dare you cross my Wards and profane my Temple! Do you have the slightest idea what you have done?"

Kiara swung an elbow into his fat stomach, broke free, and ran to Karina, who stood unmoving, staring in horror

and revulsion at something at her feet. "I think you killed
it. . . ."

Kiara dropped to knees, wincing slightly as they hit the
hard stone floor. "It" was a small amphibianlike creature, a
dark muddy-brown-gray-black color, which appeared to be
slowly melting onto the floor. She scooped it up into her
apron with one hand, grabbed Karina by the upper arm with
the other, and towed her toward the kitchen. "You need burn
ointment for your hands. What is this thing, anyway?"

"Salamander," Karina replied faintly, staring blankly
ahead of her.

Oh, Holy Mother, Kiara realized in dismay, *she's going
into shock.* She hastily dragged Karina to the kitchen and
shoved her into a horizontal position on the bench next to the
fire. The salamander still lay inert in her apron, but she had
the feeling it was not quite dead. It was *there,* in a way that
dead things weren't. She untied her apron and lowered it
carefully in the fire, putting the salamander into the center of
the flames. It was the only thing she could think of to do for
it, and maybe it would work. Then she turned away to wrap a
blanket around Karina and break off a piece of the plant she
used for scrapes and burns. She was carefully squeezing sap
over the burned areas on her sister's hands when Tarnor
limped wheezing into the kitchen.

"Fine priestess you are," he snarled at Karina, "panicking
over a little thing like that. How do you expect to get anywhere without learning to embrace the pain? Don't you
know that the universe *is* pain?"

"Save your breath!" Kiara snapped at him. "She can't hear
you anyway. And *your* universe may be pain, but *mine* certainly isn't—and I don't think that Karina's crazy enough to
want hers to be."

"She wants what I want." To Tarnor this was obviously
Natural Law. "And as for *your* universe . . ." His foot lashed
out suddenly, caught her hip, and propelled her into the fire.
Dimly she heard him continue, ". . . that can be changed."

The flames hurt excruciatingly for a moment, then all sensation went away. *I must be dying,* Kiara thought, vaguely
remembering having heard that dying of burns didn't hurt
once the shock hit. Then there was pain again, sharp teeth

digging into the side of her neck. *I must have landed on the salamander. Poor creature, what a day it's having.*

"Verily," the salamander agreed. "But yours isn't going very smoothly either."

Startled, Kiara twisted her head and opened her eyes. The salamander was next to her, filling most of her field of vision. The only other thing she could see was fire. "Is it because I'm dead that we can hear each other?"

"No." The salamander stretched out all four legs, neck, and tail, obviously reveling in the fire which ran along its body, now a glowing red-orange. "It's because we're in Fire. Earth, Water and Air transmit sound; Fire transmits energy."

Kiara thought about that for a moment. "And emotion is a form of energy, and since ideas can be expressed in either words or emotions . . ."

". . . they can transferred through any of the Elements," the salamander finished for her. "Exactly. Besides, you're not dead."

"I'm not?" Kiara looked down at herself. Her body was the same glowing red-orange as the salamander's, with the same four short legs. She stretched and twisted her head farther around to regard her long tapering tail in disbelief. "Holy Mother of All Living Things!" She went limp again, and discovered that she was floating comfortably in the middle of the fire. It did feel good, but it was going to require a little mental adjustment—to say the least.

"You didn't land on me," the salamander was explaining, "I bit you to transform you—not that I think you couldn't have done it on your own eventually—since the fire didn't kill you, you obviously have magic—but I wanted to get us out of here before the wretched wizard notices and constrains us."

"You mean he hasn't noticed my turning into a salamander? I admit he tends to ignore me, but that seems rather a lot to ignore!"

"I don't feel him noticing us, but let's get out of here before he does!"

"But my sister . . ."

"What can you do for her in this form? Her stupid phobia of salamanders is what got us in this mess—if you can remember that far back!" The salamander was thoroughly impatient. "You can't help her now, and if we don't get out of here you'll never be able to. Come!" It disappeared from view, but Kiara could feel a faint tugging. She followed it.

Kiara spent a period of time (she had no idea how long—salamanders didn't reckon time the way people did) learning how to be a salamander. What salamanders did, apparently, was to understand Fire, to celebrate it, to embody it. In a curious way salamanders were Fire and Fire was Salamander—at least that was as close as she could come to putting it in words. She learned to move through Fire and to go from Fire to individual fires in the realms of men.

Occasionally she would be summoned, not by name, but simply as the nearest salamander, by some magician in need of extra heat or illumination, but such terms of service were fixed and short. Apparently there was some sort of Law governing such things, not that it was ever written out or put into words, but some things made sense and worked in practice and others did not. She realized that this was what had been working in her when she put the salamander in the fire—it had made sense to her, and she had done it.

Being curious about these matters, she took to hanging around where she would be the one called, and began her somewhat informal study of magic—looking over the shoulders of her unknowing teachers. She discovered that while magic users came in many varieties, there were two basic flavors—those who used magic as a celebration of the beauty of creation, and those who used it for their own selfish ends.

She had two personal favorites, both of the first sort: a man who had the most cluttered workroom she had ever seen (or ever expected to see) but always seemed to have exactly the book she needed to read spread open below her, and a woman who always dismissed her with "My thanks for your aid, Essence of Fire." It was comforting to be noticed, even if not named, for being a salamander was lonely for a human—salamanders didn't care about individuality. As a person she had been unique, even as "Karina's ugly twin" she was an individual, but as a salamander, she was just a salamander like every other salamander.

Then a summons came, and she discovered to her horror

that she was in Tarnor's temple. He didn't notice her, of course; to him she was just a source of light—though she doubted that he needed light for what he and his "priestess" were doing on the black-draped high couch he called an altar. But the girl was not Karina—she was younger and blond.

"Where is Karina—what happened to her—how long have I been a salamander?!?" Kiara hovered in the corner, grimly lighting the ritual, though the amount of power she perceived in it was minimal, and thinking furiously. There wasn't much else she could do at the moment, but she resolved that as soon as she was dismissed she would slip down to the kitchen fire and start searching the place—even if she had to be a flame on every candle in the entire tower.

But she wasn't dismissed. Instead of completing the ritual with the proper dismissals and banishings, Tarnor fell asleep on the altar. The blonde sighed, slipped quietly away from him, and went to the edge of the circle where the sword lay. She picked it up and ran it widdershins around the edge of the circle to make a gap she could pass through, then left the room, leaving the gap in the circle. Kiara, shaking her head at such carelessness, followed her.

The blonde went to the kitchen, where, to Kiara's immense relief, Karina was carving a roast. She looked tired and cross, but at least she was alive and well—even the burns on her hands had healed.

"No rush on dinner," the blonde said, grabbing a slice of meat and chewing on it. "He's asleep."

Karina looked up, saw Kiara, and let out a loud scream. The blonde put a quick hand across her mouth. "Hush! You'll wake the Master." Then she turned to see what Karina was staring at with such terror. "Oh, damn. He forgot to dismiss the salamander—but how did it get across the wards?"

Something snapped in Kiara; she thought it must be her temper. While she had been a salamander nothing had touched her nearly enough to get her angry, but this was her sister, her other self, reduced to a servant for Tarnor and his incompetent new mistress. She transformed to human form, retaining enough fire about her to substitute for the clothes that had burned away that day in the kitchen fire. The stone floor was very cold under her feet. "*You* opened the circle, fool—and left it open! Doesn't Tarnor train his 'priestesses' at all?"

"Of course he does!" the blonde replied indignantly. "He's a great wizard!"

"Not as great a wizard as you are a fool—both of you!" She slapped the girl's hand away from Karina's mouth. "Being good in bed is *not* the major qualification for a priestess." Her old clothes chest still sat in the corner, and she grabbed the first dress to hand, doused the rest of her fire, and hastily dressed, hoping not to freeze to death in the process.

"And I suppose being a good housekeeper is?" Karina, apparently unable to cope with questions like "why were you a salamander?" was falling back on their old sibling rivalry. "You're always right, always perfect—but you can't even get a man!"

"Why would I want to? You've always had plenty for both of us!" Kiara snapped back, and looked at her sister critically. "But you won't be able to much longer if you hang around here being a drudge—already your hands are rough, and your hair looks dreadful, when did you last brush it?"

Karina burst into tears, the blonde stared from one to the other in total incomprehension, and Tarnor limped heavily into the room.

"What's this noise? I told both of you that I expect my priestesses to get along with one another—how am I supposed to do Great Magick with the pair of you acting like common scolds? Magick requires sacrifice, concentration, and discipline."

"None of which you possess," Kiara said coldly, drawing herself to her full height and slowly advancing on him. "You're not fit to scrub a hearth-witch's cauldron."

"I don't know who you are, girl, or what you're doing in my Tower, but obviously you know nothing of Magick." Tarnor's voice was low and sonorous, but to Kiara he was so obviously bluffing that she couldn't understand why the other girls couldn't hear it.

She didn't bother to answer in words; she simply stretched both arms out at shoulder height, pointing toward him. She noticed that they were pale and smooth (being a salamander seemed to have done wonders for her complexion), before she started the flames running down them and shooting out from her fingertips. It was a ridiculously simple trick, using virtually no energy, and not dangerous to anyone in the room; but it had most satisfying results. Tarnor fled screaming, the blonde sank to her knees in a small cowering heap, and Karina fainted.

Kiara lowered her arms, stopping the flames, stepped over her sister's body, and began to pack her clothes. After a moment Karina moaned softly, and the blonde, with a fearful glance at Kiara, fled the room. Kiara finished packing her things, then turned to her sister.

"I'm leaving this place, Karina. If you care to accompany me, pack your things."

"But Tarnor—"

"He's not going to stop us," Kiara pointed out.

"But I can't abandon him! He needs me to save him."

"Save him from what?" Kiara inquired. "That blonde girl—or his own incompetence?"

"You don't understand," Karina said. "He's really a good person underneath, but he needs my love to manifest it."

"Oh, I think I understand," Kiara said slowly. "You think that if you love him enough and stick with him, you can change him into what you think he should be. Just as I always thought that if I stuck with you long enough, you'd turn out like me."

"But I am like you, aren't I? We're twins."

"Yes, but I don't know that we're any more alike in essence than we are in looks." Kiara shrugged. "In any case, I'm going. If you want to come with me, come. If you want to stay here, stay."

"I can't leave him," Karina repeated.

"Then stay with him." Kiara sighed and picked up her pack. "Be happy, Karina." She hugged her sister, then turned and walked out the door, no longer half a pair of twins, but an individual in her own right.

About Kit Wesler and "The Bane of the Red Queen" About Deborah Millitello and "The Reluctant Vampire"

These stories—really short-shorts—were two of the stories from issue 10 that have remained in my memory. In general I am even less of a short-story reader than a writer ... and I usually have trouble writing less than a hundred thousand words. And yet, although myself a writer of novels, the longer the better, paradoxically I think the short-short story is the quintessence of writing skill. In a long story, you can fumble around, waste time, never really get to the point. In the short-short, you can't waste a word; you must know very precisely the point you are making, and make it without delay.

I am sure every writer can think of some perfect little gem of a short story; everyone will have his own favorites. Mine, I confess, for pure skill, are Ray Bradbury's "All Summer in a Day" and Arthur C. Clarke's "The Star." And among my favorites are these two presented here.

The Bane of the Red Queen

Kit Wesler

"In the bleakness of winter shall a child be born who carries the mark of Selene; and she shall be the Red Queen's bane." For the first time, Queen Caramae could recite those words, and *laugh*.

She strode lithely around the stone chamber, nearly dancing in her excitement: Caramae, called the Red Queen in part because of the glorious hair that fell in ripples and waves past her shoulders, but more because of the bloody terror of her sorcerous reign. Her seneschal and bodyguard, Glaedwyr of Glaud, stood at the window, dividing his attention between his queen and the courtyard below, the latter nearly invisible through the sleet.

It was bitterly cold in the high chamber, whose windows were neither glazed nor shuttered, and Glaedwyr was bundled heavily. Yet the queen wore only a light gown. Glaedwyr glanced at her, impressed as ever with the sheer vitality of the woman, the fierceness that he had once loved, and then hated. He looked back into the sleet. Beside his hand on the windowsill lay a crossbow, a sporting weapon, too light to pierce armor, but deadly enough in the hands of a marksman.

The Red Queen whirled toward the grim stone slab with

its rusty stains that stood in the center of the chamber, then away again, too full of malice and glee to stand still.

"The prophecy!" She laughed. "The last hope of fools and romantics! Did they think my Art could not find this child?"

"There was less art in it than thoroughness," Glaedwyr observed mildly.

She gave him an ugly look, then laughed. "A hundred mothers in this city due to birth this month. My Art found them all! Even those who thought to hide in cellars and attics. And my tower held them."

Glaedwyr nodded, still watching the courtyard, empty but for the gray weather.

"And the child is mine now!" the queen swept on, pacing feverishly. "They are bringing her now. And the blood of a child of prophecy can weave such spells as even I have not yet seen!"

Glaedwyr could not help glancing at the altar, at the blades and pincers and nameless potions on the scarred table beside it. He hoped that Caramae did not notice the shudder he could not suppress.

There was a knock, and at the Red Queen's snarl, the heavy door opened to admit a gaunt serving woman carrying a shapeless bundle. The queen cried out in triumph, snatching the bundle. Then her voice changed to a cry of fury. "It's dead! The baby is already dead!"

The serving woman shrank back. "Please, your highness, it died before I touched it!"

But the queen did not deliver the expected blow. "Is it the one?" Caramae demanded, pawing through the cloths. The serving woman looked quickly at Glaedwyr, desperate and pleading, and the tall man nodded shortly, the only reassurance he dared give.

"There!" the Red Queen said. "The moon-shaped birthmark! It is the one!"

"Thoroughness always pays," said Glaedwyr stolidly. He turned away as the queen threw the pathetic bundle onto the altar and spat, "Get out!" to the servant, who complied in haste.

As the sleet fell more heavily, Glaedwyr began to fear that he would not be able to see the expected signal. But as the queen began to pace again, muttering furiously, he saw it: a thin flicker of a lamp shone once, twice, and again, at the far gate. He quietly cocked the crossbow, and dropped an iron-tipped quarrel into the groove. But when he turned from the window, he found Caramae facing him, smiling. She held her hand breast-high before her, in a clawed gesture he knew signified deadly power.

"You fool, Glaedwyr," she said, low-voiced. "Did you really think I wouldn't know? That your men could lock up all the nobles who still support me, and disarm my Red Guard, and steal the talisman from the crypt, all without my knowing? I knew it all the time!"

With a sneer, she made a throwing motion, and said a loathsome word under her breath. But Glaedwyr merely blinked and held the crossbow steady.

It was the first time he had ever seen her face turn ugly; the first time he had seen the shock and dismay of failure in those great blue eyes.

"Your power is done, Caramae. As it was foretold."

"But the child is dead!" she shouted angrily. "The prophecy is foiled!"

"I regret that we were not quite ready in time to save the girl's life," Glaedwyr said calmly. His gray eyes were as bleak as the frozen courtyard below him. "Better to be smothered on the stair than to be given live to your spells. But it is no matter to you, either way."

"But the prophecy—"

"The prophecy said that the child would be born," Glaedwyr told her. "No one ever said it had to live very long."

Nor did the chroniclers ever mention the iron-tipped quarrel that did, in point of fact, end the Red Queen's reign.

The Reluctant Vampire

Deborah Millitello

Sharon woke with the worst headache she'd ever had, worse than her monthly migraines, even though it wasn't quite that time yet. This one was different. Her mouth and throat were dry. There was a grapefruit-size knot in her stomach. Her golden eyes pulsed in rhythm with her throbbing head. Hunger clawed her stomach like a wild animal.

Sitting up slowly, she realized she was still wearing her party dress. "What in the world did Trevairin put in my tomato juice last night?" she groaned. "Probably slipped in vodka—and after I told him I can't drink alcohol. I'm going to kill him."

When she stood, her legs felt like rubber bands. Cradling her head, she shuffled to the kitchen, opened the fridge, and took out a bottle of orange juice. The gurgle of liquid splashing into the glass echoed like Niagara Falls in her head. She popped two aspirins in her mouth, took a drink, then gagged. It tasted like mustard and cayenne pepper mixed with powdered charcoal. She ran for the toilet but didn't quite make it. When she'd cleaned up the mess, she trudged back to the kitchen and heated water for tea.

Pulling up a corner of the window shade, she saw crimson

clouds in the September sky. A glance at the clock told her it was 7:33 P.M., just past sunset. "Oh, no! Mr. Jameson'll fire me for sure. No excuses."

The fragrance of the almond-mint tea soothed her anger slightly, as she inhaled the steam. Her breath swirled tiny tornadoes above the cup until the tea was drinking temperature. But when she tried to swallow, her throat tightened. She choked, and tea splattered the table and her dress. She slowly wiped her mouth and watering eyes.

"Trevairin Drogoloh's going to wish he was dead!"

She stripped off her dress, went to the bathroom, and turned on the shower. The hot water felt good; she hadn't realized she was so cold. By the time she stepped out, she felt more alive and much less irritated. Blow-drying her short, ebony hair took a few minutes, but she couldn't wipe the mirror clear enough to use her curling iron. She threw up her hands and sighed. *Well, I'm not going over there to impress him, just to remove his head from his shoulders.*

The air outside her apartment was crisp and autumn-spicy. She knew the full moon was hiding behind the trees and buildings, just waiting for the perfect moment to rain silver light on the city.

Trevairin's place was in an upper-middle-class neighborhood, usually fifteen minutes away by interstate. Sharon made the trip in ten. Screeching her car to a halt before the large glass-and-brick house, she jumped out, slammed her door, and strode to the front porch, where she leaned on the doorbell.

The heavy oak door creaked open. Suddenly looming before her were the dark eyes and swarthy figure of Trevairin, dressed in black Levi's and shirt. He didn't look at all surprised to see her.

"Come in, Sharon. There are some people I would like you to meet." Leaving the door open, he turned around and sauntered down the main hallway.

Sharon stood motionless, the words she'd practiced all the way over gone from her thoughts. Without protest, she followed him into his den. Four men and three women lounged in casual, dark-colored clothes. When she hesitated in the doorway, they all smiled at her.

Taking her hand, Trevairin led her to the room's center.

"Tonight we add another member to our family. Sharon, we welcome you." His lips brushed her hand.

She shivered from his touch. Suddenly she regained hold of why she had come. "Look, Trev," she said, jerking her hand away and poking his chest, "spiking my drink wasn't funny or nice. I told you that alcohol makes me sicker than a dog. And because of you, I've probably lost my job. I don't suppose it matters to you, but I have to work for a living, unlike you rich people."

A slow, toothy smile lit Trevairin's face. "My dear Sharon, you do not have to work if you do not wish to. You are welcome to stay with us now."

Sharon glared at him. "That's the last thing I'd do!"

One of the women—who seemed vaguely familiar—moved toward her. "Sharon, you belong here. You're one of us. We all have the same blood."

Sharon gaped at her. "Excuse me? The same blood? Are you claiming to be my long-lost relative or something?"

"No," the woman said, a feral look in her gray eyes, "newly found relatives. Trevairin did put vodka—and blood—in your drink last night. You've shared blood with us, and now we're blood kin."

Sharon shook her still-pounding head. "This is getting too weird. Good-bye, Trev, and thanks for nothing."

She turned to leave, but Trevairin clutched her arm and spun her to face him. His narrowed eyes gleamed intensely.

"Sharon, you are my bride. At the party, I made you like myself—a child of the night."

With more force than she'd intended, she slugged him in the stomach. He doubled over, and she backed away.

"I'm not married to anyone," she began, icy calm. "If you cooked up a wedding last night, I can have it annulled 'cause I wasn't sober. As for being a vampire . . ." She flicked her long sharp nails and ran her tongue over her emerging canine teeth. She smiled as she read terror in their eyes. "Werewolves can't become vampires."

About Tanya Huff and "Be It Ever So Humble"

Tanya Huff says of herself that she dislikes telephones, store-bought muffins, and the concept of social drinking; she likes baseball, sleeping at least eight hours a night, and snow. She lives in Ontario, so it's probably a good thing she likes snow. I rejoice in the diversity of creation, having moved to California at least partly so I'd never have to see or feel snow again, having grown up with too much of it.

This story took first place in the Cauldron vote in issue 11, and we've been trying to get Tanya to write more stories about Magdelene ever since. She's still trying to come up with the perfect situation for her next Magdelene story, but in the meantime she's written us two other stories, so we can't complain too much.

Be It Ever So Humble

Tanya Huff

"**S**o, got any dirt on this place?" Magdelene asked the gold and black lizard who was sunning itself on a nearby rock.

The lizard, looking more like a beautifully crafted piece of jewelry than a living creature, merely flicked its inner eyelid closed and pretended to be asleep. Children with rocks or nets it had to do something about. Young women in donkey carts who asked stupid questions could safely be ignored.

Magdelene studied the little village nestled along the curve of its natural harbor and chewed reflectively on a strand of chestnut hair. It looked like a nice place, but, as much as she wanted to settle down, as tired as she was of constantly packing up and moving on, she knew better than to get her hopes up.

In a dozen years of traveling, she'd learned that the most jewel-like villages, in the most bucolic settings, often had the quaintest customs. Customs like welcoming wandering wizards with an axe, or attempting to convince wandering wizards to stay by outfitting them with manacles and chains, or by suggesting the tarring and feathering of wandering wizards with no better reason that the small matter of a straying husband or two. For the most part, Magdelene had found these customs no more than a minor inconvenience, although, had she known the man was married, she would never have suggested they . . .

She grinned at the memory. He'd proven a lot more flexible than she'd anticipated.

"Well, H'sak?" She spit out the hair and glanced back at the large mirror propped up behind the seat of the cart. "Shall we check it out?"

H'sak, trapped in the mirror, made no answer. Magdelene wasn't entirely certain the demon was aware of what went on outside his prison, but, traveling alone, she'd fallen into the habit of talking to him and figured, just in case he ever got out, it couldn't hurt if he had memories of pleasant, albeit one-sided, conversations. Not, she supposed, that a bit of chat would make up for her trapping him in the mirror in the first place. Stretching back, she pulled an old cloak down over the glass—no point in upsetting potential neighbors right off—then gathered up the reins and slapped them lightly on the donkey's rump. The donkey, who had worked out an understanding with the wizard early on, took another few mouthfuls of the coarse grass lining the track and slowly started down the hill to the village.

At the first house, Magdelene stopped the cart and sat quietly studying the scene. A few chickens scratched in the sandy dirt that served the village as a main street, and a black sow sprawled in the only visible bit of shade, her litter suckling noisily. A lullaby, softly sung, drifted through one of the open windows, and from the beach came the screams and laughter of children at play. Just the sort of lazy ambience she appreciated.

"Who are you?"

Languidly, for it was far too hot to be startled, Magdelene turned. A boy, nine or ten years old, naked except for a shell threaded on a frayed piece of gut, peered up at her from under a heavy shock of dusty black hair. Although he showed no signs of malnutrition or neglect, his left arm hung withered and useless by his side.

"My name is Magdelene." She pushed her hair back off her face. "Who are you?"

"Juan." He edged a little closer. "You a trader?"

"No. I'm a wizard." Over the years, she'd discovered life worked out better if she didn't try to hide that. It made explanations so much easier when things started happening. And things always did.

The boy looked her up and down and tossed his head. "Ha!" he scoffed. "Tell us another one. Wizards got gray hair and warts. You're not old enough to be a wizard."

"I'm twenty-seven," she told him a little indignantly. He was a fine one to talk about not old enough. . . .

"Oh." Juan considered it and apparently decided twenty-seven was sufficiently ancient even without the gray hair and warts. "What about your clothes, then? Wizards wear robes and stuff. Everyone knows that."

He had a point. Wizards did wear robes and stuff; usually of a dark, heavy, and imposing fabric; always hot, scratchy, and uncomfortable. Magdelene, who preferred to be comfortable, never bothered.

"I'm the most powerful wizard in the world," she explained as a rivulet of sweat ran under her bright-blue breastband, "so I wear what I want."

"Yeah, sure," he snorted. "Prove it."

"All right." She gathered up the multicolored folds of her skirt, jumped down off the cart, and held out her hand. "Give me your arm and I'll fix it."

"Oh no." He backed up a pace and turned, protecting the withered arm behind the rest of his body. "You ain't proving it on me. Find something else."

"Like what?"

Juan thought about it a moment. "Could you send my sister someplace far away?" he asked hopefully.

Magdelene thought about that in turn. It didn't seem worth antagonizing the village just to prove a point to one grubby child. "I could, but I don't think I should."

The boy sighed. The kind of sigh that said he knew what the answer would be but thought there could be no harm in asking.

They stood together in silence for a moment, Magdelene leaning against the back of her cart—perfectly content to do nothing—and Juan digging his toe into the sand. The donkey, who could smell water, decided enough was enough and started toward the center of the village. He was hot, he was thirsty, and he was going to do something about it.

As the cart jerked forward, Magdelene hit the ground with an unwizardlike thud. Closer proximity proved the sand was not as soft as it looked. "Lizard piss," she muttered a curse, rubbing at a stone-bruise. When she looked up, Juan had disappeared.

She shrugged philosophically and, following along behind the donkey, amused herself by pulling back an image of Juan as an adult. Long and lean and sleekly muscled, it was a future worth sticking around for. At some point between now and then, she appeared to have convinced him to let her fix his arm. It looked like she'd be staying, at least for a while.

An impatient bray demanded her attention and she allowed the image to slip back to its own time; they'd arrived at the well.

When the trough was full and the donkey had bent his head to drink, Magdelene, pulled by the realization she was no longer alone, slowly turned. All around the edges of the square stood the children of the village, staring at her with wide dark eyes.

"Yes?" she asked.

The children merely continued to stare.

Demons, she decided, were easier to deal with. At least you always knew what demons wanted.

"Magdelene-lady!"

The children stared on as Magdelene gratefully noted Juan approaching with an adult in tow. The old man had been bent and twisted by the weight of his years, his fingers warped into shapes more like driftwood than flesh. His skin had been tanned by sun and wind and salt into creased leather, and any hair he'd had was long gone. He followed Juan with the rolling gait of a life spent at sea, and his jaws worked to the rhythm of his walking.

"Whatcha doing sitting around like a pile of fish guts?" he growled at the children as he stopped an arm's length from Magdelene and glared about. "Untie her beast, put him to pasture, and get that wagon in the shade."

The children hesitated.

"You are staying a bit?" he asked, his growl softening, his dark eyes meeting hers.

Magdalene smiled her second-best smile—she couldn't be certain his heart would be up to her best—and said, "Yes." She wanted very much to stay for a bit. Maybe this time things would work out.

The old man nodded and waved both twisted hands. "You heard her. Get!"

They got, Juan with the rest, and Magdelene watched bemused as her donkey was led away and her cart was pulled carefully to rest under a stand of palm.

"Boy says you told him you're a wizard."

"That's right."

"Don't have much need for a wizard here. Wizards make you soft and then the sea takes you. We prefer to do things for ourselves."

"So do I," Magdelene told him, leaning back against the damp stones. "Prefer to have people do things for themselves, that is." She grinned. She liked this old man and sensed in him a kindred spirit. "To be honest, I like people to do things for me as well."

He returned the grin and his eyes twinkled as he looked her up and down. "Ah, child," he cackled, "what I could do for you if I were only fifty years younger."

"Would you like to be?" she asked, rather hoping he would.

He laughed, then he realized she was serious. "You could do that?"

"Yes."

His gaze turned inward, and Magdelene could feel the strength of the memories he sifted. After a moment, he sighed and shook his head. "Foolish wishes, child. I've earned my age and I'll wear it with honor."

Magdelene hid her disappointment. Personally, she couldn't see the honor in blurred eyesight, aching bones, and swollen, painful joints, but if that was his choice . . .

There were sixteen buildings in the village, eight goats, eleven pigs, twenty-one chickens, and fourteen boats. No one had ever managed an accurate count of the cats.

"Six families came here three generations ago," Carlos,

the old man, explained as they stood on the beach watching boats made tiny by distance slide up and down the rolling waves. Through his eyes, Magdelene saw the harbor as it had been, sparkling untouched in the sun, never sailed, never fished, theirs. "I'm the last of the first. I've outlived two wives and most of my children as well."

"Do you mind?" Magdelene asked, knowing she was likely to see entire civilizations rise and fall in her lifetime and not entirely certain how she felt about it.

"Well . . ." He considered the question for a moment. "I'll live 'til I die. Nothing else I can do."

"You didn't answer my question."

He patted her cheek. "I know."

That night, in the crowded main room of the headman's house, Carlos presented Magdelene to the adults of the village. ". . . and she'd like to stay on a bit."

"A wizard," the headman ruminated. "That's something we don't see every day."

Magdelene missed much of the discussion that followed as she was busy trying to make eye contact with a very attractive young man standing by one of the deep windows. She gave up when she realized that he was trying to make eye contact with a very attractive young man standing by the door.

". . . although frankly, we'd rather you were a trader."

"The traders are late this year?" Magdelene guessed, hoping she hadn't missed anything important.

"Aye. They've always come with the kayle."

Just in time, she remembered that kayle were fish.

"Surely you saw them on the road?" a young woman asked hopefully.

"No." Magdelene frowned as she thought back over the last few weeks of travel. "I didn't." The emptiness of the trail hadn't seemed strange to her at the time. It did now.

"I don't suppose you can conjure one?" asked a middle-aged woman dryly, tamping down her pipe.

The room rippled with laughter.

"I could," Magdelene admitted.

The room fell silent.

Magdelene cleared her throat. She might as well get it over with. "I'm the most powerful wizard in the world," she began.

The middle-aged woman snorted. "Says who?"

"Well, uh . . ."

"Doesn't matter. Would this conjured trader do us any good?"

"Probably not." A trader conjured suddenly into the village would be more likely to trade in strong hysterics than anything useful.

"I thought as much." The woman expertly lit her pipe with a spill from the lamp. "What in Neto's breath are we wasting our time here for, that's what I want to know?"

"I thought you might like to know that a stranger, a wizard, has come to the village," Carlos told her tartly.

She snorted again. "All right. Now we know." She pointed the stem of her pipe at Magdelene and demanded, "You planning on causing any trouble?"

"Of course not," Magdelene declared emphatically. She never planned on causing any trouble.

"Will you keep your nose out of what doesn't concern you?"

She had to think about that for a moment, wondering how broad a definition could be put on what didn't concern her. "I'll try."

"See that you do."

"So I can stay for a while?"

"For a while." Her head wreathed in smoke, the woman rose. "That's that, then," she said shortly, and left.

The headman sighed and raised both hands in a gesture of defeat. You heard her. You can go."

As people began to leave, Magdelene leaned over and whispered to Carlos, "Why does he let her get away with that?"

Carlos snickered, his palm lying warm and dry on Magdelene's arm. "Force of habit," he said in his normal speaking voice. "She's his older sister, raised him after their mother drowned. Refused to be headwoman, said she didn't have the time, but she runs every meeting he calls."

The headman smiled, for Carlos's speech had risen clearly

over the noise of the departing villagers. "Look at it this way, grandfather, the village gets two fish on one piece of bait. I do all the work and Yolanda does all the talking." He stood, stretched, and turned to Magdelene. "Have you got a bed, Wizard?"

Studying the muscles of his torso, still corded and firm for all his forty-odd years, Magdelene considered several replies. All of which she discarded after catching a speaking glance from the headman's wife.

"While the weather holds," she sighed, "I'm perfectly comfortable under my cart."

"And I am perfectly comfortable," she sighed again a half hour later, plumping up the pillows on her huge feather bed, "but I wouldn't mind some company." As if in answer to her request, the canvas flaps hanging from the sides of the cart parted and Juan poked in his head. "I was thinking," she muttered to whatever gods were listening, "of company a little older."

Juan blinked, shook his head, and gazed around curiously. "How'd you get all this stuff under here?" he demanded.

"I told you," Magdelene poured herself a glass of chilled grape juice, "I'm the most powerful wizard in the world." She dabbed at the spreading purple stain on the front of her tunic. "Can I fix your arm now?"

He didn't answer, just crawled forward and found himself in a large room that held—besides the bed—a wardrobe, an overstuffed armchair, and a huge book bound in red leather lying closed on a wooden stand. "Where's the wagon?"

Magdelene pointed at the ceiling, impressed by his attitude. She'd had one or two supposed adults fall gibbering to the carpet.

Juan looked up. Dark red runes had been scrawled across the rough boards of the ceiling. "What's that writing on there?"

"The spell that allows this room to exist."

"Oh." He had little or no interest in spells. "Got any more juice?"

She handed him a full glass and watched him putter about, poking his nose into everything. Setting his glass down on the book, he pulled open the wardrobe door.

"What's that?"

"It's a demon trapped in a mirror, what's it look like?" She'd hung the mirror on the door that afternoon, figuring H'sak was safer there than in the wagon.

"How long's he been in there?"

"Twelve years."

"How long you gonna keep him in there?"

"Until I let him out."

An answer that would have infuriated an adult, suited Juan fine. He took one last admiring look at H'sak, finished his juice, and handed Magdelene the empty glass. "I better get home."

"Juan."

About to step through the canvas walls, he glanced back over his shoulder.

"You still haven't told me if I can fix your arm."

His gaze slid over to the demon and then back to the wizard. He shrugged. "Maybe later," he said, and left.

Magdelene spent most of the next three days with Carlos. The children treated her like an exotic curiosity and she tried to live up to their expectations. The adults treated her with a wary suspicion and she tried not to live up to theirs. Carlos treated her like a friend.

The oldest in the village by a good twenty years, his eyes sometimes twinkled and sparkled and looked no older than Juan's. Sometimes they burned with more mature fires and she longed to give him back his youth if only for a few hours behind the dunes. Sometimes they appeared deeper and blacker and wiser than the night sky. Sometimes they just looked old. Marveling, she realized that he remembered all the ages he had been and more, that they were with him still, making a home, not a prison, of his age. This was his strength, and Magdelene placed the lesson it taught her carefully away with her other precious things.

She began to hope the village had a place for her.

In the morning of the fourth day, they'd gathered about the well—the wizard and the few adults who remained ashore due to age or disability—when the high-pitched shriek of a child jerked all heads around.

"Riders!"

Screaming out the news of their discovery, Juan and three of the other children burst into the center of the village. The chickens panicked, screeched, and scattered. The adults tried to make sense out of the cacophony.

"One at a time!" The baker finally managed to make himself heard. "Juan, what happened?"

"Riders, uncle!" Juan told him, bouncing in his excitement. "Five of them. On horses. Coming here!"

"Are you sure?"

"Yes! We were going up the track to look for gooseberries . . ." The other three children nodded vigorously in agreement. ". . . and we met them coming down."

"They aren't traders?"

Juan sighed in exaggerated exasperation. "Uncle, I seen traders before. And these aren't . . ." He noticed the baker was no longer looking at him, noticed no one was looking at him, so he let the last word trail off and he turned.

They rode slowly, with a ponderous certainty more threatening than a wild charge. Voluminous robes in tans and browns hid all but their eyes and each wore a long, curved blade. They stopped, the line of horses reflecting the line of the well, and the rider in the center let the fabric drop from his face.

Nice, thought Magdelene, continuing to stroke the black and white cat sprawled across her lap. Good cheekbones, flashing eyes, full lips, and, she realized, shoulders dropping a little in disappointment, about as congenial as H'sak.

"We have come," said the rider, "for the kayle."

Carlos stepped forward, his hand on Juan's shoulder—both to support himself and to keep the boy from doing anything rash. "What do you have to trade?" he asked levelly.

"Your lives," replied the rider, and his hand dropped to the hilt of his sword.

Magdelene rolled her eyes. She'd never much cared for melodrama.

"If you take the kayle, we will have nothing when the traders come."

"The traders will not come. The warlord rules here."

"I don't recall being conquered," Carlos snapped, temper showing at last.

The rider smiled, showing perfect teeth and no sense of humor. "You are being conquered now." The line of horses took a single step in intimidating unison.

Juan's one hand curled into a fist.

Magdelene stood, dumping the indignant cat to the ground.

"Just one minute," she began.

"SILENCE, WOMAN!" the rider thundered.

"Stuff a sock in it." She brushed cat hair off her skirt. "You're not impressing anyone."

For just an instant, acute puzzlement replaced the rider's belligerent expression. A people in the process of being terrorized simply did not behave in this fashion. With a perceivable effort, he regained his scowl and drew his sword. To either side, his men did the same.

"Kill them all," he said.

The horses leapt forward and vanished.

The saddles and the riders hung in the air for one long second, then crashed to the ground, raising great clouds of dust and more panicked squawking from the chickens.

"And as you want the kayle so badly," Magdelene said.

Steel swords became silver fish making desperate attempts to get free of the grip on their tails.

The children laughed and pointed.

When they found they couldn't release the fish, the riders began to panic.

"When you get back to your warlord," Magdelene told them smiling pleasantly, "you'll be able to let go. If I can make a suggestion, don't waste any time. Very shortly those fish are not going to be the best of traveling companions."

Throwing garbage and clots of dirt, the children chased the riders from the village.

Magdelene turned and saw four of the five adults regarding her with awe. Carlos merely looked thoughtful.

"With luck, they'll convince their warlord that this village is more trouble than it's worth," Magdelene explained reassuringly, rubbing at the beads of sweat between her breasts.

"Unless he has a wizard of his own, he'll only be beaten again if he comes back." She didn't add that even if he did have a wizard, he'd still be beaten—it sounded too much like bragging. Even though it was true.

"And without luck?" Carlos prodded.

Magdelene sighed. "Without luck, I'll just have to convince him myself. But I hope he does the sensible thing."

Carlos snorted. "Men who style themselves 'The Warlord' seldom do the sensible thing."

"Men in general seldom do the sensible thing." Magdelene winked at the baker, who had, after all, only lost one leg at sea. "Fortunately, they have other uses."

Carlos cackled wildly. The baker blushed.

". . . although you did say you'd keep out of what didn't concern you."

"My home concerns me."

Yolanda peered at Magdelene through a cloud of pipe smoke. "Home is it? I thought you were just staying for a while?"

"The village needs me."

"We neither need nor want you taking care of us," the older woman growled.

"Good. Because I wasn't planning to." Even through the smoke, she could see Yolanda's eyes narrow. The five empty saddles had been piled by the well when the fishing fleet returned. "I'll be like the seawall. Just another buffer against the storms." She spread her arms. "Without me, the persecutions your people left could well follow them."

"This warlord could send others," Carlos pointed out, pulling himself to his feet on the wizard's shoulder. "We have no way to defend ourselves."

"I can be your defenses," Magdelene insisted.

Yolanda's teeth ground against her pipe stem. "You could use your power to enslave us."

"I could . . . but why would I bother?"

She sounded so sincerely puzzled that Carlos began to laugh. "She's right," he cackled. "The only thing she'd rather do than lie in the sun is . . ." Just what exactly Magdelene would rather do than lie in the sun got lost in a violent coughing fit, but more than one stupid grin was hastily hidden.

"I thought I'd build a house on the headland," Magdelene said firmly, shooting Carlos a look that almost set him off again. "If no one has any objection."

"Humph." Yolanda's snort brought with it another cloud of smoke. Magdelene couldn't be sure, but she thought there was a smile behind it. "Well, if grandfather is so certain, I've no objection."

The headman sighed. "Does anyone else wish to offer an objection?" he asked mildly. Yolanda glared at the assembled villagers, who wisely remained silent. "In that case," he inclined his head graciously, "you may build as you wish, Lady-wizard."

Magdelene studied the designs she'd drawn on the bare rock of the headland, then checked them against the originals in the book. Although her hair and bright-yellow shift blew wildly about in the wind, the pages of the spellbook remained still and not one grain of fine white sand she'd used for the parameters of her house shifted. The moment Juan returned from the beach she'd be able to finish. She could have just lifted the last bit of sand she needed, but the boy had wanted to help. If she let him hang around, she figured she'd eventually do something he considered worthy and he'd let her fix his arm.

She turned her face to the sun, eyes half closed in blissful anticipation of actually having a place of her own. No more traveling and no more adventures. Adventures were highly overrated as far as Magdelene was concerned, as they usually included uncomfortable sleeping arrangements, primitive or nonexistent toilet facilities, and someone—or someones—in direct and often violent opposition.

"Magdelene!"

Jolted out of her reverie, she squinted at the tiny figure scrambling up the steep path from the beach. It wasn't Juan, for the child had two healthy arms he . . . no, she . . . flailed about for balance.

"The riders," the little girl panted as Magdelene reached down to pull her the last few feet. "They've come back."

So the warlord hadn't taken the hint. "Don't worry about it," the wizard advised, holding a hankie to a nose obediently blown. "That's why I'm here."

"But they've got Juan!"

"What?!" Magdelene spun around and stared down at the village, the distant scene snapping suddenly into clarity at the touch of her will. Not the same riders, but the same type, their robes of tan and brown billowing in the wind. A full two dozen men faced the well this time, a red pennant snapping about over their heads as if trying to leap from the lance time. One horse stood a little forward and Juan had been thrown across the pommel of its saddle, his good arm twisted cruelly back.

She could see the villagers gathering—the kayle run had stopped and the seas had been too high to put out for a less certain catch. Carlos—the headman and Yolanda at his back—stepped out of the crowd and spoke. Magdelene could see his lips move, although the wind whipped away the words. Juan began to struggle and squirm.

The rider's grip shifted, and it didn't take a wizard's ears to hear the high-pitched scream that rose on the wind.

"Magdelene!" The little girl tugged on the wizard's shift. "You gotta do something!"

Juan went limp.

Magdelene's fingers closed on the child's shoulder, and the next instant the two of them stood by the well. The child tore herself out of Magdelene's hold and dashed to her mother.

"Did you see, Mama? Did you see? We went poof!"

Alone now, between the villagers and the riders, Magdelene took a deep breath, clamped her teeth, and forced the wobbling world to steady. The last time she'd used the transit spell, she'd puked her guts out upon arrival. This time she couldn't give in to the nausea; retching at the warlord's feet might be unpleasant, but it could hardly be considered intimidating. When she regained her ability to focus, most of the riders still wore expressions of combined fear and disbelief.

Only the man who held Juan looked unaffected.

He smiled down at her. "You must be the wizard," he said.

She returned the smile with equal sincerity. "And you must be the warlord."

"I got your message. I'm here to give you my answer. And," his eyes narrowed, "I wouldn't suggest a repeat of the last incident, not while I have the boy."

Magdelene wasn't particularly worried. She could send the warlord and his men back where they came from without disturbing a hair on Juan's head. The problem was, they'd only come back. If she played to the Warlord's ego, she might be able to negotiate a more permanent solution. "What do you want?"

"You." His smile broadened, the scar that split one side of his mouth twisting his face unevenly.

Magdelene's brows reached for her hairline. "I beg your pardon?"

"I have decided I could use a wizard." He waved his free hand expansively. "You are to put yourself under my command."

Pompous bloody twit. He actually sounded as if she should be thrilled with the opportunity. She folded her arms and glared up at him. "Why would I want to do that?" she demanded.

"If you don't, I will kill the boy."

"And if I do?"

"I will spare both the boy and the village."

"Magdelene . . ." Carlos's voice sounded strained, all the laughter gone from it.

"It's all right, Carlos," Magdelene muttered out of the corner of her mouth. "I've got things under control." Or she would have shortly. A man who expected his mere presence to overwhelm all opposition could be dealt with.

"While I appreciate your very generous offer," she told him, preparing to launch a special-effects extravaganza that would convince him to never tangle with her village again, "I'm afraid I shall have to decline."

His smile never wavered. "Pity," he said. Throwing one arm about the boy's upper body, he grabbed the small head and twisted.

The crack sounded very loud.

Juan's body slid to the ground to lie in a crumpled heap, the head bent around at an impossible angle.

Magdelene's mouth worked but no sound emerged. She hadn't really believed he would do that. Behind her, she heard a wail of grief from Juan's mother.

The warlord's men moved forward until they surrounded the villagers with a wall of steel.

"Now," said the warlord, still smiling, "what have you to say to my most generous offer?"

The smile slipped as Magdelene raised her head and met his eyes.

"Die," she told him.

He didn't have time to look surprised. His eyes rolled up, his mouth went slack, and he collapsed forward over the pommel. Startled by this new limp weight, the horse tossed its head and shied sideways, dumping the warlord's body to the sand beside the small heap of bones and flesh that had been Juan.

In silence that followed, the breathing of the surrounding horses sounded unnaturally loud. Their riders made no sound at all, each hoping desperately that the wizard would not now turn her attention to him.

The silence grew and stretched, broken only by the sobbing of Juan's mother. Pushing her hair back off her face with a trembling hand, Magdelene knelt by the boy's body. She straightened his tangled limbs and gently turned his head until it sat naturally once again.

"Lady-wizard . . ." It was the first time Carlos hadn't used her name. ". . . this isn't to say you haven't done what you felt you had to in removing this man from the world, but . . ."

He fell silent as Magdelene took Juan's cold little hand in hers and called his name.

The slight chest began to rise and fall. Juan hiccuped and opened his eyes.

"I wasn't here," he said, scratching his nose.

"That's right." Magdelene was a firm believer in telling children the truth. "You were dead."

"Oh." He thought about that for a moment. "It sure was boring."

She moved out of the way as his family rushed forward to

claim him. He squirmed, looked disgusted, and tried to avoid the sloppiest displays of affection.

"Mama, stop it."

"Lady-wizard?"

Magdelene turned to face the villagers. They'd ask her to leave now. Or they'd deify her. Things wouldn't be the same. She stifled a near-hysterical giggle. People so often overreacted to the raising of the dead.

"If you can bring back Juan," the headman told her quietly, "you must bring back the warlord and right the wrong you've done."

"Wrong?"

"We don't believe in the taking of life." He glanced down at the warlord's body and his lip curled. "As much as we may recognize the emotion that prompts it." Behind him, the villagers stared at her, no two expressions the same.

She heaved a sigh of relief. If that was all they wanted, they were taking it rather well. Maybe she could still salvage the situation. "But what of that lot?" Magdelene shot a glance back over her shoulder at the warlord's men, who tried very hard to appear harmless and insignificant. "Cut the head off a snake and the snake dies. If I rejoin the head, then the snake lives and eats the heads of others and . . ." She frowned, lost in the metaphor, and sighed again. "Look, I don't think it's a good idea."

"If you want to make this your home," Yolanda told her bluntly, as unaffected by miracles as she was by most things, "you must respect our beliefs."

"But he deserved to die."

A couple of the villagers nodded in agreement. Yolanda stood firm. "You have no more right to decide that about him than he did about Juan. If you wish us to respect you, you must respect us."

Was it as easy as that? Magdelene wrapped her arms about herself and thought it over.

"Does your warlord have a name?" she asked the riders at last.

They looked at each other and then down at the body of their leader.

"Anwar, Lady-wizard," ventured the young man who held

the lance with the warlord's pennant. She smiled her thanks, and he began breathing again.

Squatting by the warlord's body, Magdelene took his hand in hers and called. She didn't bother to make him more comfortable first.

This time, she wouldn't underestimate him.

His eyes opened. He looked around, slowly untangled himself, and sat up. "Bleshnaggle?" he asked, grabbing for a blowing strand of Magdelene's hair.

She pulled it out of his hand and stood. The warlord pouted for a second, then discovered his boots. He gazed at them in fascination, babbling nonsense words and patting at the air with limp hands.

Everyone, the villagers and the riders, took a step forward.

"What happened?" Yolanda asked finally.

Magdelene watched the warlord trying to catch the billowing end of his own robe. "Death seems to have unsettled him a bit," she said.

"But Juan was fine."

The wizard shrugged. "Children are a lot more adaptable about . . ."

A dark-haired, pale-skinned young woman appeared suddenly beside the warlord, hands on hip and eyes flashing. "Would you make up your mind!" Her black robes hung straight to the sand, unaffected by the breeze. "What are we playing, musical souls? First I've got 'em, then I don't. You're not supposed to do that!" She spotted Juan worming his way to the front of the crowd. "Hi, kid."

Juan's mother grabbed his ear and yanked him behind her, cutting off his cheerful greeting. As far as she could see there was no one there, and her baby had been involved with quite enough strangeness for one afternoon.

"Death?" Magdelene hazarded.

Everyone, the riders and the villagers, took a step back. At this point, they were willing to take the wizard's word for it.

"Good guess," Death snapped. "Now, do you want to explain what's going on around here?"

"It's a long story."

"Look, lady," Death began, a little more calmly.

"Magdelene."

"Okay. Magdelene. Look, Magdelene, I haven't got time for a long story, I've got places to go, people to see. Let's make a deal—you can keep the kid, but tall, dark, and violent comes with me." She pointed a long, pale finger down at the warlord. Both her ebony brows rose as he pulled off a boot and began filling it with sand. "Now look what you've done!" she wailed, causing every living creature in earshot to break into a cold sweat. "You've broken him!"

"Sorry." Magdelene spread her hands.

"No you're not." Death tapped one foot against the sand. "Okay. I'm sure we can work this out like sensible women. You can keep him, just give me one of them." She swept her gaze over the riders.

One sensitive young man fainted, falling forward in the saddle, arms dangling limply down each side of his horses's neck.

"Sorry," Magdelene said again, lifting her shoulders in a rueful shrug. "They're not mine to give. Why don't you just take one?"

Three saddles were suddenly wet.

"I don't work that way." Death shook her head. "I can't take someone if it isn't their time."

"Lady?"

Both Death and the wizard turned.

Carlos stepped forward, one twisted hand held out before him.

Death's expression softened, and she smiled. She had a beautiful smile. "Don't I know you?" she asked softly.

"You should," Carlos told her. "I've been expecting you for some time."

Her voice became a caress. "Forgive me for taking so long."

When she took his hand, he sighed and all the aches and pains of his age seemed to drop off him. He stood straight for a moment, his face serene, then he crumpled to the ground.

All eyes were on the body of the old man. Only Magdelene saw the young one, tall and strong, who still held Death's hand. Lips trembling, she gave him her best smile. He returned it. And was gone.

Magdelene stood quietly, tears on her cheeks, while the villagers lovingly carried Carlos's body away. She stood quietly while the warlord's men managed to get their leader onto his horse, and she didn't move as they headed out of the village. She stood quietly until a small hand slipped into hers.

"I've got the rest of the sand," Juan told her, a bulging pouch hung around his neck. "Can we go finish your house now?"

She looked down and lightly touched his hair. "They want me to stay?"

He shrugged, unsure who they were. "No one wants you to go."

Hand in hand, they climbed the path to the headland.

"Are you going to stay here forever," Juan asked.

Magdelene met the anxious look in his black eyes and grinned. "How old are you, Juan?"

"Nine."

The image of the young man she'd pulled from the future stood behind the child and winked. She shooed it back where it belonged. "I'll be around long enough."

Juan nodded, satisfied.

"So . . . I took you back from Death today. Ready to let me fix your arm now?"

He tossed his head. "I'm still thinkin' about it."

The most powerful wizard in the world stared down at him in astonishment, then started to laugh. "You," she declared, "are one hard kid to impress."